The Secret Diary of a Checkout Girl

Samantha Rose

ISBN 9 781 84914 8245

First published in Great Britain in 2015
by CompletelyNovel

This book is a work of fiction. Names, characters, places, organizations, and incidents, other than those clearly in the public domain, are either products of the author's imagination or are used fictitiously. Any resemblance to actual events, organizations, or persons, living or dead, is entirely coincidental.

"I get knocked down
But I get up again
You're never gonna keep me down
I get knocked down
But I get up again
You're never gonna keep me down
Pissing the night away
Pissing the night away..."

\- Chumbawamba

Preface

I don't care if this ruins the rest of the book for you. I can't hold it in any longer. I'm just so happy that I managed to get out of there! Yes, that's right. I left my job as a checkout girl for Eggberts Supermarkets, and what follows is the story of how.

Guess I'd better warn you, there are no highs. No, *'I'm so lucky to have a job in this economy'*, no, *'well the job's bad, but at least I've made some great friends'*; none of that sentimental crap. What happens in this book is real, and it happens every day. It's happening right now.

Yes, this is the story of how I crawled out of a miserable dead end. But it's also the story of a multi-million pound company breaking the spirit of a young woman time and time again. The worst thing is, even though I got out, I can still hear the sound of other spirits being broken, snapped, severed. Listen closely...

EGGBERTS
Leeds 147
Tel: 0845 *** ****

Weed Killer 1ltr	£3.99

TOTAL SALE:	£3.99
CASH:	£5.00
CHANGE DUE:	£1.01

01/01/14 14:37 0287 081 1305 92

You were served by Suzanne.

Eggberts. Crackin' Deals

Please hold onto receipts.

January

New Year's Day

Happy New Year!

My name is Suzie Quesnell. It's French, and my dad did teach me a little: *'Mange tout, Rodney, mange tout'*. I forget what it means.

I'm writing to you from behind checkout fourteen in Eggberts Supermarket, Leeds, Yorkshire - my home away from home.

There is a slight possibility that I am hungover, or drunk (or hovering between the two), from last night's celebrations. Correction – this morning's celebrations!

Although, what is there to celebrate? I'm twenty-six, graduated from uni five years ago (with a first class degree in Canine Behaviour and Training, *thank you very much*), and I still work behind this bloody till.

BIG stop-gap. My whole life might turn out to be a bloody stop-gap. It certainly feels that way at the minute; and it's easily done, believe me. There are people working here one year off retirement that said Eggberts was meant to be their stop-gap. I feel sick just thinking about it. But maybe that's the Sambuca shots.

I'm not usually such a mess. In fact, I think I might be the most normal person that works here. Ever look around at your colleagues and think, '*Where the hell did they find this lot?!*' Some mothers do 'ave 'em.

Anyway, I'm normally half decent. I've come in today looking like shit and smelling twice as bad because, in case no one's noticed, IT'S FUCKING NEW YEAR'S DAY.

Who shops on New Year's Day? Honestly, it's a bloody public holiday. Yet here I am sat behind a till with no extra benefits or even an extra thank you for it.

Some people would stop me in my tracks and tell me I'm lucky to have a job. I know half of you reading this are probably thinking that right now. But I also know that you are the half that has never worked in a supermarket, and until you have, you just don't know. You just don't know.

2nd Jan

Well, you know you've hit rock bottom when you start complaining to yourself on the back of a till receipt for weed killer. I've no idea why anyone would feel the need to nip to the shop for weed killer on New Year's Day, but each to their own.

Anyway, having read through my drunken ramblings on that receipt, it's evident that I am even more unhappy than I thought. But, if there's ever a time for a new start it's January, right?

So, here and now I am going to make a promise to myself. I, Suzie Quesnell, promise that by this time next year I will not be working in Eggberts Supermarket. Or any bloody supermarket; and I won't *ever* be working on New Year's Day again either. I'm going to sort my life out. And in the meantime, I promise to spill all of the dirty secrets from the sordid supermarket world into this very diary.

Secret 1: Diaries are so much cheaper if you buy them on 2nd Jan!

4th Jan

A pigeon flew into the shop today. It pooed on a customer's head and she got all her shopping for free. My dad always says a bird crapping on you is good luck.

Nothing else to report today.

8th Jan

Happy Birthday to me! Twenty-seven, would you believe it? It's also the sixth consecutive birthday I have spent counting away the minutes on the bottom left-hand corner of my till screen.

See, the supermarket has this policy: no holidays are to be taken in December or January as it is classed as the 'Christmas Period'.

Fair enough, I understand December. But it's the 8th of January! The trees have been taken down, the tinsel has been swept under the rug, and don't lie to yourself, nearly all of the choccies are gone too. Christmas is finished.

Anyway, I'm not going to let it piss me off. Twenty-seven isn't exactly a birthday I want to celebrate, not when I'm still living the life of a teenager. I just wish I didn't have to watch the minutes go by, that's all. It's bad enough hearing that '*beep*' '*beep*' every second without having to look at the time as well.

I used to cover the time up with stickers I'd obtained from watermelons, honeydew melons, basically any melon I could find. But then the Rottweiler caught on, and she started withholding my breaks until the maximum four hours allowed by law, so I stopped.

I guess I'd better take this opportunity to expose the Rottweiler:

Real name: Christine Marshall.

Occupation: Checkout Manager/Psychotic Bitch.

Christine earned herself the nickname, the Rottweiler (in my head), because of her ruthless temper and her size. She's a big girl, and I don't mean, '*she could do with losing a few*', I mean, her main hobby is throwing shot puts.

Now, don't get me wrong, I'm a huge dog-lover; and as a dog behavioural expert, I don't like to stereotype breeds.

But, have you ever found yourself alone in a room with a bad-tempered, 150 pound Rottweiler? There is kind of like this unspoken agreement that if it wanted to, the dog could rip you to shreds. The same applies to Christine Marshall.

11th Jan

I always feel so much better when I come to work after two days off. More refreshed, you know?

Well, for the first ten minutes anyway, around which time some smart-arse customer will interrupt my daydreaming with a very loud: '*Help with packin'? I'd rather you helped with payin', love!*'

Or the even more popular: '*Do* I *need help with packing? I've got thirty years experience, doll. You're looking at the master!*'

It's amazing how many times people can use the same dry joke.

On the weekend*, my boyfriend, Nick, was supposed to be taking me out for a birthday meal. Only, when I got home from work he wasn't there. Our housemates were though – two lads, both students. I managed to get the gist of '*he's in the library*' over the sound of computerised aliens dying horrible deaths at the hands of a PlayStation controller.

Nick is doing a PhD, so it's not uncommon for him to be studying. He's so much more successful than I was at his age (he's 23), or than I am now. I'm ever so proud of him, when I'm not livid with jealousy.

As the clock struck 9 p.m., I knew that Nick had forgotten all about my birthday. I cracked open a bottle of red wine from the *Eggberts' Indulge* range and drank it alone in our room.

---

* In supermarket lingo, 'weekend' refers to any two days off in a row. It's a rare occurrence, and the chances of it happening between Friday and Sunday are slim to nothing.

I tried to shrug it off. *'He's busy'*, I told myself. Plus, it's not uncommon for people to forget a January birthday. No one wants to celebrate so soon after Christmas and New Year's Eve. Still, there are a handful of people that I can always count on to remember my birthday, and Nick used to be one of them.

I had polished off the full bottle of wine and fallen asleep by the time Nick eventually got home. He shook me awake, furious at the state I'd got myself in to (did I forget to mention that I threw up on my side of the bed, then slept on his?). But when he had the cheek to miss my birthday, there was no way I was letting *him* be the furious one.

I let him have it! He didn't half look sorry for himself when I'd finished. He kept going on about how he got so involved in his assignment. I wasn't listening though; I'd heard it all before. But then, something made me prick up my ears.

'*Andrea*'.

Her name lingered in the air like a bad smell (and let me tell you, with my puke on the sheets the room already stank more than enough).

He spends all bloody day and night with this '*Andrea*', his '*research partner*'. I know she's a fraud and I've told him so countless times. No one can be that leggy and blonde, AND be interested (or talented) at chemistry.

'It's not biologically possible', I told him. 'You're a scientist, surely you get that?'

He walked off at that point, but not before uttering three dangerous words: 'You wouldn't understand'.

Well butter me up and call me a jacket potato! Doesn't he know that I am educated to degree level too? Not only do I have one, it's first *bloody* class. Now, I know spending all day facing a screen that's only interesting function is showing twenty-five different varieties of apples is killing my brain cells, but they're not all dead yet!

I wouldn't bloody understand?! No, *he* wouldn't understand! The bloody cheek of him. I should have said: 'No, *you* don't understand, pal. *You* don't understand the real world, and let me tell *you*, it's boring, it's painful, and there are more apple varieties out there than X-Factor finalists!'

***

Ooh, the Rottweiler has put the closing sign on my till, must be my break already! Time really does fly when you're complaining. She's starting to get wise to my diary though. I don't know what her problem is. I always finish my sentence when I have a customer waiting...

***

Now, where was I? Oh yeah, my weekend. Well, Mum and Dad came over the next day. Nice of them to drive the hour or so from the other side of the Pennines, I kind of wish they hadn't bothered though. I woke up to my dad banging on the door like a heavy weight boxer, always a great way to awaken with a hangover.

'Oh dear', he giggled, 'someone had a good birthday'.

My mother's large behind pushed him out of the way. She cocked her head to one side in pity, 'Oh Suzie, look at the state of you'.

Then she barged past me and tried to find a seat on the couch that wasn't already taken up by crushed Wotsits. She waited for me and my dad to join her, and then she rolled her eyes around the whole room, clicking her tongue a few times, 'This is no way for a twenty-seven year old woman to live'.

I muttered something about brews and hid in the kitchen for a while. I caught my reflection in the microwave and it was safe to say I looked like a right bloody mess. Nick was nowhere to be seen either, back at the bloody library already. *Good birthday you ask, Dad? Yeah, top notch!*

I finally went back in the living room and perched on the arm of the sofa.

'Where are the brews, pet?' Dad said.

I told him I forgot and was about to get up to make them when Mum chirped in.

'We're not staying', she said. 'The stench of teenage boy is unbearable. We've brought your presents'.

I went over and got them, dodging my mother's hands that morphed into a washcloth and comb the minute she clapped eyes on me.

My gifts were... interesting. Two things from my parents: a book titled *'101 things to do with an animal degree'* (that one had my mum written all over it), and an electronic xylophone, clearly my dad's idea. He followed it with his usual, 'I think you mentioned that once'.

See, my dad's hobby is visiting his local auction house at least once a week and bidding on all of the lots that no one else bids on. He justifies it by saying, *'I just can't let anything go to waste!'*

Now, you might find this cute or quirky, but let me tell you this: everyone mentions EVERYTHING at least *once*!

The xylophone went in a drawer alongside my light-up yo-yo, my Super Mario N64 game cartridge, my size nine Homer Simpson slippers (I'm a size five), and ten sheets of personalised 'Robert' wrapping paper (my ex-boyfriend's name).

But I knew they both meant well, so I thanked them and hugged them.

Mum recoiled, 'Ugh, you smell like off-meat!'

Nice.

The last present I opened was from my sister. She's three years younger than me and never made the mistake of going to university. She's now Head of 'something or other' at a Publishing House in London.

I turned the tiny gadget over in my hand, confused. She'd got me a pocket organiser. I looked up at my parents, 'Does she know I work in a supermarket?'

'Maybe she thinks it'll help you manage your time more efficiently, so that you can apply for more suitable jobs'.

'I apply for jobs all the time, Mum'. I lied with such force that it actually frightened me. But I've always been defensive when it comes to my sister. Ever since she was born she has been more successful than me. It's her name, I think. Renée Quesnell deserves to be Head of 'something or other'. *Renée* would never be caught dead behind a grotty checkout. Suzie Quesnell, on the other hand, slots in to that space quite nicely.

My dad's always been a peace-keeper, so he tried to change the subject – bad idea. 'What did Nick get you then?'

'Nothing...'

I saw Mum roll her eyes and swiftly added '...yet'.

'Everything alright?' My dad peered at me from under his furrowed, grey brows.

I nodded, not wanting to lie out loud again. Dad didn't believe me though. He stood up, patted me on the shoulder and said, 'Come on, love. Let's go down the pub'.

Despite his quarter French origin, my dad is a true Lancastrian at heart. He believes there is nothing that a pie and a pint can't fix. And in that, he's right.

14th Jan

You know how checkout girls sit back to back?

Well, if you've ever been in a supermarket you do. Anyway, I'm sat back to back with one of those old lady-types. The '*I only work here because it gets me out of the house*' types. And she has extreme flatulence. They aren't even silent ones either. I've given her a few dirty looks, but it just doesn't work when you're looking at the back of the person's head.

17th Jan

Urgh! Dear Diary, I am blue (and not just because I'm wearing this ridiculous navy bubble jacket and tabard).

Nick and I have had yet another argument. I was trying to tell him about this creepy customer who gave me her money one coin at a time, when he cut me off.

'Can we not talk about Eggberts for once?'

'What's that supposed to mean?' I said.

'You never shut up about the bloody place'.

'Well, I do spend nine hours there every day'.

'Yeah, and then you spend the rest of the day talking about it'.

He went on like that, sniping at me, until he grabbed his coat and walked out. He's good at doing that.

It's so much easier for him when we fall out because he can hide away in the library and confide in *Andrea.* But what about me, where can I go?

Eggberts Supermarket.

Who can I confide in?

No one.

I thought of a very depressing fact today: I must interact with hundreds of people sat behind this till and yet, I have no one to talk to. Instead, I have to sit here smiling and reading from my memorised script, whilst the speakers in the sky play twelve songs on repeat *all* day – one of which is Dolly Parton's 9-5. If only, Dolly! Today I'm on a 12-9.

I thought the fact that it's Friday and the store is heaving would help the evening go faster, but everywhere I look I see friends giggling, chatting – I even saw a few arguing and I'm still jealous!

All of the friends I had back in Lancashire have forgotten about me, and all of the BFFs I met whilst at uni here in Leeds have buggered off back to their hometowns. Not even a glance back over their shoulder at poor old Suzie in her blue bubble jacket and tabard.

I have *tried* to make friends here.

Okay, that's a lie.

I came in like every other student: thinking I was better than everyone else and already planning my next step before I'd finished my first shift behind the till. But it's not entirely my fault that I can't fit in! As a graduate in this environment, you're *made* to feel like you don't belong. The brief conversations I have had with colleagues usually end with them saying, *'What?! You're a graduate?'*

At which point, I nod, clench, and wait for the crushing blow: *'And you work here, with me?!'* (Or the ever-devastating, 'you work here *for* me'), usually followed by such interjections as, '*Me and my brothers didn't get a GCPE between us!*' Oh dear.

Now, I know I'm not the only graduate in this position: earning minimum wage, on the same part-time contract I had when I was a student, despite working forty-five hours a week like an Iranian donkey – Hey, maybe they should have an emotional advert appeal for us, with heartbreaking music and the Rottweiler barking in our faces:

'*Your donations can stop this cruelty. Hire a graduate today...*'

This place is filled with graduates. In fact, I think the entire fresh food department is made up of qualified lawyers. But the difference between them and me is that they've given up. They *must* have. I see them hop in here every day: smiling, laughing, *interacting*. They've accepted it. They've accepted that their degree was for nothing. I am the only one that strolls in no sooner than five seconds early, with a face like a slapped arse and an attitude like...well, like I've got an attitude problem. I do this is a silent protest, and if I were allowed to wear a sandwich board, or carry a placard, it would say: I SHOULD NOT BE HERE.

I guess what I'm trying to say is, I'm pretty tired of protesting alone. It's lonely, you know?

I'd say there are three people at Eggberts who I actually have conversations with (four if you count The Rottweiler, but all she ever talks to me about is taking my nail varnish off and cleaning my till).

There's Carl (or Creepy Carl, as my wondrous imagination has dreamed up). A scrawny, sweaty, mop-headed, cheesemonger* that looks like a pubescent teenager, despite the fact he is coming up to thirty. Obviously, he is not a person that I particularly enjoy talking to. Our conversations usually go like this:

Creepy Carl: 'Hey *sniff sniff* Suzie *sniffle*, you doing anything this weekend? *sniffle sniff*' (I probably should have mentioned he sounds like Chuckie Finster).

Me: *Not giving eye contact, ever!* 'Working. Your hay fever playing up again?'

Creepy Carl: 'Oh, no *sniff sniff* this is a sinus problem. I have some nasal spray'.

I usually stay silent at this point to give him the opportunity to leave. Mostly he will, but not before uttering his famous catchphrase: 'Need a hug?'

I will *never* need a hug that bad.

When he does leave, he doesn't get further than the next till, and the next poor checkout girl. His persistently pathetic attempt at mating everyone, combined with his pasty white skin and curly hair, sort of reminds me of a Bichon Frise that seriously needs groomed, and neutered.

---

*This is actually his job role, not a pathetic attempt at an insult like the rest of the words in that sentence.

The second person is someone that I used to be very close to. Her name's Clare Connor. Clare has an arts degree, like most shop assistants in the UK.

Clare and I went to the same university, and even graduated on the same day. We were also both hired by Eggberts on the exact same day. In theory, we should be the best of friends. In fact, we were once, but I pushed her away like I did all the others when I started calling Eggberts my 'full-time' job.

Now, I've already mentioned that I disassociate myself from other graduates because of their bright acceptance of this cruel existence, but I pushed Clare away for the opposite reason.

She works on the self-scan machines, so she gets to wander about a bit, and at least twice a day she'll walk past me and ask, '*Applied for any jobs yet?*' with a kind of sickening enthusiasm that makes me want to thump her.

She's like one of those overly eager border collies that just keeps scurrying back with the ball, despite the fact that you don't want to play anymore. The worst thing about dogs (or people) like this, is that they are so harmless and happy you can't stop yourself from throwing that stupid ball.

My reply is usually, 'No, have you?'

Then I take myself off to a faraway place whilst she goes on and on about the jobs she's applied for, the interviews she's been on, the interviews she's going on, and so on. Listening to her trying so hard for over five years makes me exhausted and depressed. So I've stopped listening.

I've saved the best person 'til last, and for once, I'm not being sarcastic. Number three is Paul the Basket Guy. He's 53, as thick as an oak tree, and twice as wide. But I wouldn't change him. He is possibly the most sweet-natured human being I've ever met. Think of a bumbling St Bernard/Great Dane puppy (what a crossbreed that would be!) with thinning hair and legs it hasn't quite figured out how to use yet, and bingo: you have Paul.

My friendship with Paul began unusually early in my 'career' (God, help me) with Eggberts, when I was still a pretentious student. He would always smile, wave, and say '*Hi Suzie*' every time I walked past him, even if no longer than sixty seconds had elapsed since the last time he saw me. I always smiled back because he remembered to call me Suzie, despite the ridiculous 'Suzanne' name badge that I was, and still am, expected to wear.

I was in the canteen one day (between hangovers) eating last night's kebab, when a shadow loomed over me. Had my liver finally packed in and sent the grim reaper for me?!

No. It was just lovely, old Paul. Although, back then I didn't think he was lovely, old Paul at all. I thought he was weird and creepy, old Paul.

'Can I sit here?' He said as he sat down opposite me. He placed a plastic One Direction lunchbox on the table, opened it, and took out some carefully wrapped peanut butter sandwiches.

'Nice lunchbox', I snorted.

'Thanks!' Paul shouted and clapped his hands together clumsily. 'I just love all their songs, they're so happy...'

He continued to blab about the band, but I was too busy trying to hide my embarrassment to listen. I glanced around the room and saw a few people whispering and giggling. When I turned back to Paul he was tucking into his peanut butter butties without an air of unease. He saw me watching him and felt the need to say, 'My mum makes the best butties'.

I heard more snickering and was beginning to get the picture (or so I thought). 'Okay, who put you up to this?' I said.

Paul the Basket Guy looked truly perplexed.

I elaborated, 'I mean, why are you sitting here?'

Paul put down the crusts of his first sandwich. 'You're the only one that smiles back at me when I wave. My mum says that makes us friends'. He picked up the next sandwich and began eating.

It was then that I realised Paul was special in more ways than one, and suddenly, I didn't feel embarrassed because people were giggling at us, I felt furious. I shot a few daggers at everyone on surrounding tables, making countless enemies, but that didn't matter.

'Yeah, we're friends', I said.

20th Jan

It's 8 p.m. I've been inside the confines of Eggberts Supermarket since 11:59 a.m., and in the entirety of that time I've had two 100ml cups of water. I seriously think I'm dying.

The Rottweiler rallied us around yesterday and said one of the managers (not a department manager like her, but a real manager) has decided that we are not to drink at our tills anymore, ever. Apparently, it sickens them to see us 'swigging away' on the job.

I wouldn't really call it 'swigging away', more like keeping hydrated in order to survive but, whatever.

Obviously, the Rottweiler was greeted with outrage and protestation for telling us this, but she just shrugged: *'Don't like it, leave'*. A very typical thing for a manager in a supermarket to say, and so bloody annoying too because we're all thinking, *'If only we could leave!'* If bloody only.

We all went back to our stations and did what every normal supermarket worker does when their human rights have been violated (and it happens more than you'd think). We ignored the bitch.

The Rottweiler was crafty though. That manager must have really put his or her foot down on this one. Yesterday, the Rottweiler confiscated four bottles of water from me alone, and I'm on minimum wage; I can't afford to buy water I'm not allowed to drink.

So today I have only been allowed to drink whilst on my breaks, and I do not feel great. Having leftover pizza for my dinner couldn't have helped. I could practically feel each glass of water I drank being soaked up by the salt from my pepperoni stuffed crust.

I'm so glad I started this diary because this is exactly the kind of stuff I wanted to expose. This is a real-life problem that is happening right now in a first world country!

It's getting ridiculous. Every time I breathe in, the dusty air-con air is adding another layer of dryness to my throat.

21st Jan

So, I fainted yesterday.

Thank God I shoved my diary in my inside pocket. No one from Eggberts seems to have read it. But I think the nurses have had a little read, they keep smirking at me.

I'm in hospital. I've been here since last night. I fainted thirteen minutes before my shift was over, would you bloody believe it?! If I'd known I was going to faint I would have done it as soon as I walked through the door. Anyway, it's done now, and at least I've had today off, and I'm not at death's door anymore.

When I woke up, I was in a hospital bed, with a doctor on one side and Nick on the other. The doctor said my dehydration was close to being fatal, but I'd be alright after a few hours on a drip.

Nick stayed with me all day. In fact, he's only just left my bedside so he can get me some chocolate. It's the longest amount of time we've spent together since, well, I can't even remember. But at least he spent today with me. He looked dead concerned, bless him.

After he'd apologised, like, a million times, for being a neglectful boyfriend, we watched *Babe: Pig in the City* on my tiny hospital TV. I fell asleep halfway through the film, but he was still there when I woke up, holding my hand. He told me that Creepy Carl had been to visit whilst I was asleep – I don't know whether that's a blessing or not. He left some cheese that I gave to the German woman in the bed next to me. She can't speak English, but she seems to really love cheese.

Clare also came to visit. My back tensed up as she walked through the door. I was just so sure she was going to skip over to me and say in her sing-song voice, 'Applied for any jobs yet?'

But instead, she just sat next to my bed quietly. She stayed for an hour or so, and brought flowers – they were from the reduced section, but still.

When Clare arrived, Nick left to get some dinner and call my parents. So we got a chance to chat like we used to, when we were on the cusp of becoming good friends.

She told me that the Rottweiler's face looks permanently sunburned from her embarrassing telling off from the doctor - even if it's not her fault I'm hospitalised, she's a jobsworth and deserves it all the same - and now, not only are we allowed to drink water at the checkouts, but it is to be provided to us. A nice cold bottle every four hours to prevent this from happening again!

Wow. I feel like I've started a revolution. '*Poor people gonna' rise up, and get their share...*'

23rd Jan

Back to work and back to my twisted version of reality. I have received no apology about what happened to me, only annoyed grunts from various members of management that now have the terribly difficult chore of making sure their staff are hydrated.

I'm actually glad to be back – *Did I really just say that?!*

Nick and I had been kind of falling over each other. It was nice to spend some quality time together, but it started to feel forced very quickly. As soon as we arrived home from the hospital, I could tell that he had somewhere to be, some work to do. He was dying for me to dismiss him, but I couldn't. He is my boyfriend and he needs to start acting like it. So, I made us sit in awkward silence whilst we watched game shows and tried to think of things to say to one another. Not exactly how you would expect an evening with your boyfriend to be.

It's strange. Like, I've spent over four years in a relationship with this man – or boy, whatever, and every night we sleep next to each other, our skin touching, but that's all I see of him. I know he's studying really hard for his PhD, but he must have some spare time. He *must* have. And the sad reality is, he doesn't want to spend it with me.

28th Jan

Woohoo! Pay day! Finally a happy day where I won't moan at all, right? I wish!

Ever open your wage-slip and think, '*What the f#@k?*' If you answered yes to this question I will assume that you have worked in a supermarket at one point or another.

I started this diary on New Year's Day. I *worked* on New Year's Day - a public holiday! When it emerged (about two days beforehand) that the store would be open on New Year's Day, management assured us that working was a voluntary option (lie number one).

When no one volunteered, they soon changed their tune. I was one of the unlucky people that was forced to work. In return, I was told I would get an extra paid day off in January (lie number two).

So, whilst I loathed New Year's Day, I was happy when the time came for my extra paid holiday. Why then, does my wage slip today state: 'Two hours holiday – £12.64'? And that's before tax!

I stormed into the personnel office this morning and could see I wasn't the only one kicking up a fuss. There were so many people in there that the personnel manager closed the door and called it an 'emergency meeting'.

He so *kindly* explained to us that in the small print of our employee handbooks it states that when a member of staff gains an extra holiday from the company, the pay obtained is a fifth of their contracted hours. My contract, although I've worked full-time for over five years, is one of the lowest at ten hours.

So, I was *forced* to take a day off for £12 instead of working and earning around £50, just so Mr Eggbert could sleep easy about having his stores open on New Year's Day! I spent more than that on my bloody day off!

My colleagues and I have once again become victims to the many loopholes in the system. I bumped into poor, old, Paul the Basket Guy on my way out of the office. He was grinning as usual and telling me it's better than nothing. Sometimes I envy that dumb bastard.

***

As if I wasn't in a foul enough mood already today, Creepy Carl has been hovering around me like a fly around sticky toffee pudding. He tends to be more persistent when the Valentine's Day stock gets put on the shelves.

‘Suzie Q, why so blue?’ He giggled to himself at his unbelievably clever poem.

I was serving a customer so I had to play nice, and he knew it. ‘You’re a poet, and you didn’t even know it’, I said with absolutely no enthusiasm.

He laughed until snot ran out of his shiny, swollen, snout. He swiped at it with his shirt sleeve.

I smiled until the customer was out of earshot and then I said, ‘Look, get lost Cree--Carl, I’m not in the mood’.

It’s not the first time I’ve snapped at him. He’s practically immune to my scoldings now. Like any training technique that is overused, snapping at him has become ineffective.

‘Well, why don’t you let me know when you are in the mood and I’ll come straight back, sugar’.

Sugar? Who says things like that?!

Another customer started loading her shopping on my conveyor belt and there was a frying pan within reach. It was about time I changed tactics and showed him who the Pack Leader was. But, luckily for him, the Rottweiler came over, ‘Stop flirting you two’.

I rolled my eyes whilst he ran back to his stupid cheese counter, giggling his stupid schoolgirl laugh.

February

1st Feb

I'm in the mood for secret spilling. Well, not really. I'm just in the mood to finish this last twenty minutes of my shift as quickly as possible; and writing passes the time much faster than staring into space worrying about whether my relationship has a future.

So, *secret alert* did you know that supermarkets are incredibly dirty?

Yes, you probably did. But I can't think of anything else to keep me occupied for the next nineteen minutes, so I'll tell you anyway.

I'll start with the floor. Everyone expects that to be dirty anyway, right? Hundreds of shoes walking around on it all day and night: shoes from muddy fields, shoes that have splashed in dirty puddles, shoes with vomit on them – all kinds of dirt. And it's not just shoes: prams, the paws of guide dogs, and don't even get me started on the trolley wheels!

Think about all of those germs multiplying the next time you bend down to pick up a rogue pepper, or let your child practise crawling down the health and beauty aisle – supermarkets are death traps.

Let me think now, what else is dirty?

The toilets of course, but that's obvious to anyone who has been unfortunate enough to use them.

The conveyor belts and self-scan machines only get cleaned around once a week, and even then it's poorly done. They probably have about the same amount of germs on them as a thirty year old penny, leading me on to the next problem: money.

Money is everywhere in a supermarket, and it is touched by everyone. My face is practically covered in spots because

I'm not allowed to leave my till to wash my hands, nor do I have the time to squirt a dollop of hand sanitizer on them before another customer comes along huffing and puffing. So if I have an itchy nose, I have to scratch it with three decades worth of germs under my nails. Lovely!

Next up are the food preparation departments: the butchery, the cafe, and the bakery. Obviously, there are more departments that prepare food than this, but these three are by far the dirtiest. Don't tell me you trusted them all to be clean?!

The butchery is full of those lazy, middle-aged men that let the others in their age group down. The kind that don't know how to turn on the washing machine, or how to cook a steak (*irony*), or that need their wives to tell them to keep their finger out of their nose. Unfortunately for our customers, their wives aren't around when they are preparing the meat.

The cafe has a similar hygiene problem, but the department is mainly made up of women. Overweight, middle-aged women with various levels of alcohol dependency. They also have a varied range of habits: There's a nose picker in there too, a girl who likes to give her flaky scalp a good scratch, and an old lady who licks her fingers after every sausage butty she makes.

However, the bakery is the most disappointing for me – possibly because of my infatuation with tiger bread. Unfortunately, I can't eat tiger bread anymore. I swore off it completely after seeing the bakery manager use his '*meat and two veg*' as a way to warm up his hands before kneading the dough.

Well, I think that's enough horror stories for one day. I hope you weren't eating whilst reading. If you were, I assume you've stopped either one or the other by now.

5th Feb

I have good news and bad news.

The good news is that I got to finish work two hours early yesterday, something about trying to cut back on shifts because of all the extra money they spent working us like dogs over Christmas. Imagine how skint they'd be if they actually paid us proper benefits like other companies?

Anyway, the bad news is that when I arrived home, I saw Nick and Andrea entwined on the sofa playing what my mum calls 'tonsil tennis'.

It was Andrea that spotted me first. They stopped kissing as Nick began to unbutton her jeans, and she saw me as she rested her head on his naked shoulder. She let out a scream and then covered her silky, purple bra with her hands. All of my bras are cotton white, or grey from wear and tear, and I could tell that hers cost more than all of mine put together. Just like that, I was the one that felt self-conscious.

'What the hell are you doing here?' She hissed at me as she put her jumper back on.

Nick just stared at me, and then back at Andrea, his face blank with shock.

The rage that I usually reserve for Eggberts found a voice, 'I fucking live here'.

Andrea has only seen me a handful of times, and she's never seen me in full-blown checkout girl mode*. She was scared and I knew it. It was surreal to suddenly find triumph in a situation as dire as that, but somehow I managed it.

Andrea gave Nick a rage-filled look and exhaled sharply. She started putting her boots on, 'My God, Nick. Grow a backbone!'

As she stormed out, Nick finally managed to speak, but instead of saying my name he muttered, 'Andrea'.

---

* My checkout girl mode, in case you haven't noticed, is 'I hate the world and everything in it!'

She turned before leaving, 'Choose, Nick. Is it that difficult?'

There was a pause in which I wasn't sure what was happening. I was happy to see Andrea in such a state: shocked, angry, and spitting out words. She's not the beautiful, majestic creature she would have all other women believe, she's just like the rest of us.

When Nick didn't 'choose' she let out another haggard exhale and stormed out of the house. Nick retreated to our bedroom (*his bedroom?*) and I was left with the rest of the house. I kept waiting for him to come down and apologise. I even played with the fact of running upstairs stark naked and trying to reignite our relationship. But, after seeing him with Andrea, I wasn't in the mood.

I wasn't angry at him at all. I knew I was expected to be though - at least that's what rom-coms have taught me. But, my instinct told me to just let him be. I slept on the sofa in my work uniform, so I didn't need to bother him.

I suppose the real reason I didn't bother him is because I wanted to look like the sane option. Long-term girlfriend who doesn't shout at you and give you ultimatums, or new slut that does?

I know, I'm pathetic. But without him, what else do I have to show for these past few years?

Oh, bloody hell! If those bra burning women could see me now I'd be in for a slap.

7th Feb

Dumped. Dumped. Dumped. Dumped. I've been dumped by someone younger, smarter, more ambitious...Oh God, kill me. Kill me, kill me, kill me; or fix me.

Well a few minutes have passed, I've served fourteen customers, and no lightning bolt has come down to electrocute me to death. No thief has come and threatened to stab me for the till drawer, and believe me, at this moment in time I'd let him. Wouldn't that be a story for the papers?! *'Noble Checkout Girl dies protecting cash drawer...'* Nope, her life was just so miserable that she chose the easy escape.

But, seeing as nothing has killed me perhaps God wants to fix me after all.

Oh great, the Rottweiler is making a bee-line for me. Well, who knows, maybe she is doing God's bidding. Maybe she's on her way over here to tell me that I'm going to leave this life behind to become rich and famous on a brand new TV show: *The only way is Eggberts.*

***

God's bidding? Yeah right, that mutt has devil written all over her. I'm currently sat in the canteen trying to control my sobbing.

The Rottweiler came over to inform me that I'd short changed my last three customers. She tried to find out what was the matter, but the nosey cow got nothing out of me. Then, she sent me around to clean the empty tills, an even more thankless job than my current position. But to be honest, I was quite enjoying the change. Keeping busy stopped me from evaluating the broken shards of glass that are my life. But then *he* came along.

Grrr! I could rip all of the pubescent hairs out of his exceptionally flat scalp! I am referring of course, to none other than Creepy, desperate, nasal, (*word for someone who makes your skin crawl*) Carl.

I was just minding my own business, trying to lift a thirty year old milk stain from a conveyor belt, when I felt a cold touch on my shoulder. I jumped, turned, and there he was in all his runny-nosed non-glory.

I think I muttered something like, 'What do you want?' as I turned back to my cleaning. I sprayed much more of

Eggberts' Sparkle Spray than I needed to because his aroma of blue cheese and desperation was making me want to retch.

'Just checking in on Suzie-Q. How are you?'

Now, I don't know if I've mentioned this already, but I *detest* being called Suzie-Q, and with the foul mood I was in, I was in no position to hide my feelings – they had come too close to the surface.

'I'm fucking fine', I said, scrubbing harder than ever. Miraculously, the milk stain was starting to disappear. But unfortunately, I didn't stick around to finish the job.

Sniff sniff 'You need a hug?'

Things became a little fuzzy after that, but I remember that time seemed to stand still as I thought of all the reasons why I needed a hug now more than I ever had done. When I came back to reality, I was crying and screaming abuse into Creepy Carl's face which was dripping with Eggberts' Sparkle Spray. That's when the Rottweiler practically man-handled me into the canteen and told me to calm down. So here I am, calming.

Oh Lord, Creepy Carl just walked in. Heart-rate back up to 200 bpm. I swear, if he manages to leave this canteen without my fist imprint on his face then miracles do happen.

12:30 p.m.

Miracles don't happen, and I've been sent 'home' for the day. Of course, if I do go 'home' I'll probably bump into Nick and his new beau, finishing what they started on the sofa the other day. So now I have to move out and I have no money to do so. *Great.* That's just one more thing for me to think about.

But I've put off thinking for the time-being. Instead, I'm sat alone in McDonalds eating a Happy Meal and trying not to cry. Oh irony, how I loathe you.

7:00 p.m.

This feels like the longest day in history, but at least the tables have turned for me. I'm just having one last drink at 'home' before Clare and some other girls from work pick me up in a taxi. We're going clubbing. Me, clubbing! And with fellow checkout girls too! My tables really have gone full circle.

Clare and her friends came into McDonalds on their lunch hour and inevitably saw me sobbing into my McChicken nuggets. In seconds they surrounded me with girly talk like:

'You're too good for him'

'He'll come crawling back'

'Treat 'em mean, keep 'em keen' – I didn't really understand the relevance of this one, but I said thanks all the same.

Clare's suggestion of a night out appeared to be the perfect solution for three reasons:

1. I could dress up and make Nick jealous
2. I could dance off the fat and chemicals I'd just consumed
3. I could drink my troubles away.

I looked at Clare who, in spite of everything, has actually been a consistent friend to me throughout the years. I threw down my empty McFlurry pot and said, 'I'm in'.

I scuttled back to my shared 'home', thankful that no one was there, and I've been drinking, getting ready, and hiding in the bathroom ever since. Ooh, that's a taxi I hear! Bye bye Diary, don't wait up. Xxx

??? a.m.

I don't... I mean...What? Oh, life is just...Shit, work in morning, orlate shift? Sick.

8th Feb

Well, it's safe to say last night is a total blur. My head is banging with every beep the till makes. Yes, I'm back behind the till and nothing has been said about my incidents the day before, or the fact that I reek of vodka. That's the good thing about supermarkets, they can't be arsed hiring more people so they just let things slide.

You hit a member of staff in the face? Who cares?!

Your vodka breath knocked out a little child? Fine by us!

As I was saying, my memories from last night are very foggy. But one of them is distinctly vivid, just like the worst one always is.

I remember being in a club and looking around – everyone, and I mean everyone, except me, Clare, and her friends, was younger than twenty. I felt grubby even dancing among them. Naturally, I thought more alcohol would cure this feeling. But of course, alcohol never cures, it only numbs. So every now and then some other baby-faced, bright eyed kid would catch my eye and I'd feel all kinds of horrible things: guilt, disappointment, anger, jealousy. But I just kept drinking my feelings away, and then The Rembrandts came on singing their only song and I couldn't take it anymore. I just ran from the place, and kept on running until I was sat on the ground in a back alley and Clare was standing over me.

I was sobbing loudly and I felt like I had to justify myself, so I slurred, 'I don't want this. I don't want my life to be like the F.R.I.E.N.D.S. theme tune!'

Clare crept up beside me then and put her arm around me. It felt nice, reassuring, until she opened her mouth, '*So no one told you life was gonna be this way. You're job's a joke, you're broke, your love-life's...*'

And that is when it finally defeated me. With those few lines, all of the unhappiness and failure I'd felt for years came pouring out of me in vodka induced gasps. I mean, I was *balling*. I think it knocked Clare for six. I remember her patting my back and repeating 'Oh no, oh no' over and over again. I'd always been so happy at uni, when she'd known me. When I was friendly. When I had purpose.

I calmed down eventually and then she whispered, '*I'll be there for you, when the rain starts to pour. I'll be there for you, like I've been there before'*.

I looked up at her and started crying all over again. Clare joined in that time. It was like something from a cheesy, straight-to-DVD movie. My cheeks are burning just thinking about it.

However, (if she can ever make eye contact with me again) it's safe to say I've made a best friend, and that's a lot more than I had yesterday. Things will get better.

12th Feb

Thankfully, I haven't seen Nick since he dumped me for Dr. Whore, not that I saw him much before that. In fact, I've spent most of my time at bloody work. I did a fourteen hour shift yesterday, and I'm doing one today and tomorrow, too. I'm not sure if that's legal, but I'll be happy when I get paid.

***

I'm twelve hours, sixty seven minutes into my shift, and I don't know if it's the tiredness talking, or if they've been spraying something wacky into the aircon, but I just had a thought so outrageous it might be true. And now I'm scared.

I think Eggberts Supermarket might be hell. Not, *'I don't like it here, it's hell on earth',* but quite literally, hell. Like, real hell.

I read a Stephen King book recently (yeah, checkout girls read too you know), well it wasn't a book, more of a short story (I said we read, I didn't say we excel ourselves). It was called: *'That feeling, you can only say what it is in French'*.

I was probably attracted to it because of my French roots, and obviously, just by reading the title, I knew the story was about *Dave-Jar-View*.

It's a good book, I'd recommend it. It's about a woman that is in her own version of hell, which is the constant repetition of a horrible moment in her life.

Sometimes I look around and get a chill: same songs, same customers with the same questions, same jokes. Just:

Beep beep

'Do you want help packing?'

Beep beep

'Nice weather'.

Beep beep

'Thank you, bye'.

Beep beep

'Please place the item in the bagging area'.

Beep beep.

Hell.

13th Feb

I've packed up my things and moved on with my life.

It turns out Clare wasn't as disgusted in my crying outburst as I thought, and we have become a lot closer in the past week. I realise that we could have always been this way if I'd only been a bit kinder, or more approachable. But enough about the past, in fact, fuck the past! I'm done with it. I've moved out, and now I'm going to get a new job and be a successful, independent woman that never cries or moans, or has to eat microwave noodles for breakfast, dinner, and tea because she has no money.

It's actually Clare that I've moved in with, can you believe it? She's been an absolute Godsend. Of course, I still have my doubts about her. She hasn't asked me her infamous question in a while because of all my other troubles, but I hear her asking other graduates all the time.

'*Applied for any jobs yet?*'

I also see their reactions, they mirror my own – a slight rolling of the eyes, a shake of the head, and a sarcastic smile.

There's no denying she's annoying, but she's a nice annoying, like, you know she would never kill you in the night. And beggars can't be choosers.

Clare's flat, or I guess I should now be saying *my* flat, is not as disgustingly plain as I thought it would be. In fact, it's gorgeous – especially for the money.

A simple front room with large windows that allow the sun to gleam on everything, although, there's not much to gleam on: a small, lime green leather sofa, a coffee table, and a couple of beanbags. The kitchen is tiny, but the worktops have that black, glittery effect that's really fashionable at the minute. Both bedrooms are decorated the same: sky blue walls and white decor. Everything is *so* bloody vintage! My room has one of those dainty birdcages on a stand, and Clare's has one of those plush decorative mannequins. I wanted to sell them for extra cash, but Clare said the landlord wouldn't like it.

So yeah, everything is pretty lovely. There's not a PlayStation controller in sight.

I've got the kind of butterflies you get on the first evening of uni, when you realise that you are actually alone.

This is my space, and this is my fresh start. It will be a fresh start won't it?

Only time will tell...

14th Feb

Woke up at 10 a.m. to the smell of buttery crumpets. Before I fully switched on, I thought Nick was surprising me to a Valentine's Day breakfast, and then I remembered I have no Nick, and no Valentine. Oh well, at least I have breakfast.

Turns out me and Clare both have the day off today*, and my new roomie made breakfast to celebrate. But, that's not all she planned for us today...

'Okay', Clare began. She starts a lot of sentences like that. 'Okay, I've planned it out perfectly...'

'Should I get my pocket organiser?' I said, but Clare decided we don't need my gadget with a shake of her head. I haven't used it once yet.

'...all we're going to do is spend the morning writing your CV, and maybe tweaking mine a bit. Then we'll treat ourselves to a nice dinner.

'After that, we'll spend the rest of the day sending our CVs to job adverts. When we've applied to twenty, we can go out for a meal and some drinks. Okay, so it's like chore, treat, chore, treat'.

Now, up until that moment I have to say I was thinking I had made a big mistake moving in with irritatingly organised, *'Applied for any jobs yet?',* Clare. But what a perfect plan: chore, treat, chore, treat!

'Brilliant!' I told her. 'Just one problem; I've only got £7.94 in my bank account'.

I felt guilty until Clare admitted she only has minus-£10 in hers.

'We'll cross that bridge when we come to it', she said.

***

Today was the most productive day I've had all year, or even in this decade! I've applied for 24 jobs! I feel brilliant, and

---

* Let's just take a moment to celebrate the odds of this happening. If the odds of winning the Lotto are 1 in 14 million, then this is 1 in 14 billion!

I've not even had a drop to drink! Mind you, it has been a long, HARD day. This was my first attempt at a CV:

CV Writing for ~~The Damned~~ Checkout Girls

Education: Instead of boring you with letters and numbers, let's just say I'm exceptionally over-qualified.

Work Experience: Checkout girl from 06/08 – eternity.

Skills:
Smiling at people I want to kill
Handling more cash all day than I'll earn all month
Sitting (for long periods)
Being able to differentiate between twenty-five different varieties of apples
Watching AB FAB re-runs in my head
Exceptional at making small talk about the weather

Personal interests:
Crying myself to sleep over my wasted degree
Daydreaming about what life would be like if I was *insert useless z-lister celeb here*
Drinking enough alcohol to numb all nerve-endings
Listening to my mother lecturing me about failure

Referees:
The Rottweiler.

Seriously. We spent a lot of time brainstorming, and relying on Clare's massive imagination that got her that pretty, little performing arts degree before we could come up with an acceptable CV. By the time we had done that it was like 3 p.m., so it was strawberry ice cream and cola bottle sweets for dinner.

After that, it was time to look for jobs on the old interweb. I was so shocked at what we found! People kept on whinging about the recession, so I just assumed that getting a job was next to impossible, but when I typed in 'Animal jobs' the search showed 1,469! My jaw nearly fell off.

Of course, I was only qualified for like 30 of them, and some of them were in pretty sad places, I mean, Burnley? No thanks.

By around 7ish, I'd applied for 19 jobs that I am defo qualified for and 5 that I'm not - but you never know!

You should have seen the salaries for some of them: £30,000+. My heart is racing at the thought! It would literally be like winning the lottery, except, well, I'd be working for the money.

Ah, going to bed happy for once! Pure bliss!

P.s. I'm sleeping with my fingers crossed!

15th Feb

Far too many men have come in today buying the reduced Valentine's Day items. They all look so shameful too. The way I see it, at least their girlfriends are getting something – whether it's a day late or not – they should be thankful.

Wow. It's not like me to go on about 'thankfulness'. I must be desperate.

20th Feb

The productiveness of our day off has had me and Clare floating through work this week. I think my blood pressure may actually be back to the normal level, no palpitations or anything!

The Rottweiler doesn't share my newfound zest for life. In fact, I think she's doing her best to break me. She's had me cleaning everything this week. I'm just back from scrubbing a questionable stain from underneath one of the customer loos. And you thought checkout girls just sit on their arse and daydream all day – how naive.

However, now I'm back on my till I guess there's nothing left to do but daydream! There's one job in particular that I really hope I get. It's in London, so I'd be close to my sister, or at least I think I would. I've never been to London so I don't know how big it is, can't be too big though, can it?

The job pays a whopping £28,000 plus benefits! The benefits could list working in the nude and I'd still love it. I'm not really sure what the ins and outs of the job are though, typical dog training job, I suppose.

Clare keeps taking our phones to the loo. She's got more leeway about wandering off because she works on self-scan. She can grab someone on the way past, tell them to cover for her and she becomes a free-range chicken. But me, I'm just a full on battery hen.

She's been checking our emails for replies from employers. So far, we've only had 5 responses between us – all rejections. According to Clare that's a good turnout, she says most companies don't even bother to reply! I'm optimistic though, we've applied for loads of jobs, so we're bound to get one eventually. It's just a matter of time. The bad thing is we work in a place where time stands still.

24th Feb

Don't get too excited, Diary, no word on the job front yet, this entry is purely a RANT!!!

I hate customers, in case you didn't already know. Now, they aren't the worst part of the job, but they certainly don't make it any easier.

Let's compare working at Eggberts to being abandoned in a scorching desert. So if you can imagine that unbearable heat, unquenchable thirst (the water every four hours policy has gone out the window), and that feeling of no escape, you'll know exactly what I'm talking about. Now, let's say lots of flies start buzzing around you, maybe even biting you, irritating an already awful situation. Customers are these flies.

I'd say on an average day around eighty percent of customers don't even know I exist. They just pack their shopping, pay their bill, and dart out. The image of my face has already faded by the time they reach their car. And I'm fine with that. It's the other twenty percent: the rude, lonely, 'witty', obnoxious (or whatever else their problem is) customers that get on my wick!

There are so many problem customers that I'm going to have to document this in list format.

Oh, and if you read any of these and think, '*Ha! I do that!*' Go to hell.

First up, we have the customers who spot Uncle Derek down an aisle and wander off in the middle of the transaction to go and play catch up on the last ten years. Leaving me with their unpaid for, unpacked shopping, and a queue full of angry customers. Yes, it gets awkward. Verdict: **RUDE**

Then there are the customers that rip something whilst packing, or put two of the same item in the trolley, and hand said item to me saying, 'I don't want this'.

I, in turn, end up with a Jenga tower of crap in my already suffocating work space. Great! Verdict: **RUDER**

And of course, there are those customers that think queues do not apply to them. Verdict: **RUDEST**

Rudeness brings us across to awkwardness, and up there with the best are the customers that decide they want to pay separately seconds before the end of a transaction:

'Uh, so, there are six of us and we spent £60. Should we split it?'

'Yeah, but how?'

'I've got £7.01 in cash'.

'And I have £13.49 left on this card and a couple of pennies in my back pocket...'

Verdict: **IDIOTS**

Then there are the customers that tell you to look in 'the back' when a product they want is not on the shelf.

Did someone start a rumour about the back being this magical place where everything your heart desires grows from the ground? Because I'm continuously asked to go and look in there when I know that the only products in the back are shrink-wrapped to an eight foot tall pallet, and there's no way of opening them up just to get one product out for one customer. I normally just wander in there, count to twenty, and then come back out shaking my head. Usually, customers decide to have some sort of stare-off with me at this point, as if an intimidating glance can make the six pack of Mini Cheddars they so desperately desire suddenly appear.

Verdict: **MISGUIDED WEIRDOS**

And finally, awkwardness brings us on to *Kelis* screaming: '*I hate you so much right now*!' The following interjections have been said by real individuals on more than one occasion (I've also included what I reply to them in my head, just for shits and giggles, and to pass this final half hour of my shift):

- 'Do you take cash?' *Har har. My fake laugh is now so realistic and more frequently used than my normal laugh that I fear it has replaced it.*
- 'You look bored'. *Actually I was just taking a break from three non-stop hours of BEEP.BEEP.BEEP. But sure, bring your bulging trolley over here.*
- 'Do you work here?' *No, I just look hot in a tabard.*
- 'I just made that fresh this morning'. *Sir, if you had the ability to make fifty pound notes, I don't believe you would smell the way you do.*
- 'Oh 1066, that was a fine year'. *I said ten POUNDS sixty six, but thanks for letting me know you're the world's oldest prat.*
- 'Smile love, it might never happen'. *It already has, Jackass!*

27th Feb

It has been a hard, hard day. My legs are aching, and I think I have pneumonia. It's only 7 p.m. and I'm tucked up in bed with a hot water bottle under my knees.

I don't know how Clare manages on that self-scan till all day. There's nothing to even lean against, let alone a place to sit down. Plus, the constant draft from the entrance doors has had my nose running all day.

The Rottweiler put me on there today, seeing as Clare is off on a day trip with her mum. Now, I've never previously worked on the self-scan machines before, but I wasn't offered any training, why would I be? Wouldn't want to waste a manager's precious time now, would we?

Turns out, they're not the hardest things to navigate anyway. In fact, self-scan wouldn't be that bad at all, if it weren't for the bloody customers! Six of them at one time. I'm used to serving just one at a time, and they are used to having the full attention of a checkout girl, and let me tell you, they're not shy about showing it. A click of the fingers here, an '*Oi Love*!' there, someone even nudged me in the back to get my attention. Actual physical contact! Do you want to know what his big emergency was? He wanted *me* to scan his shopping through and place it in the bags. Yes, he did know that he was on *self*-scan, he was just too rude and bone-idle to care.

As if six customers mithering me wasn't enough, I had to deal we that posh, polite, bitch of a voice in my ear *all* day:

'Please place the item in the bagging area'.

'Insert cash or touch 'Pay with Card'.

'Unexpected item in bagging area, remove this item before continuing'.

Just so you can further empathise with my situation: the item was in the bagging area, the customer was inserting cash, and the item wasn't unexpected, and it had already been removed!!!

At least I can be happy that after a long, hard shift at work I'm not coming home to her. Can you imagine hearing that voice all night?!

'Please place your dishes in the sink'.

'Insert your keys into the door, or ring the doorbell'.

'Unexpected item in toilet, remove this item before continuing'.

Even when the self-scan machines were empty I couldn't get a moment's peace. Whenever I had a gap in customers, Creepy Carl was there with his usual overwhelming, rotting cheese smell and nasal catchphrase, *'Need a hug?'*

At one point during the day he actually did hug me! I didn't realise how vulnerable being out in the open was. My ice-cold skin is still crawling.

I was so traumatised that when Paul came past and accidentally wheeled the baskets into me, I leapt three feet into the air.

That was the only positive about being on self-scan, Paul would come by every half hour or so to collect the baskets and we could have a little chat. He updated me on his upcoming doctor's appointments, and what he bought his mum for her birthday, and how when they reduce the Teenage Mutant Ninja Turtle lamps on the home and leisure dept. he's going to buy two for his bedroom.

But Paul's visits were not enough to make self-scan an enjoyable experience. I used to envy Clare with her freedom to walk about the store and chat with other colleagues, but the reality is that you are confined to a 12x12 square, and colleagues only come by to pester you (well, most of them do). I'll never take my little pen of a checkout for granted again. Until about ten minutes into my shift tomorrow.

March

3rd Mar

Oh shit! Shit on a brick! Shit on it! Shit on it! Bloody shit!

Well, shit. Me and Clare have hit a brick wall. Can you guess what's smeared all over it?!

We were so optimistic. February practically flew by due to our massive optimism and our even bigger denial.

Clare took our phones to the loo this morning, and when she came back I could tell by her expression that something had happened. She couldn't get over to my till, and all sorts of possibilities began to run through my mind:

a) She's got an interview and doesn't know how to break the news to me
b) I've got an interview and she's gutted
c) She's dropped my phone down the toilet.

Twenty minutes passed – a lifetime when you're on a till, and even longer when your friend is keeping a secret from you. Clare stopped trying to make eye contact with me, until the Rottweiler told her to go for her break. Then, she stared at me for a few seconds – that haunted expression still etched upon her face – and she headed for the canteen. She wanted me to follow her. I just had to find a way. Instinctively, I flashed my light and started bouncing around on my chair. The Rottweiler came eventually, dragging her big paws behind her.

'What?' She grunted.

'I'm bursting for a wee'.

'Nice try, Suzanne'. She obviously saw Clare's 'follow me' look too, my wee routine usually works.

'It's fucking Suzie!' I shouted in my head as she wandered back to her little podium of authority.

‘You gonna take my money, or what?’ A huffy, stay-at-home mum with five kids swarming around her was holding out a crumpled, not to mention sticky, tenner to pay for the nappies I’d just scanned.

I took the money, and on turning back towards the till drawer I saw my plan B, a sign that said five magical words: This till is now closing. I passed it to the last customer in my queue and started to scan everything as quickly as I could. But, not even thirty seconds had passed when a dark cloud arrived at my till, and it smelled like wet dog.

‘Don’t push it, Suzie’, the Rottweiler said as she took the sign from me.

I smiled innocently; at least she’d got my name right.

I glanced at the time, fifteen minutes had passed. What a bloody joke! Why does time only fly when it’s not convenient?

Clare was on a thirty minute break, so I had no time to spare. I looked at the shopping on the belt and spotted exactly what I was after. I put the first of the items through, made pleasant conversation; I practically acted like one of those jobsworths from the training videos. Then I grabbed the bottle of red wine and said, ‘I’ve never seen snow in March before’. When the customer turned to look out of the window I did what any self-respecting person would do, I smashed the wine bottle on the till, making sure I got as much red on me as possible.

‘Oh sugar’ I said, as though it wouldn’t melt in my mouth.

‘Oh dear. Are you alright, love?’ The customer’s concern almost made me feel bad. Almost.

‘I’m fine. There’s no glass on me’, I replied. Then I flashed my light again.

The Rottweiler came over, using all her might to keep from swearing. ‘Get cleaned up and then come straight back’. The deadpan tone of her voice was actually quite frightening.

I scurried through the aisles and ran straight into the staff canteen. Everyone looked up, seeing the panic on my face and the red on my shirt. 'Oh, it's not blood, just wine', I shouted and sat opposite Clare. She was alone; a rarity for her, and her face was still as gloomy.

'What is it? I don't have long'.

She passed me my phone, 'Okay, you got an email, and it said...'

She stopped talking as I began reading it myself:

'Dear Miss Quesnell,

Thank you for your interest in this position. However, without the attachment of a cover letter we cannot consider you for this role.

With respect, I add that most employers will decline an application without the presence of a worthy covering letter. I hope this helps you in your future ventures...'

I didn't read the rest. 'What the bloody hell is a covering letter?'

Clare shrugged.

'So we've wasted all that time applying for jobs we have no chance of getting?'

'Yes. It's alright for you, you only wasted one day. I've been doing this for more than half a decade'. Clare sipped the water she'd got from the vending machine and looked down at a stain on the table. I didn't like it. It was my job to be depressed about everything, and her job to be annoyingly upbeat. I reached my arm out to comfort her, but before I made contact I heard a bellowing noise from behind me.

'Suzie Quesnell!'

Safe to say that everyone stopped eating their dinners to gawk at the Rottweiler dragging me to the personnel office.

It's also safe to say that my face went as red as the wine on my collar.

I'm reciting all of this to you from the comfort of my bed. It's been such a long day. I was made to work the rest of my shift with the red wine stuck to me. I also wasn't allowed a break, because apparently I'd taken the 'unwanted innovative to create my own break time as I saw fit'. *Whatever.*

So, for three hours straight I had to listen to every single customer's unoriginal red wine joke:

'Should I call an ambulance?'

'It's meant to go in your mouth, love'

Or the most popular, '*You've got red on you'*. Yes, we've all seen Shaun of the Dead. Bravo.

Clare's been quiet for the rest of the day, but coincidentally, we're both off again tomorrow, so I'm going to try and do what she did for me last month. I might even get up early and make crumpets. We'll relive our day of productivity, except this time we will actually be productive, by writing cover letters, or covering letters, whatever they are.

4th Mar

Would you believe the cheek of it?!

I got up super-early this morning, (well, 09:30) made crumpets and coffees, and I even stretched to putting a few biscuits out. But when I went to knock on Clare's bedroom door she came out in FULL uniform.

'What the bloody hell are you doing?' I said to her.

'Oh, and "Good Morning" to you too', she glided past me, buttoning the left side of her tabard. At least she was back in her annoyingly happy mood.

She started eating the crumpets. I sat down opposite her. 'It's your day off. You've not lost the plot have you?'

‘Okay, I told Angie that I’d cover for her. It’s her kid brother’s birthday or something’.

‘But I had an entire productive day planned. We were going to write cover letters’.

‘Oh, I suppose we do need to make a start on that. Well, I’m only working until half four, so we can do it later if you want?’

‘Yeah, I suppose’, I said, even though I doubted she’d have the energy to do anything productive after work, I never do.

Clare stood up to leave, ‘You can get a head start. Find out what the bastard things are’.

I’m pretty sure it was the first time Clare had ever sworn in her life, it suited her. ‘Right, I’ll do that’, I said, with all the best intentions.

4 p.m.

Do you know how distracting the internet is? Bloody very!

As soon as Clare left today I sat in front of my laptop and typed ‘Cover Letters’ into a search engine. But, an ad popped up on the side of the screen for bicycle covers. I don’t need a bike cover, on account of I don’t have a bike, but I did like the leggings that the girl was wearing in the ad, so I clicked it.

Five hours later and here I am. I’m none the wiser about cover letters, but I have watched two hours worth of prank videos, read several articles on celeb breakdowns, and looked through all 158 photos from one of my old friend’s trips to Ibiza.

My eyes are stinging, but I need to research cover letters before Clare gets home. Her happy-go-lucky attitude is annoying, yes, but her silent sadness is even worse, so I can’t let her down.

Panic over. It's only taken me 10 minutes, and I now know exactly what they are! Cover letters are letters about the qualities and strengths that you believe make you better suited to a job than other applicants. It sounds similar to the personal statement I wrote for uni, but I had a lot of help from my college tutors with that one. The examples I've seen look simple enough, but boring as hell. An ideal one appears to be at least a whole page long!

10 p.m.

Clare walked through the door a few minutes after I finished writing the paragraph above, and as I'd guessed, she was too tired to do anything. In all honesty, I was tired too, from all the videos I'd watched. My eyes couldn't have handled the bright, white sting of a word document.

Instead, we collapsed on the beanbags with a tub of ice cream each and watched Coronation Street repeats on the internet.

6th Mar

Well, I'm actually glad to be sat on my till for once! Time's flown today, and I think the main reason is because I've been working on a different department. But, after spending six hours in the Cake-Shop I can't decide which is worse, being stuck on a till where every minute lasts an hour, or being stood behind a counter, where yes, every minute only lasts a second, but you end up smelling like off-cream!

Suppose I'll start from the top. Two people called in sick, one from the Cake-Shop, and one from the Deli (unfortunately it wasn't Creepy Carl, he's still alive, well, and repulsive as ever). When something like this happens, checkout girls *always* have to fill in. Always. And if I'm available, I'm always chosen, mainly because the Rottweiler can't stand the sight of me. For some God-given reason she decided to put me in the Cake-Shop, and poor, old, Gina from checkout 6 was sent to the smelly cheese counter.

The first thing I noticed about the Cake-Shop was that it smelled worse than the Deli. The smell was like old wallpaper that had been yellowed by decades of smoke damage. The frightening thing was that the walls weren't producing this smell, the Cake-Shop manager, Kathy, was.

She's a decrepit little woman. She makes me think of a turtle that's lost its shell. Nicotine literally seeps from every pore in her body, and I've eaten a lot of Eggberts cakes in my time. Great.

'You from checkouts?' was the first thing she said to me.

I nodded. Her breath smelled like her throat died last month.

'Spread jam on those sponges'; she pointed to a desk behind her. There was a pile of round sponges packed in plastic bags in one corner, and a pot of jam next to them.

I opened one of the sponge packets and then I realised I hadn't washed my hands. I looked for a sink, not wanting her to open her coffin of a mouth again. But, when I couldn't find one I spoke with my back to her. 'You got a sink?'

'A sink?'

'Yeah, to wash my hands. I've been touching money'.

There was a pause in which I thought maybe I should look at her, but if I did I knew it would only be a matter of time before I told her to check her throat for road kill.

'Ha!' She was loud and sarcastic. 'Sink's around the corner, *princess*'.

I heard a loud sniffle as I walked towards the sink, and I turned around just in time to see her wipe up some snot with her index finger. She was making chocolate éclairs, my favourite. My ex-favourite.

From then on, the Cake-Shop was just as dull as the checkouts. Just spread, sprinkle, dollop. The reason time went so quickly is because there was always more work to do when I was finished. I could work as fast as I wanted and more cakes would come. It's not like me to work fast, but I thought if I showed potential I might be upgraded to millionaire's cheesecake, or at least meringues.

I might have actually had a chance to work on the more advanced cakes if it hadn't been for the stupid cream machine!

Kathy told me to fill some piping bags with cream. She didn't offer any advice on how to use the cream machine, and I didn't ask, so maybe the result is partly my own fault.

Anyway, I went over and pressed the bright, green button (sensible enough) and nothing happened. So, I did what any normal person would do, I pressed harder. In hindsight, maybe I pressed a little too hard. The cream exploded out and covered the entire front of my uniform. Of course, that's never enough for Suzie-Q. Oh no, it had to be stale, lukewarm, stench-ridden cream.

The next thing I remember I was wriggling, retching, and screaming, 'Oh my God! Oh my God!'

Kathy peered over at me as I slipped out of my tabard, 'Oh, it does that sometimes'.

'Oh does it now? Fucking does it now?!'

'No need for swearing. Oh fuck, you stink, girl. The machine must be on the blink. Get back on them checkouts'.

Needless to say by this point I'd lost my rag. My rag had well and truly vanished! 'I stink?' I shouted as I stormed off. 'You smell like the Grim Reaper's Grandma! And you look like her an' all!'

My punishment for speaking the bitter truth is sitting behind checkout 14 without being able to wash off the cream which is now crusted to my uniform. Serving customers whilst caked in food and drink products is really becoming a regular occurrence; maybe I should add a skill like that to my CV.

Later that night

I am in the bath. Finally. And yet, I'm not relaxed at all. Do you want to know what my lovely, chummy, roommate has been doing all day? She's been writing *perfect* cover letters and applying for *perfect* jobs! How dare she do that without me?

'Okay, well I thought you were going to write yours yesterday on your day off', she said when I walked through the door.

'Okay, well...' I mocked, but then I had nothing to back me up. I'm just a lazy cow with the attention span of a gnat. '...I'm getting in the bath', I finished.

I walked past Clare on the way to the bathroom and as soon as I closed the door behind me I heard, 'Oh God!' And then the unquestionable burst of air freshener.

Still got it.

9th Mar

It's four minutes to nine, four minutes before the shop closes and I can go home, and four very annoying reasons why I hate my life just waltzed in wearing miniskirts.

They're all giggly, and tipsy, and full of life. They're probably nipping in to get some more alcohol because their night hasn't even started yet. Even worse, they're all drop dead gorgeous: shiny hair in ringlets, sexy false eyelashes, teeny weeny bird legs. And I'm just...ugh.

That's it. It's three minutes to nine. I am flashing my service light.

It's one minute past nine. The Rottweiler came trundling over within seconds of me flashing my light, but when I asked for a closing sign she dismissed me just as quickly.

'These girls are paying customers, and we've still got two minutes until closing time'.

'Can't they just go to Gav's till? He's here 'til half nine to clean up anyway', I protested.

'They'll choose whatever till they please'.

They chose me. Yipee! Now they are loading a trolley full of boxed wine onto my conveyor belt.

***

It's twenty-three minutes past ten, and I've just got home. Not one of the girls had I.D, and up close it was easy to see why: stuffed bras, no bags under their eyes, braces. If they did have I.D., I have a feeling it would have exposed them as being born in the noughties. God, that makes me feel old.

Anyway, there was a big uproar. They were clearly intoxicated. Tears were shed, their parents were called, and at the end of it, as the Rottweiler locked the door behind me, she said, 'You won't be getting paid over-time'.

So, on that note, I'm off to bed. It might seem a bit early to be going to bed, but my mind takes a while to switch off these days, despite how desperately tired my body is. Instead of drifting off to sleep like my limbs, my brain likes to think for about two hours first. Do you know what I'll be thinking about tonight? Why must people enter a shop at bloody closing time!

14th Mar

I finally got around to writing a few of those cover letter dealies, so I finally applied for some jobs that I actually stand a chance of getting. Oh, and I reapplied for some of the previous jobs that I 'forgot' to add a cover letter to. I hope that's okay. I'm still quite new to this whole job applying etiquette.

I've broadened my horizons. In fact, I couldn't have gone much broader. I've applied for kennel cleaning jobs, dog walking, dog babysitting – the kind of things I would have been thrilled to call my job when I was 14. I just want to do anything to get out of Eggberts. I mean, it's not like the money is keeping me there, so why not do a job that I love for minimum wage, instead of one that has me screaming into my pillow at least once a week?

Even if I end up working long hours for hardly any cash, I'll be happy as long as I am surrounded by some dogs.

I was always around dogs at uni. The course was so practical. We were working with rescue dogs around three times a week – a breed all their own, and the most grateful, hardworking breed I've ever come across. I didn't realise how much I would miss the company of canines, but I do.

We had a family dog when I was little. She was called Scooby Doo, along with millions of other dogs in the '80s and '90s, no doubt. We used to call her Scoob for short. She was just a little Yorkie, but bursting with energy. She passed away years ago, but by that time I was already immersed in dog studies at college, and then I went to uni, so I feel like this is the only time in my life when I haven't had the company of a dog.

When I come home from yet another shitty shift on the checkout, my bum numb, my brain frazzled, I crave the company of a dog. I think work would be a lot easier if I knew I had a wagging tail and smelly breath waiting for me at the end of the day. But of course, first you need the luxury of time, only then can you afford the luxury of a dog's company.

17th Mar

Maybe I'm just in a really good mood from all my productive job applications, but I've thought of something tremendously interesting about this job. Ever wondered what it would be like to be a fly on the wall? Then become a checkout girl. Honestly, people treat supermarkets like their extended homes or something. I get a free front row ticket to couples arguing:

'I paid last time'.

'Yeah, and I've paid every time before that. Courtney, you said things were going to change...'

'Okay, sorry, but I forgot my purse. I'll pay next time sweetie, sorry'.

'You forgot your purse? I just saw you take it out and show the girl your I.D...'

Good luck to Courtney.

Creepy teens talking sex tactics:

'You know, maybe we should just get one pack of condoms and split them. That way we look cooler, you know, like we've had so much sex that there's only half a pack left'.

'But I thought we were going to put the max performance condoms in the pleasure seekers box, so that they don't know we're using performance enhancing condoms?!'

'Good point. So question is, which one of us gets the pleasure seekers box?'

'Maybe we should buy a pleasure seekers box each.

'Wait, so we're buying three boxes of condoms when there's only a slight possibility that we're going to have sex'

'Slight? Dude, it will defo happen, we've got more than enough vodka. Maybe we should put the lube back though?'

Now, you may think that both of the examples above are pretty weird conversations to have in a public place. But no one can do weird better than kids.

If you have kids, or even if you were one once, you'll know that most kids have a variety of personas. There's the, *'I'm a little angel at Grandma's house'* persona, and the *'I'm a little angel at school'* persona, then there's the *'home'* persona. For some reason, the latter persona is the one that kids always bring to the supermarket.

'Mum, I need this!'

'No, you don't need it'.

'I do, I do!'

'Tammy, you are seven years old, you do not need mascara'.

'Everyone else has it!'

Next, Tammy will no doubt open/break/eat the mascara, leaving her poor mum to pay up. But, at least Tammy's mum knows the word 'No', unlike a lot of other parents I encounter.

There are the ashamed parents: *'He's had too much sugar today'.*

The defensive parents: *'It's your ridiculous marketing campaigns that have forced my little angel into wanting to eat this rubbish!'*

And of course, the down-right pathetic parents:

Child: *'I WANT THAT DVD AND I WANT TO GO HOME AND WATCH IT NOW!'*

Pathetic parent: *'Please don't shout Freddie. I've told you twice now; we can't afford that DVD today'.*

Child: *'BUT WE CAN AFFORD STUPID GRAPES? I HATE STINKY, STUPID GRAPES!'*

The child throws the grapes on the floor.

Pathetic parent: *'Freddie, clean that up right now, or else you aren't getting any chocolate biscuits'.*

Child, whilst stomping on the grapes: '*Yes I can! I always get my biscuits!*'

Pathetic parent, beginning to blush furiously: *'Shush. Here then, here. Take your biscuits, but eat them quietly on the bench'*.

Looking for a way to make sure your teenager doesn't get pregnant? Get her a job in a supermarket.

18th Mar

Well, my good mood from yesterday has flown right out of the window.

Clare has an interview. It's brought out all of those ugly feelings in me that everyone tries so hard to pretend they don't have – envy and jealousy being the top two.

It's such a strange situation. I've tried to think of something to compare it to, but it's just so odd. It's like, on my left shoulder is a mini angel-Suzie who is *so* happy for Clare and proud that her hard work has finally paid off. But, on the other shoulder is mini devil-Suzie and she is a malicious, jealous monster. I've never felt jealousy so pure; and I feel a little bit hurt too, like, how could Clare leave me here?!

She hasn't even gone for the interview yet. Lord knows what I'll be like if she gets the job!

***

I just cannot believe that Clare is back at the flat, prepping for her interview, and I'm stuck behind checkout 14 listening to Paul the Basket Guy updating me hourly on the physical attributes of his varicose vein.

To make matters worse, I've just come back from my break with the fresh knowledge that I've been rejected for three jobs, one of which was a kennel cleaner vacancy!

Apparently, I'm *'over-qualified'* – well, duh?! Anyone who can read my CV will see that! It doesn't mean I don't want the job though, does it? I think the fact that I took the time to apply might give away that clue!

I need to calm down. This is ridiculous. I don't even *want* to be a kennel cleaner. I would never have been satisfied with it; and the bloody interviewers knew that before I did! I just want out of here; out of this clammy, sticky-tiled, stinking hell-pit.

It's only now that I'm realising it was my own fault. I set myself up for a fall. Every graduate does it.

We never listened when older people said, '*It's a big, bad world out there*', or, '*It's tough to get a job*'. We were invincible. We took our degrees and held them up like tickets to our dreams coming true. Of course, the more time you spend off campus, the more uni seems like a dream in itself. What's the point of having a ticket to your dreams coming true if no one will take the time to look at it?

21st Mar

Clare didn't get the job, and now I wish that my last diary entry, the one written by a hulk-shaped bitch, could be stricken from the record.

She came home in tears, bless her. They called her before she was even on the bus home to tell her that she hadn't got the position. I don't know whether that's a good or a bad thing. But I suppose it would have been a little better for her confidence if they'd at least waited an hour or so. I force-fed her vodka and ice cream until the tears stopped, and then she told me all about it.

When she arrived there were seven of them in the room. No, not seven other candidates, seven interviewers. Seven people. Fourteen eyes judging your clothes, your body language, your height, your weight. And fourteen ears listening intently to every syllable as they roll out from between your chattering teeth.

But according to Clare, that wasn't even the worst bit. The worst bit was the stupidly awkward questions, like:

'Tell us about a time when you've had to use your better judgement to handle a situation'.

Or,

'Have you ever been trusted in a position of authority? If so, explain how you dealt with it'.

Clare would obviously reply with examples from her role at Eggberts. But they kept cutting her off: '*No, we don't want to hear about the* supermarket. *Don't you have any better examples?*'

Working at the supermarket is the only real job both Clare and I have ever had. After taking a few minutes (which apparently felt like an eternity) to try and think of appropriate examples from uni, college, or school, Clare had to admit that she could not answer the questions. They sent her home thirty-five minutes before the interview was due to end.

I gave Clare lots of hugs and kept saying things like, *'At least you know what to expect for future interviews'.*

I didn't even believe myself, but Clare seemed to and she cheered up really quickly. Or maybe I'd given her a bit too much vodka, who knows?

We spent the rest of the night thinking of what to do about our CVs. Our fears had been confirmed: no employer would take supermarket work experience seriously. It was Clare that eventually came up with the solution: volunteering. We can do our ideal jobs for free in our spare time, so that we've got something better to put on our CVs.

Clare is adamant about it, but I'm a bit sceptical. I mean, not only will I have to work 45 hours a week at Eggberts; I'll also have to work another job for free, plus spend my spare time applying for jobs! It seems nigh on impossible to me, but Clare is determined to give it a go, so I am too, I suppose. I mean, if I work non-stop for a few months, and then get a great job at the end of it, it'll all be worthwhile, right?

23rd Mar

I just want to get something down in writing, you know, 'for the record'. There's a saying going about these days: Boomerang Generation. As far as I know it refers to people that left home to go to uni, only to end up back at square one in their childhood bedroom straight after. They left home, and like a boomerang, came right back again.

The reason I am mentioning this is because I think a lot of people feel sorry for this 'boomerang generation'. But I don't. I feel sorry for me. You see, I should be part of the boomerang generation. I left home to go to uni and I graduated with no prospects and even less money. I should be back with my mum and dad, sorting myself out, finding my way. But I'm not so lucky.

Two things have stopped me moving back home in recent years. Firstly, I couldn't get a transfer to an Eggberts store near my parents' house, nor could I find another job. Going back jobless was out of the question, as they made it very clear that I would have to pay my way. The second factor that stopped me moving back home was more permanent.

Mum rang me one day, out of the blue: 'We're selling up', she said, 'Downsizing'.

'Oh', was all I could muster as I saw my childhood flash before my eyes.

'I managed to fit all of your things into two bin bags. There wasn't much left. Do you want to keep it? If not, I'll drop it off at the skip now for you'.

'Well, what's there?'

‘Oh, I don’t know. I just sort of shoved it all in’, was her reply. Then I heard a car beeping and I knew my dad was sat waiting to drive to the skip that very second. I just told her to bin it all.

But anyway, I’m getting sidetracked. The point I’m trying to make is that these poor ‘boomerang-ers’, aren’t poor at all. They’re living with their parents, possibly rent-free, and most of them, I imagine, job-free. They have the freedom to wait for the right job to come along, go travelling, or even save up for a house deposit.

Meanwhile, those of us who aren’t so privileged are working to the bone just to make ends meet. We’ve hit the big bad world in a big bad way, and let me tell you, we’re praying for something to boomerang us back.

25th Mar

I’ve received 11 job rejections in the past week. Eleven! And here is the gist of what every single bloody one said:

‘We regret to inform you that on this occasion you have been unsuccessful. This decision was made based upon your lack of experience...blah, blah, blah, yada, yada, yada!’

Lack of experience?!

If I hear that phrase one more time I’m going to rip my first class degree in half and flush it down the lavvy pan, because it obviously counts for jack shit!

I swear, the more I think about it, the more I am beginning to realise that the only decent thing I got from going to university was a bloody student card! Well that, and the fact that I got to spend three years of my life doing something I loved. But still, what am I left with? One measly certificate that no one outside of my family takes seriously, and a mound of debt. Brilliant, bloody brilliant.

31st Mar

Another month gone and I am still here. When I first started this diary, I think I genuinely believed that I'd be shot of this place by Feb. I also thought I'd have a mortgage and be engaged to Nick.

When will I stop being so naive? I mean, 27 years old is supposed to be 'grown-up' territory. When I was a kid, I thought 27 year old me would have a house, a husband, two kids, two cars, endless cash. Laughable.

In case you're wondering why I'm so reflective at this time of the year, it's because April is a strange month, and I KNOW that it will pass within a blink of my eye. I can't decide whether that's good or not. April brings:

The Easter Holidays (two whole weeks of a packed shop, screaming kids, and pissy parents). BAD

And, Profit Share (we get a percentage of our wages back as a bonus) GOOD. But I need to use the cash to pay for a filling. BAD.

And that's on top of everything else that's going on. Me and Clare have barely spoken since her job rejection. Not through any discomfort or anything, but simply because we're so petrified that the other one will get a job first. Our conversations go something like this:

Me: 'Heard from any jobs?'
Clare: 'No. You?'
Me: 'No'.
Unbearable silence whilst we both think '*Thank God!*'
Clare: 'How was work?'
Me: 'Shit'.

It doesn't help that we keep getting put on different shifts, and she has more friends than me, and thus more places to be. It doesn't bother me particularly because all her friends are checkout lovers. But, it's not a great feeling being stuck in an empty flat all night. Despite all of this unnecessary sadness, I'm determined not to go back to the heartbroken, self-pitying, alcoholic lowlife I was at the beginning of February.

On the upside, I booked tomorrow and the next day off as soon as I was allowed. I suppose I better explain how holidays work in supermarkets.

First things first: holidays renew on March 1st and have to be booked by May 31st. Yep. Just two months to plan out what you're doing for the entire year. That's so generous, don't you agree?!

Work first, family second – that should be Eggberts' new motto. To date, I have missed countless birthdays (three milestone ones), two weddings, one funeral, and three christenings – all because I was forced to book up my holidays before the end of bloody May. If only I could say: 'Sorry Nan, please could you just pencil down a date that you think you might die so I can let work know', life would be so much easier.

It's funny really. Eggberts, like all supermarkets, put out this 'family friendly' vibe. They have to do that, because families are their main customers. But, it's hilarious how much of a lie it is. I mean, I'm complaining at the things that *I've* missed, but there are some poor parents and grandparents here who've missed pinnacle family moments because they were here scanning people's shopping. I remember one year Doris from the Café burst into tears because she missed the birth of her first grandchild. I also heard on the grapevine that Ashtray Kathy from the Cake-Shop missed seven wedding anniversaries in a row (because she wasn't allowed to take time off in December – Christmas Period, remember!) and on the eighth her husband left her!

It's despicable what people are forced to give up just so they can have a job. When did money become so important, ey?

On top of that, because I'm signed up to a part-time contract, I am only allowed to take 'part-time holidays'. That means whenever I have time off, doesn't matter if it's two days or two weeks, I get paid 10 hours per week.

So, say I take one day off. I'll get paid ten hours for that day. Which is great, right? I mean, I don't even work ten hours in the day, so I'm getting paid for an extra hour. Ker-ching! But it's not all great. That one day off still counts as one week off, because my contract states that I work ten hours each week.

It's like I have to choose between taking a lot of time off and being paid nothing for it, or a little time off and getting paid modestly for it.

Don't worry if you don't understand it, I'm not even sure I completely understand it, but of course, we're not supposed to. Eggberts like to make things as complicated as possible, so that they can get away with pulling all of their nasty tricks.

April

5th Apr

I'm back at my usual post after four days off (two holidays and two actual days off. I don't know what I did to deserve them all in a row, and I'm not going to ask).

It's been quite an eventful couple of days. It started with a phone call from my dad at 8 a.m. He called to tell me that he'd won £12 million on the lotto.

When I started sobbing uncontrollably about how I'd never have to work in a supermarket again he could barely bring himself to say 'April Fool's'.

My parents were at my front door within an hour (my dad was definitely guilt-speeding). I was still whimpering when they got here, so they didn't even come in to have a look at the flat. They just took me back to their house like I was an injured kitten they found on the roadside.

It was the first time I'd been back to Lancashire in about four years. My sister goes every Christmas, but I'm always working on Christmas Eve, and then again on Boxing Day, so I can never get a train or anything. It's part of Eggberts plan to take every ounce of joy away from me until I snap.

I'm pretty sure it was only about two hours into my stay when my mum started to regret it. She came over to me all cheery and said, 'Why don't you give your friends a ring, love?' whilst plumping a cushion that I was sitting on.

I couldn't ring any of them though. I was a real fun-lover when they knew me. There was no chance I was letting them see the hollow shell I'd become after working for a corporation. Plus, socialising almost always costs money.

Mum spent the rest of the day cleaning things that were already sparkling and walking her Toy Poodle, Jakey. By the fourth time, the dog refused to get out of its bed, so she went shopping for ingredients to make us a roast dinner instead.

Me and my dad spent the day watching Only Fools and Horses reruns. He loves that show because the main character likes buying random crap, like he does. I also think he's part French, like us.

We had some beers in the evening after my mum took a cheap magazine into the bath. We played a few card games as well. A nice day really – I don't think I thought about Eggberts, job hunting, or even Clare, at all.

The next day was even better! My sister came up from London to surprise us, and surprise us she did – she's engaged! To a French cockney like that guy on the tele, would you believe it? His name is Claude and everything! I didn't have the chance to speak to him much. My dad took him out for a beer and a 'man-chat', so we were left with my hysterical mother. She rang all of her friends and her two sisters to tell them about the engagement. Within minutes, she had arranged a celebratory dinner at a posh restaurant. I was just about to tell her I hadn't brought anything nice to wear when she said, 'You don't mind keeping an eye on Jakey whilst we're out do you?'

Thankfully, my sister jumped in, before hundreds of profanities started pouring from my mouth. 'I'm not having an engagement dinner without my sister'.

My mum glanced at me whilst putting on her fancy earrings, 'Well, she hasn't brought anything suitable to wear'.

'She's right', I said. I was still wearing my Donald Duck pyjamas, but even they were better than the old jumper and tattered jeans in my bag.

'Well, we'll go and buy you something then. My treat', Renée said with a smile.

If anyone else said that I think I would've screamed the house down about not being a charity case. But it when it comes to my sister, I'm as soft as butter. I guess I just constantly feel like I owe her one because she stepped in to be the ‘big sister’ when we both realised that I was incapable of doing it.

I can’t believe she’s three years younger than me. She’s half a foot taller, half a foot thinner, her hair is always sleek like on the L'Oréal adverts, and she dresses like a celeb. I should hate her for it really. I mean, if she had been as big a failure as me then we could’ve shared the stick from my mum, but here I am, left to carry it all. Still, it’s hard to be mad at someone who buys you a £60 dress for *their* engagement dinner when all you’ve got them is an 89p ‘Congratulations’ card.

After that, my time off went pretty much downhill. My dad drove me home the next morning. He handed me a Poo-chi (you know, one of those electronic dogs that everyone had in the ‘90s) as we pulled up at the flat because, ‘I mentioned that once!’

I spent the next two days just lounging around and trying to get Poo-chi to stop barking. I got rejected for a few more jobs, and I applied for a few more too.

I watched a few more episodes of Corrie with Clare as well. I never realised how good soap operas were until I reached my late twenties (urgh! *Late* twenties).

7th Apr

Do you know what’s worse than sitting on your arse all day? Standing up all bloody day!

Some skank has robbed my chair. And there is no way of telling who, they’re all identical. The chairs I mean, not the checkout girls. Supermarkets haven’t ventured into the dark world of cloning...yet.

It’s one of the most soul-destroying things to come to your till and find it lacking a chair. Sometimes you can run off and find one before a customer comes along, but I'm never that lucky. I had a snooty cow waiting for me at my till before I'd even logged on.

'About time they put someone else on', she said, straight to my face, didn't even have the decency to mutter it under her breath.

I've been trying to nip off my till ever since, but I've not had a minute. And the Rottweiler considers herself far too busy to help me. She's just standing there counting postage stamps – doesn't look that busy to me. She won't sympathise with me because she has to stand up all day, every day. But it's different for her 'cause she gets to walk about. I'm glued to one single spot. I feel like all of the blood in my legs has collected in my feet and turned into sand.

I know what I'm going to do. I'm due my break in 25 minutes, so I'll take it, have a lovely sit down, and then I'll come back and find a chair. No chair, no checkout girl – that's my new rule.

***

I couldn't find a chair. I was not so kindly told that my break time was over, and I don't, nor will I ever have, the authority to make up rules.

No chair, no dignity, no happy.

8th Apr

Here's a sentence I never thought I'd say: 'I'm going on a date with Creepy Carl'.

My life is becoming so hilariously pathetic that I feel like I'm just at the centre of a sitcom for God and his pals. They'll just be up there, sharing a bucket of popcorn, laughing at my misfortune. I shouldn't have watched The Truman Show last night.

Suppose I'd better tell you how it happened, because, for the record, I want to say that this was one big accident!

Creepy Carl came over to my checkout, as usual, only this time he came to help a customer.

'Here's the Emmental you were after *sniff sniff*. The very last piece'.

The customer was a middle-aged woman with a huge smile. She was one of those motherly women that think anyone younger than them is a precious child to be spoiled.

'Oh, you're a star!' She pinched his cheek (cliché of the day), and then turned to me. 'I'm making Cordon Bleu. Silly old me was going to use Edam until this lovely young man helped me out. Isn't he a star?'

I don't have a clue about cooking and couldn't care less about this posh nut's cheese issues, but a customer is a customer, so I gritted my teeth and said, 'The brightest'.

That was my first mistake – complimenting him. After that he felt the need to stay and help the lady pack her shopping, and try and get all three of us involved in a conversation about fine dining. The customer was having the time of her life, but I zoned out and daydreamed of running my own dog agility class. There was a very yappy Bichon Frise that I was about to put a muzzle on when Creepy Carl disturbed my thoughts. I jumped back to reality. The customer was gone, and Carl's mucus filled nose was inches from my face.

I recoiled, 'What the hell?'

'The American Diner, how about it?'

I racked my brains to try and remember what he had been saying. I must have been sleeping with my eyes open. I guessed he meant he wanted to open one someday or something of that nature, so I just said, 'Yeah, great idea'.

I had another customer by this point. A grumpy business man who was having a meeting with his Bluetooth earpiece whilst unloading his basket.

'Cool', Creepy Carl said, 'Pick you up around 7?'

‘What?’

‘Or we could meet at the restaurant *sniff sniff*. Your choice’.

‘What are you talking about?’ I said, as the business man loudly cleared his throat. The unmistakable ‘hurry up’ sound. But I had bigger fish to fry. I glared at Creepy Carl.

He giggled that stupid, squeaky laugh, ‘I’m talking about our date, silly Suzie’. He laughed until it turned into a coughing fit.

The business man cleared his throat a little louder.

‘You’ve got to be bloody kidding...’ I started.

Carl cut me off, ‘Stop playing hard to get, Suzie’. He rubbed my arm, and I sank my nails into the cushion of my chair to stop myself from punching him. Punching the same person twice in one year would definitely lead to a disciplinary.

He continued, ‘This diner has *sniff* the *best* cheeseburgers. My treat’.

Suddenly, the customer spoke loudly into his Bluetooth device, ‘No. Still waiting to be served whilst two bratty kids decide which shack they are going to eat at this weekend’.

I had to get rid of them both. I started scanning the businessman’s shopping and turned to Creepy Carl, ‘Fine. Pick me up at 5. I like to eat early’.

I usually eat later than that, but I didn’t want to risk a busy time in case anyone we knew came in. Plus, I’ll need about a shower or ten after a date with Creepy Carl. But, free food is free food when you’re in my position. And I do love cheeseburgers.

I felt sorry for the businessman after he left. He only bought a ready meal, some black socks, and a bottle of beer. I know what it’s like to work hard all day and go home to nothingness. Still, he was wearing a suit and a Bluetooth headset so he must enjoy his job a hell’ov’a lot more than I enjoy mine.

10th Apr

Clare's started *volunteering*. Of course she has. *Super-Clare!*

She works (for free) at the local theatre on Friday nights. When she applied for a job there, they told her there were no vacancies. When she said she'd work for free however, lots of thankless jobs suddenly popped up. She takes tickets beginning at 6 p.m., then she does odd jobs whilst the show is on – passes actors their costumes, holds brushes for hair and make-up, that kind of thing. She even sells hot dogs during the interval. Then, when the show is finished, she stays behind to clean up. Overall she spends about six hours every Friday night working for absolutely nothing, and that's after working 8-4 at Eggberts during the day!

Now, you're possibly thinking what I thought when she told me she had started volunteering, '*How the hell is she getting every Friday off when she works on a pathetic rota in a supermarket?*'

Simple. People like her.

She told the Rottweiler that because she has started volunteering she can no longer work Friday nights, but she promised to work every Friday day time. And the Rottweiler was just fine and dandy with that.

If it was me on the other hand, even if I was flying to Africa every Friday to aid starving children, the answer would be a resounding NO.

Maybe I'm just using that as an excuse *not* to volunteer. I'd like to think I'm not that selfish though. I guess there are loads of dogs out there that need my help. I might even enjoy it. Clare certainly does. I suppose you'd have to be mental to work for free on Friday nights if you weren't enjoying it.

Okay, I'm going to try it. Right now before I change my mind. First I'll find a place to give my time to, and then I'll tackle the Rottweiler and her incompetent rota-writing skills.

3 hours later...

My God, is that the time?!

This volunteering lark is already proving to be too difficult. I have literally spent the past three hours trying to find a place to volunteer at – no pee breaks or anything. I even skipped dinner so I'm going to be starving on my checkout tonight!

Anyway, I suppose it wasn't a complete waste of time. Although, most of it was. First I looked online and found a big list of kennels, twenty-two altogether. Then I whittled it down to sixteen that most needed help for free – family run charities and whatnot. After that, I called them all and offered my free service. Dog helper Suzie to the rescue! And would you believe it, fourteen of them gave me a flat out, 'No thanks!'

They either had enough volunteers or not enough dogs (which is the only positive in all this). However, all of them said they wouldn't refuse a monetary donation. Well, who would? I could do with some monetary donations myself!

Thankfully, the other two kennels I called seemed more promising. One was a definite yes, if I can come between 9 a.m. and 12 p.m. on Tuesday mornings (perfect, because I normally get Tuesdays off anyway!), and the other said she'd have to ask her boss and get back to me.

So, now I've just got to bring down the big dog. Wish me luck.

13th Apr

It's Friday the 13th – not exactly a great omen for my 'date' with Creepy Carl. I tell you what, these cheeseburgers better be good. I've taken a lot of stick over the past few days for agreeing to go on a date with the local Desperate Dan. I made it very clear to everyone that I'm only in it for the free food. In fact, I'm pretty sure even Creepy Carl knows that, but unfortunately it hasn't made him change his mind.

Clare had some Sambuca leftovers that she said I could drink before the date. There was only enough for two and a half shots, so I just downed it out of the bottle. I don't feel any better yet though. Oh well, there are people out there doing worst things than going out for a free cheeseburger. I need to get over myself.

***

I'm back, and it's not even 8 p.m. Plenty of time for post date showers, although, it wasn't as bad as I thought. Don't go getting any ideas, he's still annoying as hell, but other things on the date made up for that.

It didn't start too well. He picked me up in a yellow Nissan Micra that practically embodied a block of cheese. I was so sure that the car would smell like cheese too, but surprisingly, it just smelled like car. Even Creepy Carl didn't smell like his usual cheesemonger-y self. The sour smell had been replaced by aftershave. The cheap kind that hurts the back of your throat when you breathe in, but hey, anything is better than Eau de Babybel.

The conversation, however, remained sour. He pulled out all of his usual topics: his health, the cheese counter, and his favourite subject in the world, hugs. I just stared out of the window the entire ride there, trying to memorise the route in case he attempted to abduct me.

But he didn't. And the diner was amazing! Great decor, cool music, the *best* cheeseburgers, and hot waiting staff. I'm definitely dragging Clare back when we get paid.

I stared at the waiter all night. He was Hollywood gorgeous, but he had one of those names that's easy to forget, like Ben, or John, or Mark. He smiled at me a few times too, but that's as far as our relationship went. Eating a double cheeseburger isn't exactly my best look.

I'm lucky that Creepy Carl likes to talk about himself so much. Most of the night, I got away with completely ignoring him and just saying 'yeah' when there was a few seconds of silence. The only time I turned to face him was when I had to bat his hand away from my leg or arm. It happened around seven times.

I've come home feeling quite sorry for him. I mean, he's just a sap, isn't he? A sap that has learnt about romance by watching Dear John and The Notebook. He just wants a Juliet. His biggest problem is his desperate attitude: 'anyone will do'.

Well, it's an attitude like that that's had him well and truly used by a bitch like me. But I don't think he minds. It got him out of his parents' attic for a few hours at least. He even bought dessert for me *and* Clare. I told him I'd like to take dessert home as I was 'feeling tired'.

Strangely enough, it would have passed for one of my best dates ever if he hadn't finished it with, 'Let's hug it out'.

The last thing I said to him was, 'Let's not', before slamming the door in his face.

P.S. The Rottweiler said no to me volunteering when I asked her the other day. So that's the end of that.

Apparently, because Clare is already doing it that is more than enough for now. She finished it off with one of her favourite lines: '*I can't organise this rota around everyone's personal lives you know!*'

She could at least try. Bitch.

15th Apr

Have you any idea what it's like to work in a supermarket called Eggberts around Easter? No, I don't suppose you do.

Our motto is already: *'Eggberts. Crackin' Deals'*. But around Easter the campaigns get even more pathetic:

'Have an Egg-cellent Easter with Eggberts!'

'Eggs-press yourself with our Easter Cards'

'Eggs-tra savings at the Easter Bunny's favourite place to shop!'

You get the idea, and in case you don't, it's just a lot of terrible 'egg' puns.

Every year.

And Easter is bad enough with all the kids running around hopped up on chocolate and buzzing from the school holidays. Sitting at my till looking at the hideous Easter signs and pretending to smile at customers' hyper-active children was tortuous enough. Now I've been lumbered with putting Easter stickers on each of the checkouts. Of course, I'm not doing that right now. Currently, I am sat on the toilet and writing in this diary – taking five, as some call it.

Like all supermarkets, Eggberts put their Easter decorations up in Feb, as soon as the Valentine's Day stock was gone. But the offers are constantly changing so that Eggberts can stay ahead of competitors. The Rottweiler volunteered me to put stickers on all of the checkouts letting everyone know that our eggs are now 98p. One pence cheaper than Asco (our most direct competitor).

So, I'm on minimum wage and it's 98p for an Easter egg, or £2.99 for a ready meal – I know what I'm having for tea tonight!

17th Apr

We get this thing called 'profit share' every year, which means a small percentage of the stores profits gets put in our wages in April. It's like the only incentive we have. And it's great for people like me, who work so much more than they should do according to their contracts, because this is calculated by how many hours you actually work, not how many you're contracted to.

It's never a lot of money, but mine is usually enough for me to get my dental work done. So last year, I got a filling that was long overdue, the year before that I paid for a scale and polish, and so on.

I'm due another filling, so I expected that my profit share would cover it, but when I opened my wage slip it said: Profit Share: 0.1% = £17.03. That's not even enough for a dental check up! I also think it's a huge lie, how can last year's Profit Share have been 3.2% and this year's be 0.1%. A profits dip like that would surely have a supermarket close to closing down, right?

I'm past caring anyway. I don't need handouts from millionaire scumbags like Mr Eggbert. I'll just go without my filling and be toothless by the age of thirty.

***

Oh my God! I've got an interview! Ahhhhhhhhhhhhh! I'm so excited! I found out five hours ago and this is the first time I've been actually calm enough to sit down and write about it.

I had just swiped my card to clock out when my phone began ringing. I answered it as I walked out of the store, and before I reached the exit I was told I had a job interview! I felt like I was starting my day all over again. I ran home to tell Clare but she wasn't in, so I called my sister instead who was thrilled for me. She also told me that she is having her Hen do in August, so I must remember to ask for it off work.

Anyway, where do I begin?

It's an on-site behavioural specialist role at the RSPCA in Lancashire (my sister is transferring the train ticket money to my bank account as we speak – bless her heart!) It's more money than Eggberts pay, *and* the contract is full-time. Can you believe it?! The way they go on at Eggberts it's like full-time contracts are being rationed throughout the country, and here is an employer ready and willing to give one away, and all they're asking in return is for me to work those hours! Well, you can't say fairer than that! Especially since I have spent the last God knows how many years working full-time hours on a measly ten hour contract.

My interview is on the 19th! Just two days away! I'll have to decide what to wear. When Clare got home she said she'd do my hair in a French plait for me, so it will be slicked back and professional, but still pretty. She's been so much more supportive than I was when I found out she had an interview. She's been on a few more since then though and had no luck, so she probably thinks I'll be the same. But I'm determined. I am not leaving that kennels without a job.

19th Apr

So, you have to prepare for interviews these days? Well, no one told me! The most preparation I did was ironing a blouse, and I didn't even do a good job of that!

Oh it was awful. Just a terrible, terrible experience. They asked questions like:

'What motivates you to get out of bed for work in the morning?'

Erm...the fact that I want to keep a roof over my head? What is anyone in my position supposed to say when asked that?!

I didn't want to talk about Eggberts at all. I mean, it can't possibly be relevant to a behavioural specialist role at a kennels.

Another hum-dinger that I remember all too vividly:

'Talk us through your weaknesses'.

So, I began by telling them that I am not as assertive as I'd like to be around some dogs. If their characters shine through I can't help but smile or laugh, even if they're being naughty. I like to think of this as one of my more charming traits, but I was cut off...

'No, no, your weaknesses in the work place'.

I just sat there. Face blank, thinking, I know I have so many weaknesses in the work place, but do I have any that I can mention?

I hate customers
I don't give a shit about the rules
I don't interact with staff members

I just sat there in a daze until I was asked to leave. I'll wait for their call.

22nd Apr (Easter Sunday)

You'd think a shop that cared so much about Easter would close on Easter Sunday, but oh no, the doors are wide open. Anyway, introduction over, I have a confession to make.

Has your life ever been so bad that you don't know whether to cry, or just laugh at how ridiculously unfair your situation is?

I'm sure we've all done it at some point: wallowing in self-pity because on getting home you find out KFC got your order wrong, or sulking because there's only one seat left on the train and it's next to the blocked lavatory.

Well, my situation is worse than both of these things put together. My situation is so grave that there is a name for it: sexual harassment.

Sorry if my writing is scruffier than usual today, but I'm petrified this will be the day the Rottweiler robs my diary from me, and this is the one entry I don't want anyone to read.

Surprisingly, the sexual harassment is not coming in the cheese-scented direction of Creepy Carl. It comes from a more unexpected source. He's a new ADM (Assistant Deputy Manager). He's been here for a few weeks and I guess I never marked it in my diary because...well, who gives a shit? Managers come and go all the time; apparently they're the only ones who can leave.

Anyway, he's new, and let's just refer to him as Mr Y – as in WHY did this have to happen to me?!

I guess before I mention how it started I should tell you that he is bloody fit, a real looker – for a fifty year old! He's got dark skin from splitting his time between the UK and his Spanish Villa; his hair is shocking silver, but there's quite a lot of it; and, although he always wears a suit, his body must be good because he runs the London marathon every year. There, I think that's enough detail. Any more and you'll start to think that I fancy him, which I don't. Everyone else on the other hand, well, they'd kiss his feet if he asked. There's one large lady in particular that holds a candle for him (probably one that she's made with her grubby ear wax and mammoth dog hands), and that's why it's dangerous. You guessed it, my manager loves him, and she *never* shows affection to anyone – I've seen her kick her own mother in the shin.

It all began two days ago, in the warehouse. A wretched customer spotted me walking down the milk aisle on the way back from my break.

'Excuse me, have you got any Eggberts gin?'

I looked around and yes, we were definitely down the milk aisle. I swear, customers don't even bother looking anymore. Since she was only a little, old lady I didn't have a go at her, I simply lead her to the spirits aisle. But as it turned out, we actually didn't have any Eggberts gin.

So, she said what they all say, as if gin is a massive necessity, 'Can you check in the back for me?'

I wandered into the dark and cold cave of the warehouse and surprisingly there was a box of gin there. I was beginning to think that this was some supernatural shit. The warehouse was totally bare and there was this box of gin, just sitting there. I didn't hear Mr Y walking in and chatting on the phone, and I don't think he saw me about to bend over and pull a bottle of gin from the box.

Just at the moment he walked into me, I bent down. My arse, his crotch. He ended his phone call and I felt a warm, hard bulge pressing against my pants, and through the mere shock of it, I just stayed there! Dumbfounded! I bet he thought I was loving it. After a long second I finally snapped out of it, grabbed the gin, and came to a standing position. I tried not to look at him as I stormed off.

'I hope that's for a customer, otherwise you're a very naughty girl', I heard him shout.

All I could think was, *oh shit.*

I gave the lady her precious booze and then shuffled back to my till. I found it hard to walk due to the fact I could still feel that warm imprint on my bum.

Since then it's been little things, like winking, and saying my name in a really strange way like he's tasting all the letters or something. The only person I've told is Clare and she's too busy laughing at me to offer any advice.

27th Apr

It's my dad's birthday today, and miraculously it has landed on one of my days off. And I actually had enough money to get him a present – money that everyone in my family knows I will have to borrow from my rich sister again in a few weeks, but still, it's the thought that counts, right?

I got him a bottle of whiskey, just the Eggberts kind, and only the 35cl, but like I said, it's the thought.

My parents came to me so I could wish my dad a happy birthday as I'm too poor to travel further than Leeds city centre. They like coming to visit me anyway. They see it as a day out; well, my dad does. My mum usually sits cross-legged and loud mouthed until it's time to leave. But today, they get to see the new Suzie - the Suzie that lives with her sophisticated friend in a swanky flat, and applies for jobs. The Suzie anyone would want as their daughter.

My dad came through the door first and kissed me on the cheek. He moved out of the way so that when I said, 'Happy Birthday, you old git!' I was actually facing my mum.

My dad hates any kind of attention; he always shuffles on his feet and looks around the room, pretending he can't hear you. Knowing this, I simply handed him his present and went in the kitchen to make the brews.

'Nice flat, love!' My dad shouted in.

Even my mum couldn't hold back a compliment, 'This is exactly the kind of place I imagined you living in, Suzie'. She sounded genuinely pleased and it made me feel really happy. Happier than I've felt in a long time, and all it took was a little approval from my mum– how sad!

I hadn't even taken a sip of my tea when the happiness frittered away.

'So, Nick dumped you?' my mum said, calm as anything as she sipped her drink. My dad glared at her, but she took no notice.

Clearly, Renée told them. I wouldn't have told anyone, it still mortifies me. But Renée actually calls and texts me and asks questions, and I can't just lie to her – at least, not about everything. I nodded in my mum's direction, 'So, where is Renée anyway?'

'You're not changing the subject that easily –'

'Oh yes she is', my dad butted in. 'Renée is at a book signing today. She's coming to visit us next week'.

Thank God it's my dad's special day, if it was my mum's birthday we would have spent hours on end going through the shards of broken glass that are my ~~love~~ life. And she'd probably have said it was the best birthday she's ever had, too.

'Maybe Renée will come and visit me whilst she's up North'.

'I doubt it', my mum said. 'She's a very busy woman, you know'.

'I'll mention it to her though, love', Dad said.

Our mugs were empty by this point, and there wasn't really much more of the flat for them to see, so I asked my dad what he fancied doing for his birthday.

'Thought we'd head to Chester zoo'.

My mum rolled her eyes, but I couldn't care less, I love the zoo! My dad isn't a huge fan though. 'Are you sure?' I said.

'Oh, yeah! There's a special thing on about the wild dogs. They've just had a litter apparently'.

African Wild Dogs are my favourite animal! And the thought of seeing the puppies caused me to let out one of those annoying girl squeals. I wrapped my arms around my dad's neck and said, 'You're too soft on me, you know'.

Simultaneously, my mum said, 'You're too soft on her, you know'.

That made my dad laugh, 'More similar than you think, aren't you?'

My mum looked the other way, slightly blushing, and I ran to get my coat.

Before I came back into the living room I heard my mum say, 'She needs to learn to fend for herself. She's not a child'.

My dad replied, ‘She fends for herself every day. It’s a tough world out there on your own you know. And she is a child, *our* child’.

He really is too soft on me. But I don’t care; I got to see wild dog puppies! Wonder if I’ll be able to put it on my CV? Close encounter with ferociously cute puppies!

May

1st May

Another bank holiday spent scanning the contents of other people's picnic baskets. It's all strawberries, crackers, and ice cream on my conveyor belt today.

My life is like a conveyor belt if you think about it: Hi, scan, bye. Hi, scan, bye.

Do you know what, if I leave one piece of decent advice in this diary it will be this: Never, and I mean *never*, agree to sign a part-time contract.

Even if you only need part-time work, you might as well sign up for full-time because, believe me my friend, that's exactly what you'll be doing!

Monday is not a contracted day of mine. The only days and times I am contracted to work are Sunday 12 p.m. – 5 p.m. and Monday 4 p.m. – 9 p.m. I know what you're thinking, who would sign a contract like that in the first place? Someone who was desperate, that's who!

Anyway, if I so much as dared to turn around and say to the Rottweiler: 'I'm not coming in on Bank Holiday Monday. I'm not contracted to work it, and I've made plans'. She would hit the roof and I would lose my job.

The reason for this is that in most part-time contracts (in very, very, very small print) it states: 'You will work *blah blah* hours per week **and also extra hours as the management team see fit.**' – Or something like that.

And they *always* see it as fit. There's just *always* something. I didn't realise how many public holidays there were until I had to work on every single one of them. It's always Easter Sunday this, Bank Holiday Monday that, Bonfire Night, CHRISTMAS, Eid, the Royal bloody Wedding, the pointless World Cup – need I go on?

3rd May

I cannot wait to get home today. It's been sexual harassment central.

It was bad enough when Mr Y was just looking at me funny and saying suggestive things, but now for some reason he thinks he has the right to *touch* me. A slight tug on my ponytail, or squeeze of my arm, at one point he dropped some holiday slips right in front of me and told me to, *'bend over and pick them up'*.

My skin is crawling, and for once I don't have to check under the till to see if the reason behind my itchiness is another ant infestation. *Shudder.*

***

Finally home, and I haven't laughed so much in years! I cannot believe Clare! She's taken a very, shall we say, '*Avant Garde'* approach to applying for jobs. I can't blame her really. I mean, the old way wasn't exactly working. But that doesn't mean that this new way of hers will work, not by any stretch of the imagination!

She's applying for this three-year contract in London. It's to be a character in this play; I can't remember the name now. Anyway, to be 'imaginative' she revamped her cover letter. It goes like this (sorry if I screw my writing up with laughing too much):

The Checkout Girl

I'm the best actress you'll ever find,
I'm so believable it will blow your mind.
I am the girl who is polite and smiling,
But whilst I pack your bags, my soul is dying.

...I can't remember the rest, but you get the picture. I don't know why I find it so funny, because it is so depressingly true. Maybe that's why I'm laughing – laugh or cry, right?

I shouldn't be so harsh really. I've put Clare in a right mood. I do hope she gets the job, she knows that. I also think she is going the wrong way about it. The *really* wrong way. Like, '*my soul is dying*'? That doesn't sound like a stable employee to me. Mind you, maybe I should start begging for jobs like that. Lord knows I'm past the stage of being too proud. In fact, I don't think I was ever at that stage.

7th May

Everyone's got a reason to drink today – even the people that don't have bloody I.D. I've refused two customers in the past hour, both situations got pretty ugly, and now I'm stressed. I can physically feel my hair turning grey.

There is a rule at Eggberts: if a staff member refuses to serve a customer for a valid reason, for example, if they have no I.D., then all other staff members have to stand by that original decision. Well, united we are not.

The first person I refused to serve was a heavy-set girl, with even heavier make-up. She wouldn't look out of place on the Jeremy Kyle show. Anyway, she came up to the till by herself, and placed a bottle of cider on the belt. She was on her phone when I said, 'Hi, help with packing?' (Yes, we even say that when there's only one item. It's a habit). She didn't even look at me. That was her third strike. Strike one: heavy make-up. Strike two: only one item. And, strike three: no eye contact. Now, I knew she must have been about 22, but as you may know, you have to look over 25 to be served without I.D. in a UK supermarket. And, as you may not know, if a checkout girl is caught selling alcohol to someone under 25 without asking for their I.D., they risk receiving a fine up to £5,000. Yes, that's right - £5,000. It's not worth the risk.

She didn't hear me the first time, so I had to say 'excuse me' to get her attention. I could tell by her eyes that she was going to be trouble.

'Don't be daft. I'm 26!' She shouted after I asked her.

I began reading from my well-rehearsed script: 'I'm sorry, but I can't serve you if you don't have any I.D'.

'I don't need I.D., love. I already told you, I'm twenty bloody six'.

'Sorry, but if you look under 25 then you need to present valid I.D.'.

'But I don't look under 25'.

'You do to me'.

'Well, you look about 12. You stupid little cow'.

She stormed off at that point, only to be served on self-scan a few minutes later! I flashed my light and told the Rottweiler, but the money had already exchanged hands. I half-hoped the police would walk in and give a fine to the idiot lad that served her, just so I could be right. But they didn't.

The second customer, or should I say customers, was every checkout girl's worst nightmare: a group of rowdy teenage lads – six in total. This is the type of transaction that makes a checkout girl's stomach flip as soon as they join the queue. You know that they're going to try and embarrass you, whether they have I.D., or they don't. The problem with rowdy groups like this is that every single one of them needs I.D. It's just the law. Unfortunately, most customers, these lads included, don't understand that. I could tell they were a group of freshers, splashing their student loan payment on a ridiculous amount of booze, only to be borrowing the same amount back from their parents in a few weeks time.

I tried to act blasé, 'Got any I.D.?'

Two of them started pinching one lad's cheek as he handed over his I.D. 'Ooh, baby face'. He ignored them, and I was glad to see there was at least one quiet one.

The next guy to show his I.D. winked as he handed it over, 'As you can see, I'm fully legal for any and all adult activities'. This made his new friends erupt into a roar of laughter. In fact, they only stopped laughing to say, 'You gonna scan our stuff or what?'

'I need to see I.D. from everyone'.

'You what?'

This was the hostility I had been waiting for. It's strange how quickly customers can turn on you – one minute you're laughing together about last night's episode of Coronation Street, and the next they're biting your head off because you were 'too rough' with their eggs.

'When people buy alcohol in a group, I need to see I.D. from everyone'.

'Oh yeah, I'm sure you do. So, when a woman comes in with her three kids and buys a bottle of wine, do you refuse her an' all?'

'No, because there is no indication that her kids are going to drink the wine'.

'Well, what's your 'indication' that I'm gonna drink this?' One of them piped up.

I was starting to lose my cool. 'Oh, I dunno, maybe when you said "we're gonna get so trollied tonight, lads"'

They weren't expecting me to talk back, so they changed their tactics. 'Look, we've got student cards if that helps?'

'No, I'm sorry, that's not a valid form of I.D.'.

'Why not? You have to be 18 to have one'.

'It's just not'.

'Now you're just being a spiteful bitch'.

That's when I flashed my light. I'm not trained to deal with people calling me a bitch. There's only one way I know how to retaliate to that kind of behaviour, and it would definitely get me sacked.

The Rottweiler didn't take long. 'Yeah?' she said.

'These customers are getting aggressive because I won't serve them'.

'Aggressive?!' one of them shouted. I could feel everyone's eyes turn to look. 'You lying little slag!' My cheeks started to burn through a mixture of embarrassment and anger.

'Oi! If you're going to talk to my staff like that you can get out and stay out!'

Wow. The Rottweiler actually sticking up for me. I was blown away.

The lads changed tactics again. 'We just think she's being unfair. We've shown our uni I.D. – that's proof we're old enough'.

The Rottweiler hesitated. She knows the line, I know she does. She's the one that taught it to me: *'That's not a valid form of I.D.' 'That's not a valid form of I.D.'*

The Rottweiler looked at my conveyor belt. There was over one hundred quid's worth of booze on it, and that swayed her, 'Alright. Just this once'.

And so, I served them whilst they snickered, celebrated, and whispered about me. It was one of the most humiliating things to happen to me whilst working here.

Sure, I could've kicked off. Could've refused to serve them. Could've told a senior manager that the Rottweiler went against protocol. But what's the point? No one cares. The best thing I can do is vent in this diary, and thank God for that.

9th May

I banged my head on a door today. Not deliberately. I'm not that depressed – yet.

10th May

Payday! And Friday! This can only mean one thing: ALCOHOL.

I finished work two hours ago, but Clare still has another three hours left, so I'm chilling the Eggberts value cider in the fridge for her. When I had no friends, I just started drinking whenever, wherever, but it only feels right to wait for Clare. Plus, whilst I'm sober I can catch the bitch up on job applications! She's always one step ahead of me. I'm getting pretty good at applications myself, at least I think I am. I reckon I'll be able to get six done before Clare gets home. It's so much easier to be optimistic when you've got cash in your pocket isn't it?

At a time unknown.

AHHHH. AHHH. Oh my. How can I even...What is happend is not the greatnest. Oh dear.

12th May

Suppose I'd better explain my previous ramblings. I would have done it sooner but I've been showering for two days straight. Yep, it was one of *those* mistakes.

It was a perfectly amazing night. I was too drunk to comprehend the music I was dancing to, and the hours were flying by like minutes. But then, Clare met up with some of her other checkout girl mates who I don't really get on with. I mean, all they talk about is work. Who wants to listen to that?

So, I was kind of drifting off on my own when I saw those two, the 'perfect' couple: Nick and Andrea. They were having a quiet, romantic drink in the corner; so typical of sensible, science types like them.

They didn't spot me swaying in the crowd, or maybe they did and chose to ignore me. For some horrid reason, I couldn't take my eyes off them. Andrea was giggling coyly, and Nick stroked her arm gently, tucked hair behind her ear, anything to have his hands on her. When I saw him lean in to kiss her, I knew I'd never seen two people so...content. Pressure started to build up in my stomach. It travelled up my chest, tightening everything along the way, and when it reached my head I just burst into pathetic, single, checkout girl tears.

The next thing I remembered, I was running as fast as I could, I was still crying, and I'd found my way outside. The wind was cold on my bare arms and legs, but my face was hot with…embarrassment? Disappointment? Who knows.

Then I ran into a brick wall, and the brick wall wrapped his arms around me.

I woke up a few hours later, my hair stuck to my cheeks by leftover tears and my head thumping to a tune I couldn't remember.

The first thing I saw upon opening my eyes was a wide back covered in a pale blue shirt. Then a full head of grey hair. I gasped, and he turned to face me, smiling smugly.

'Morning', said Mr Y.

I leaned over the side of my bed and vomited onto the used condom in the bin. Thank God for small favours.

'I'll tell Christine you've called in sick', he said on his way out. It took me a minute to register that he was talking about the Rottweiler, and by that time, he'd gone.

I expected to cry, but apparently I'd used all my tears the night before.

'You little minx', Clare suddenly appeared on the edge of my bed and I hid under the duvet. 'Maybe you'll get a pay rise, or at least better shifts. Yeah, definitely better shifts. You should use this to your advantage'.

'What possible advantages can come from this situation?' I said. But I'm pretty sure all she heard were muffled whimpers.

She tried to pull the duvet off me, but I clung on for dear life. 'Come on, Suz. We've got work in two hours, and you need at least an hour in the shower'.

I peeked out on hearing the word *shower*. 'I don't do this kind of thing', I told her, feeling more pathetic with every word.

Clare shrugged, 'You do now'.

Let me tell you, nothing has ever stung more than those three tiny words. *You do now*.

I looked around my room and thought about who I am now. I'm nearly 30, I work in a dead-end job on minimum wage, and to top it off, I've had a one-night stand with a colleague old enough to be my dad.

I got an overwhelming want for home at that point –for my dad, and even my nagging mum. I decided I'm going to stay with them for a bit. I've got a week's holiday left so I'll just book it ASAP.

Yeah, that was the plan: I'd bite the bullet, go home, and let my mum nag me to success. But first, I needed a shower.

I looked back at Clare who was busying herself by pulling a thread on her sock. 'I'm not coming in today, probably not tomorrow either', I said as I got out of bed and grabbed a towel.

'Oh, okay', she got up to leave. 'Perks of fucking the boss, I guess'.

I've decided swearing does not suit Clare anymore, not one bit.

I'm finally going to pluck up the courage to go back to work again tomorrow. But first, another shower.

13th May

It feels like I've never been away from my till. I'll only start to feel the comeuppance of my days off when I get paid. Did you know that if you work full-time whilst on a part-time contract, you don't get paid for sick days, and you barely get paid for holidays?

I don't suppose you do unless you're in the same boat as me, which is slowly rowing up shit creek.

As I said yesterday, I've still got a week, or 10 hours, of holiday left to take, and despite me having time to think about it, I'm still crazy enough to want to spend it with my parents. However, when I went up to the Rottweiler today my luck was out, AGAIN.

At first I thought she was just being a cow with me because I took two days off sick, so she eventually let me have a look at the rota myself, and she was right: no full weeks left at all. The best I could get was 4 days off in September and 3 in October – won't be going back to my roots any time soon!

At first she didn't even want me to take a week, 'Why not just take ten hours off, it's all you get paid for anyway, and it's obvious you need the money'.

If looks could kill I'd be spitting on her grave right now. When you're faced with one measly day away from the sticky floors and questionable smell of Eggberts Supermarket, or one week, you take the week – always!

So, the result is that I will be paid five hours for my September holiday, and five for my October one, resulting in a measly £35 each time. But I'll cross that rickety bridge when I get there.

In other news:

- Mr Y is off work today (*Phew!*)
- I've been rejected for two jobs, thirteen are still pending.
- Paul the Basket Guy found another varicose vein on his leg. He's keeping an eye on it.

16th May

I'm finally sat on my sofa, in my flat, in my clothes. And what I mean by that is: I am finally sat on *Clare's* sofa, in my *rented* flat, in clothes that aren't in Eggberts brand colours. I'll never wear blue for leisure again. Shame, it suited me.

Nothing terribly dramatic has happened today – thankfully. I'm just exhausted. It's weird really because what do I have to be exhausted about? I sit down all day, and I certainly don't use my brain. But, I'm beginning to think that doing the same thing every single day can take a toll on your sanity. After all, what is that saying? Insanity is doing the same thing over and over again and getting the same results? Something like that anyway.

That's why working in a supermarket drives people insane. It's not just checkout girls, look at the others: Paul the Basket Guy and Creepy Carl. I love one and hate the other, but I could never totally verify the sanity of either of them. The old ladies that work there '*just to get out of the house for a few hours*' are definitely off their rocker too.

So, maybe that's it. Maybe I've lost my mind. It's kind of an anti-climax if I'm honest. I don't feel any different, just more...tired. And more like...I can't be bothered. I think it generated from me receiving a new name badge today. It still says bloody Suzanne instead of Suzie, but this time it says 'six years service' underneath. It sounds like I'm doing a stretch in prison; feels like it too, I imagine. No, that's not fair. Prisoners get their meals made for them, I have to go home and make my own. Still, it's been the highlight of my day: chicken noodles on toast.

Yep, everything was pretty routine, until about ten minutes ago when I received a text message from a number that I didn't recognise. As soon as I read it, I knew who it was from. It said: 'Hey naughty. Hope you aren't avoiding me. We need a repeat of last weekend!'

Well, after reading that my tea almost repeated on me! I wish I could show someone the text and get the bastard sacked, but the truth is, I just don't want people to know that I woke up next to that fossil.

Come on, God. If you're up there, give me a little hand will you?

18th May

Mighty God has reached out his hand to me, and nestled inside his giant palm was a promotion! Would you bloody believe it?!

Of course, it was Mr Y who set it all up as some kind of desperate cry for attention, but I'd rather forget that minor detail.

As of tomorrow, I will be: Suzie Quesnell, Administration Assistant! It's actually crazy how happy I've been since I found out yesterday. Since then, I've told like a gazillion people (the Rottweiler was the first to find out. I wish I'd taken a photo of her grumpy, red face! She looked like a toddler who'd dropped his lolly in the potty whilst suffering his first bout of constipation!), and I've already updated my CV, and applied for six admin jobs that pay better than here, and have normal 9-5 hours. One of the jobs is even within a boarding kennels, so it's almost relevant!

Anyway, enough about the very uncertain future, I need to start enjoying the now. However, there are some cons to this lovely new set-up:

1. There is no pay-rise or rise in my contracted-hours. I will still be working 45 hours on a 10 hour contract and will be paid minimum wage, a whole £2 per hour less than the rest of the admin staff.

2. It ties me closer to Mr Y. I mean, if he asks me to go out for a drink am I now obligated to say yes? In fact,

the job ties me closer to everyone since the admin staff regulate every department. That means making small talk with the likes of Creepy Carl and Ashtray Kathy.

3. I'll actually have to use my brain for this job, something I've not done in a long time (well, since I perched my bum behind till 14 all those years ago).

2 a.m.

There's a fourth con. I start at 6 a.m. tomorrow, or rather, today, and I can't sleep!

23rd May

What a week! And it's not even over yet! I thought staring at a checkout all day was exhausting until I started working in admin. I must walk about ten miles every day whilst doing this so-called 'office job'. I literally collapse in my bed after every shift, which is why I haven't had time to spill all the details of the job into this diary! On the plus side, with all of this added walking and no time to eat, or energy to cook, I've lost 6lb!

This is the first day off I've had since I started my job as an admin assistant, and I'm planning on spending all of it in bed!

So, where should I begin? I suppose I'll begin with Monday. The admin dept. is very regimented, (unlike the rest of the supermarket) and there are separate jobs for each day. On Mondays we start at 6 a.m. because that is the only time available for us to put up all the promotional signs for the items that are on offer. I asked the admin manager why we can't just do it on Sunday when the shop closes early and I was informed that Sunday is for taking all of the promotional signs down for items that are no longer on offer. So, every Sunday I'll be working until 8 or 9 p.m. and every Monday I'll be starting work at 6 a.m. The admin manager smiled as he told me this, it's the kind of smile I imagine the devil gives people when they arrive in their new eternal home.

The other specific Monday job is testing the food probes. I'd never seen a probe before Monday. They are like knitting needles made out of sharp metal, connected to little brick computers that document the temperature of whatever it is you are stabbing. As I carried them all to the admin office in one giant bucket, I looked down cautiously at the needles sticking out in all directions. I was convinced that someone, or something, was going to trip me up and I would fall face first into the bucket and come out looking like that guy from Hellraiser. I had a close call when Mr Y made me jump by pinching my bum on his way to the canteen, but I survived. I'm dreading having to do it all over again next week.

Tuesday was less frightening, but not easier. On Tuesday, I had to take weights to every checkout in the store and test the scales of each till. I did all this before the store was even open! Who knew all this went on behind the scenes, eh?

After that I had to do some more scale testing, but this time on different departments. So I weighed 25 pizzas of various sizes in the Fresh Prep. Dept, which meant I got to spend some quality time with the resident crazy old ladies: June/Julie (I don't know her actual name, but I'm sure it's one of those) and Marie. They asked the usual question, '*How's your new job?*' and then went back to their crazy lady banter:

'I got my Mike a Magic Mike costume the other day'.

'Who's Magic Mike?'

'Oh, you know, he's a stripper, from that film'.

'Oh yeah. Ooh, he's nice he is. I'd eat this tuna and sweetcorn pasta off his chest any day'.

'But, you don't like tuna'.

'Well, that's the point, Marie. Oh, never mind'.

That was the mildest conversation they had. I didn't want to document anything stronger. I shuddered all the way to the next department: The Deli – home of Creepy Carl.

'**Sniff sniff** Hey Suzie **sniff**'.

It was the first time we'd spoken properly since our 'date'.

'How's your new **sniffle** job?'

'Fine, thanks', I said, barging past him so I could weigh the cheese and olives, and leave.

Creepy Carl served a few customers and then his counter was empty. I could feel his eyes staring at the back of my head.

'I've got a girlfriend'.

'Good for you', I muttered. I was quite surprised but didn't dare show it, he'll say anything to spark up a conversation.

'It's that new girl on the fish counter'.

'What lovely smelling children you will have'. It just slipped out, but thankfully Creepy Carl burst into a fit of laughter and sniffles. With everything I've said to him by now he could probably get me sacked. Then again, I could probably do the same to him; he's such a pest.

He slowed his laughter to a stop and then stepped closer to me. I tensed. I could literally feel his stale breath blowing on the curl of baby hair that was too short for me to tuck behind my ear.

'She really likes me, and **sniffle** I was just wondering if you knew, and you could **sniff** tell me, how to do it?'

I finished weighing as soon as he finished speaking. When I swung my head around, our noses touched – that's how close he was. He stepped back and sneezed from the contact, and I attempted to dart off. But then the admin manager walked past with Mr Y (who is apparently his best friend).

'Suzie, you have to put all of the stock back on the shelves once you've weighed it'.

So, I turned back towards Creepy Carl and started to collect the products. Carl picked up a few too and walked down to the cheese aisle with me.

'So, can you tell me how to do it?'

I shoved everything on to the shelf, in no particular order. 'Do what?' I sighed.

'You know, sex', he hissed.

'What?!' I dropped my clipboard with all of my weight findings on. Lots of people turned to look as I bent down to get it, probably because Creepy Carl bent down with me – it does not take two people to pick a clipboard off the floor.

'Just tell me, is it easy to put in?'

I could not believe what I was hearing. I snatched my clipboard and ran to the next department. Even still, he shouted after me, 'Does it hurt?'

Good Lord, we are not close enough for him to say things like that to me. He's lucky I won't be telling the whole store.

The final department I tested the scales of – after getting in the way of some chauvinistic pigs in the butchery and partaking in the most unbearable awkward silence with Ashtray Kathy at the bakery – was fish. I put it off until last because:

a) It stinks, and
b) I didn't want to bump into Creepy Carl's new girlfriend.

His new 'girlfriend', and Eggberts' newest fishmonger, is a stunning nineteen year old from South America. She is doing an exchange year with one of the students at Leeds University.

I could not get over her looks, she looked photoshopped! I just stared at her blankly for the first ten minutes.

She had pouty red lips, big brown eyes, and lovely chocolatey waves of hair that, if it wasn't tied up in a hair net, would probably fall just around her narrow waist.

She seemed quite shy, but eager to ask me questions about...well, everything. It was me that brought up Creepy Carl.

'So, Carl says you're going on a date?' I thought that sounded a lot better than, *'So, Carl says he's losing his thirty-year old virginity to you?'*

'Date? No, he's just been showing me around. He's a friendly guy, reminds me of my step-brother'.

After work I went back to the counter and gave her my rape alarm. A pretty girl in a city she doesn't know should not be giving guys like Creepy Carl the wrong idea. I also didn't like the sound of her step-brother.

On Wednesday, I spent most of the day in the office. Finally doing what I thought the job entailed – messing around on a computer and answering the phone. The manager takes Wednesdays off, so the girls just do this every week apparently.

The admin girls are people I could really see myself getting along with. They are just as moody and bitchy as me. The only problem is that they do it in the high-pitched squeaky way, like the girls from *Mean Girls*, whereas I'm more like the '*Am I bovvered?*' girl from *The Catherine Tate Show*.

Oh, and the other problem is, they *love* Mr Y. Like everyone else in this bloody shop. They spent half the morning daring each other to call him on the phone, or shout him over the tannoy. It was embarrassing just watching them. At one point, one of them took the fact that I wasn't joining in with their stupid game to mean that I fancied him more than all of them put together. Once she suggested that, the rest of the gathered around me like a pack of wild dogs around prey, and, as much as I willed my body not too, my face started to turn pink.

'Oh my god, you *do* fancy him', one of them said.

'It's nothing to be embarrassed about. He's fit!' said the bitch that started it all in the first place.

If only they knew the real reason I was blushing. I did contemplate telling them just as something to talk about, but they would either be super jealous and hate me, or start all that high-pitched girly squealing: '*Oh my god! Tell us all about it!*' Both options I could not be bothered to deal with.

They were finally moving on from the subject and showing me how to use the tannoy when Mr Y walked in. I had just finished my first tannoy announcement: 'Staff call. Christine Marshall contact administration please'. I put the silly microphone down, quite pleased with myself, and found Mr Y standing inbetween the admin girls. His arms folded in the same schoolgirl way as them.

'You've got the perfect voice for that you know', he said, all suave, before walking out and leaving the girls practically swooning. You'd think he was James bloody Bond.

26th May

I think I'm finally getting the swing of things in admin. I don't get massive headaches during my shifts anymore so my brain must be used to the extra activity, and it's great to have such freedom to walk about the store.

Whenever I want to get away from it all, I can just hide wherever I want. Down the spirits aisle, in the toilet, in the warehouse, in the admin office itself, you name it and I am allowed to be there without someone saying '*What are you doing?*'

Don't get me wrong, I still hate working in a supermarket. I'm still underpaid, underappreciated, and overworked.

I've started applying for some more jobs though, admin related ones. I've found a few that are admin and dog related, such as Kennel Receptionist, and an admin post at the RSPCA.

So, moving to admin has been a vast improvement in many ways. Although, there is one distinct disadvantage that springs to mind: Mr Y has upped his game. I knew he would. The problem is, these days I spend a lot of the time in work before the store opens, and after it closes, which means no customers to interrupt him, and lots of cold, dark corners for me to get trapped in.

Why did he have to pick me? Of all the people. I don't want to come across as having low self-esteem but, it's not like I make much of an effort with my appearance, and the stress of working here has definitely taken its toll on my looks. I think I even found a grey hair the other day.

The worst thing is that I feel like I have to be a bit more polite about it now, I mean, he did get me this job, which will make it easier for me to get out of here eventually (I hope). I've just been smiling at him whenever he does something disgusting, like whispering, stroking, or grabbing. But I haven't smiled naturally for years. For all I know, I could just be baring my teeth at him. If he asked me to go for a drink or a meal or something, I would go. But only through pure obligation because he got me this promotion, and because I'm not in a position to turn down free food. But, it's never that. Instead, he always has something perverted to say, like most perverts do.

This morning he practically dragged me behind the cooked chicken counter, but at that time in the morning it was the raw chicken counter and the smell made me want to gag. He started going on about how it's been too long since he woke up in my bed and we need to relive it. He really likes to hear himself talk. Then he started going on about the admin manager, his best mate, and Clare. So I pricked up my ears, thinking he meant double date. I know Clare wouldn't say no to free food either. And also, if I dragged her into it, I wouldn't be in this disgustingly sticky situation alone.

'So, the four of us could, you know, get together', he said.

I started to suggest a new Italian that has just opened round the corner when he cut me off with his chiselled stage laugh, '*Har-Har-Har*'. 'Not that kind of get-together, love'.

At that point he grabbed my hand and placed it on his crotch. Luckily, one of the other ADMs appeared on the other side of the store and shouted for him to come and help her. Ugh! I washed my hands for about fifteen minutes, until they started to hurt. I'm done being polite to that sick bastard.

30th May

Mr Y has been caught! I would feel so relieved if only the affair was dealt with a little more privately. But, when you work in a supermarket environment, nothing is private. Everyone knows who's slept with who, who fancies who, who hates who...everything.

He was caught yesterday, by the Rottweiler of all people. I was tidying the signage cupboard – some idiot had put all the '£1' signs in the 'half price' box, and all the 'half price' signs in the 'two for one' box and, well, you get the picture – when Mr Y walked past. I knew he couldn't let an opportunity like this slide: alone together in a cupboard, oh how romantic! My upper lip started to sweat, I had managed to dodge him since the unfortunate incident at the cooked chicken counter, but there was no escape here.

'Hey', he whispered as he slipped in. He tried to close the door, but my foot was firmly pressed against it. 'Oh, so you want everyone to see us, do you? I didn't know you lived so dangerously, Suzie'.

He tried to curl a strand of my hair around his finger, but it was sticky and knotty from when I accidentally dipped it in my yoghurt at lunch, not quite the romantic gesture he was hoping for. He ended up pulling it instead.

‘Ow! Get off!’ I shouted (no more Miss Polite Suzie). I pushed his hand away.

Then, something about him changed. He grabbed my wrist and squeezed it, hard – really hurting me, intentionally hurting me. My heart started racing. For the first time in a long time, I wasn’t the bitchy checkout girl who shouted her mouth off no matter what the consequences; I was a damsel in distress. But I’d die before showing Mr Y that. ‘Get off me right now’, I said with all the authority I could muster.

‘Not so tough now are we, Suzie-Q?’

I moved my arm sharply to try and loosen his grip, but he just laughed it off. Then he went to move my foot from the door. And that is when the Rottweiler arrived. I’ve never been happier to see her face. In fact, before that moment I had literally never been happy to see her face. She came through for me today though. She may be a psychotic bitch that gets a thrill out of working her staff to the bone, but she is dedicated to her job, I will always give her that.

She realised, in that split second before Mr Y let go of my wrist, what a monster this Mr Perfect really was. At first, I was sure she would take his side, being one of his many admirers. But, true to her nature, she marched straight to the personnel office, ignoring his pathetic pleas: ‘Christine! Christine, wait!’

After he was found out, there was a meeting in personnel with me, him, and the Rottweiler. Then just me and him. Then just me. And finally, just him. He came out without a job. I didn’t want it to go that far, and I didn’t expect it to. It’s no secret how hard it is to get sacked from a supermarket. But Mr Y managed it. He left in a dignified fashion. Breaking the hearts of all the disillusioned girls as he walked away – I think one of the girls from the frozen dept. even cried.

So, as he left, looking like a wounded hero. I remained, looking like a heartless bitch. I’ve been more of an outcast than usual since it happened. Even Creepy Carl has kept his distance! No one from admin has spoken to me since, apart from to tell me what to do and when to do it. Still, it'll pass. Someone else will air their dirty laundry soon enough and mine will be forgotten about.

June

3rd June

Dear Diary,

This has been one bad Sunday.

I have been demoted. Back to the checkouts I go. It happened this morning. Well, I was *told* this morning.

I went into the office and the girls were in there with the manager, Mr Y's best mate. I could tell they were talking about me by the way they all silenced and sat up straight when I entered. I tried to ignore it and be cheery, 'Right, I'll get started on the increased price tickets', I said, picking up a clipboard. The manager snatched it from me and held it tight to his chest.

'No, I'm afraid you won't. The girls and I have been talking amongst ourselves and we're just not sure that you're cut out for this department'.

'What do you mean?' I was humiliated and furious. Can you imagine any manager having this conversation in front of his entire staff, even if his entire staff only consists of three people?

'After today, you'll be going back to the checkouts. I've informed Christine'.

I laughed, 'So, this is what I get for standing up to your perverted mate? Well, at least your loyal, I'll give you that'.

He turned plum purple as he felt everyone's eyes on him, and I couldn't help it, I smirked. So, what was my punishment? There was always going to be a punishment.

I spent my last day as an admin assistant taking down every single piece of POS by myself: the posters and banners outside, the posters that hang from the ceiling, the stickers on the floor, the offer signs down the aisles, you name it, I took it down or put it up today. It's usually a three person job, but the rest of the admin staff went home at 6. I worked until 10 to get it all finished. And now, at 11, I'm finally home and in bed, waiting for my next shift, bright and early at 8 a.m. behind checkout fourteen. Just like the good old days.

4th June

So, here I am, back on checkout bloody fourteen. Home, sweet, home. Someone's messed everything up too, but I'm determined not to let it get to me. Surely I don't care enough about my job to be annoyed when someone else uses my work station. Even if that person has stuck gum to every possible space under the counter, *and* stolen my bag sponge.

A bag sponge, for those of you lucky enough to have never served time in a supermarket, is a cheap scrap of sponge in a little sandwich box with a dash of water inside – enough to wet my fingers and open bags rapid-fire.

Yes, that's right, we cheat. And we still have the cheek to look at customers in disgust when they lick fingers or spit on their hands to open a bag.

We've been cheating for years. As far as I know, a lady named Bonnie Baggers (no joke, she's like William Henry Hoover or Thomas Crapper) invented it seventy years ago. Apparently they are widely used in supermarkets all over the world now, but Bonnie wouldn't have gotten any thanks or praise for it. She would have been made to sit silently and scan shopping until she retired on a minimum wage pension. Some hot-shot manager would've taken the credit for her idea, no doubt, and then retired to Fiji with all of the millions he made from it.

Anyway, back to the real problem. I have no bag sponge. No chance of getting another one from anywhere. Everyone has been horrible to me since I came back from admin, well, even more horrible than usual. Stupid remarks like:

'Back slumming it with us lot are you?'

'Thought you were too good for the checkouts'

Stupid, jealous jibes like that. So I know that if I ask for a bag sponge, I'll be greeted with the same spitefulness.

There is another way to easily open bags – probably the best kept secret a checkout girl can spill, or at least the most useful.

So, listen up. You hold up the bag, one hand on the tip of each handle, and then pull outwards – swift and hard. *Voila!*[*] The bag is now open, or ripped because you were too forceful. Even so, you now have the skills to open bags at the supermarkets, without licking your germ-ridden fingers. Who knew such wisdom lurked within me?!

But it's probably too late for that little life lesson, right? Most people just use reusable bags now. They bloody stink those reusable bags – God knows where customers are keeping them. I myself, do not use reusable bags. Hear me out before you shoot me.

Let's think about it. Supermarkets all over the country make these bags out of non-recyclable plastic. Then they make you, or me, the consumer, feel terrible for using them. We have signs up all over the staff canteen telling us about the damage of plastic bags piling up in landfills, or how plastic bags cost 2 pence per person and the supermarkets give them out for FREE – God forbid they give something back to their loyal customers for once. They do this to guilt-trip us into guilt-tripping customers into using reusable bags that are, coincidentally, sold by the supermarkets.

Eggberts, or any supermarket, could start making bags out of recyclable paper if they wanted to - if they *really* cared about the planet. But they don't. Instead, they shift the responsibility to the everyday man and woman, the average Joes that certainly aren't mass producing plastic bags on a weekly basis. What I'm getting at here is, global warming: blame the supermarkets.

---

* That's French for 'There you have it!' – At least, I think it is.

7th June

I like to think me and Clare are best friends. So, why is it that everyone loves her and hates me?!

She's only gone and managed to get a week off by giving, like, a day's notice!

Okay, maybe that is deceptive. She hasn't been given a week of *paid* holiday. I'd drop dead of a heart attack if Eggberts agreed to that at short notice. No, she's been very tactful indeed. I'll have to remember her scheme in case I *ever* get another interview.

She's got a week-long interview in London for that play she applied for. So they didn't laugh at her cover letter after all, or maybe they did and they want to mock her in person.

She's planning to call in sick for the first three days. She'll call up and tell management she has sickness and diarrhoea. The reason for this is because it is absolutely, diabolically, illegal for a supermarket worker to come in if they have such an illness. We touch so many other people's food that we could start a nationwide epidemic. But that still doesn't mean management don't expect you to drag yourself out of bed and crawl to your checkout, especially if there is a holiday going on. Last year, I came in to work when I had a very real case of sickness and diarrhoea because, as I recall the Rottweiler screaming: 'There's only sixteen working days left until Christmas, and if you're not here you'll be lucky to get coal in your stocking!' I must have been a bit delirious from my illness because I asked her to elaborate and obviously she meant: get here, or get sacked. Still, Clare's managed to pick a convenient time of the year to be 'ill', so although she'll get scolded, she'll still be allowed to keep her job. How generous of our superiors.

After three days off sick, she then has two days off anyway. The problem after that was getting people to cover the remaining two days. I'm the lucky sap that is covering one of them. I'm hoping that it will send me some good karma. One of her other friends is covering the next one, although I'm the only person that knows where Clare is actually going. She's told her other friends that she is off to visit an old relative, or something stupid like that. They bought it.

You can't tell anyone that you're applying for jobs in this place. You'll be battered with remarks of jealousy, and spiteful comments like, '*You'll never get out of here, you know*', every time you get rejected for an interview. Then they'll start to look down on you and say things like, '*It's not that bad here. I've survived thirty years, what makes you special enough to leave?*'

We've seen it happen to many people, most of them all still work here, their spirit broken beyond repair. They haven't made peace with an eternity of 'stack, stack, stack' or 'scan, scan, scan', they've fought with all they have and been beaten, badly. No fight left in them. It scares me a lot.

10th June

Currently hiding among several boxes of bananas. Don't know why I'm choosing this as a moment to write in my diary, possibly so that it keeps my mind off the fact there could be a Brazilian People Eater spider lurking about in the bananas. It's always in the news stuff like that, isn't it? Urgh. Makes me shudder.

***

So, yeah, I've spent a lot of my day hiding. One of my university tutors came in to the shop, and I would rather be caught streaking down the street than in this supermarket wearing this uniform that says: My degree was a waste of time.

It was that one tutor that I never got along with – typical. And she came in for a massive shop. She must have spent well over an hour in here. If she saw me, I just knew she would say something smug, so I did the adult thing – hid in various places until I was sure she was gone.

It's not the first time it's happened to me. I'll just be walking down the coffee aisle minding my own, and then bam! An old uni friend is in the area to speak at an alumni meeting because she's had so much success with her degree. Seeing anyone you know whilst working here just makes your heart sink right down your chest, fall out your pants, and splat on the floor.

Today I've hid in the warehouse, down the wine aisle, in the butchery freezer, and of course among the bananas. Thank God I wasn't sat on my till when she came in. She would have definitely come to my till, even if the queue was three miles long. I don't get that about people. My mum does it all the time. She'll see someone she knows working behind a till and she'll go: 'Oh, let's just see how she is'.

I'll tell you how she is Mum: she's miserable because she has to work here, and you've just made it all the worse by asking her to serve you.

Know someone that works in a supermarket? Never 'pop in' and see them. Every time you do, another piece of their soul dies. Luckily, I hardly have any friends, so my soul is still pretty much intact. My dignity, however, not so much.

***

Mere minutes before my lunch hour was over and I was about to head back to the place where I would be spending the next three hours, and will probably spend the remainder of my life (*think positive thoughts, think positive thoughts*), my mum called with great news.

'Hello darling'.

Oddly cheerful for my mum, but she's been a bit more upbeat since Renée announced she was getting married. 'Hi, Mum. What's up?'

'Nothing, nothing; I'm just ringing because I'm about to book a last minute deal thingie on the internet to see your grandma'.

By my grandma, she means my dad's mother. My grandma is like an even more insufferable version of my mum, but she lives in five bedroom house in Marseille, so she's a lot easier to put up with than my mum, who only lives in a bungalow in Lancashire.

'We're going on the tenth of July for a week. Just wondering if you're free?'

Err – Yes! I am always free for a holiday. Well, this was my initial reaction, and then in the following five seconds I realised I could never get that much time off, could I? Maybe if a few people covered for me – Clare, and June/Julie, and so on. Yeah, why not?

'Course I'm free. Well, I'll work something out and make myself free!'

'Great! So you can watch Jakey then?'

'Jakey?' The thought bubble of me sunbathing in Gran's back garden suddenly popped.

'Yes, you know he doesn't do well in kennels. He likes home comforts. Plus, you can put it on your CV!'

My mum chuckled to herself whilst I swallowed a big lump in my throat, 'Yep. I'm free to watch Jakey. Have a great time'.

I must have been a real bitch in a past life.

13th June

It's Friday the 13th again! I'm not a very superstitious person, but Friday 13th is something I wholly believe in. That, and full moons. Both of which have the same effect: making the weirdest of the weird crawl out of their hideaways and venture into the nearest supermarket.

So far today, a baby has spat strained peas in my eye; I've tripped over a wet floor sign; and a woman has had a very heated argument with me because she thought Colgate toothbrushes were only 25p. And it's not even lunchtime yet. Things will get worse, mark my words.

If that wasn't enough, my tooth (the one that's needed filling for like, two years) is in constant pain today. I've practically drank a full tube of Bonjela. It seems every part of my mouth is numb except that one tooth.

***

Today has gotten a lot better, but it's still Friday 13th, no doubt. The good news is, my sister is coming to visit me tonight! I read her text on my break:

'Surprise! I'm on my way to your place! I'll be there by 7. I know how you feel about Friday 13th so I thought I'd bring you some good luck for a change ☺ Renée'.

She is so sweet! I cannot wait to see her. My first thought was, *'I am definitely going to have to call in sick tomorrow'.*

Fortunately, or unfortunately, I won't need to. This is where Friday 13th really punched me in the boob. I read my sister's text on the toilet. Now, I don't know if you've ever been to the toilet in a tabard, but you have to lift it up and out of the way before you squat – like a dress. I was so excited by the text that I forgot to lift it. Yes, I weed on my own clothes. At that moment in time, I would have welcomed Jason running into the store wearing his hockey mask. But, after a couple of minutes fretting, I didn't hear any blood curdling screams, so I had to leave the cubical. I managed to dry my tabard under the hand-dryer before anyone else came in. But I couldn't get rid of the smell of urine. I didn't have any perfume on me or anything. With my quick wit, I decided to take a detour down the fragrance aisle on the way back to my till, but of course all of the managers had chosen that aisle as a gossiping spot, because it's Friday the 13th and the universe just loves fucking with me.

So, I went back to my till and tried to pretend I couldn't smell anything. But, after six people mentioned a smell lingering around me (*including Creepy Carl!*), I decided to tell the Rottweiler. I flashed my light and as she walked towards me my tooth panged so painfully that I couldn't help but cover my mouth with my hand, which gave me any idea.

'What?' The Rottweiler said. I could tell by the way her nostrils flared that she had smelled me.

'I've got a problem with my tooth. I think I've got a fungal infection or something'.

'Can teeth even go fungal?'

I shrugged. She inhaled deeply, immediately wishing she hadn't. 'I suppose you'd better go. Don't come back until you've had that seen to'.

For a few seconds I just stared at her in shock. I was allowed to leave?! When I finally clicked back to reality, I ran home.

I'm now sitting on the sofa watching cartoons. Cartoons seem to be getting rid of my toothache. I hope it leaves soon; my sister will be here in three hours.

One hour later

I'm so super-duper excited to see my sister tonight! With Clare in London, the only people I have spoken to today have been colleagues and customers. Hence the nerdy, not to mention, desperate: '*super-duper*'.

Despite being excited, I also feel slightly nervous, if that's even possible. It's just strange because when we were younger I was the older one, and automatically called the shots. Obviously, I am still older, but my twenty-three year old sister is a big-time executive publisher. She wears pant-suits, and drinks chardonnay, and always looks immaculate.

I feel like the younger one now. The less responsible, train-wreck sibling. She can't possibly look up to me anymore.

Oh well, she's still a laugh.

One hour later

Do I clean? Or do I pretend I've been ill and hope my sister will clean for me whilst showering me with sympathy?

One hour later

I decided to clean. I figured if I said I was ill she might tell me to slow down on the drink, and right now it's possible that I am more excited to see a decent bottle of wine than I am my own sister.

I'm exhausted after all this cleaning, and all I have in the cupboards are out-of-date breadsticks, a tin of mushy peas, and a questionable jar of peanut butter. I'm hoping she brings food, too.

Ten minutes later

Where is she? Stupid Friday the 13th has probably cancelled her train or something.

Forty minutes later

Renée is here! She is just getting changed out of her 'travel clothes'! God, she's so posh!

The first words out of her mouth were: *'I'm starving! Let's go to the fanciest restaurant in a five mile radius, stuff our faces, and drink 'til they throw us out'* - I feel so proud of her.

Winner, winner, FREE chicken dinner!

14th June

It's 7:32 a.m. and I can't get back to sleep. Ever woke up after a night out drinking and felt like someone's rubbed sandpaper all over your tongue and throat?

Of course you have. Well, when it happens to me I can never get back to sleep, not without drinking a gallon of water anyway. So, I'm sat on my toilet seat doing just that.

Renée is snoring away in Clare's bed. She spent £200 on us last night. I'm trying not to think of all of the other things I could have bought with that money.

We chatted about all sorts yesterday, but as with most human beings, every topic managed to find its way back to the subject of work.

Renée *loves* her job and is insanely good at it. I hate my job, a monkey could do it better than me, and it would definitely be more polite. But, being around my sister always makes me feel motivated. We thought of a million things I can do to achieve my dream. First I just have to remember what we said...and find a dream.

I want to work with dogs, I know that much, and I thought a degree in Canine Behaviour and Training would help, but it hasn't. I just assumed I would walk out of uni with my degree and a stranger would come up to me in the street and say, 'Wow, a canine degree! Want a £30,000 a year job?' And I'd just shrug my shoulders and say 'sure', and get on with my *real* life. But of course, this is real. This is real life, and as Renée so bluntly put it last night, I'm wasting it.

I did try to defend myself, telling her I have applied for a few jobs. And I do work 45 hours a week, which makes it difficult to fit anything else in.

Renée didn't accept this. 'Anything is possible', she said.

So, today is the first day of the rest of my life – again. Today we're going to sort my CV out, allocate specific times that I can apply for jobs, and also try to think of a way I can volunteer whilst working to a stupid rota. My sister seems to think I haven't shown enough willing to find a voluntary placement.

'One thing I look for in a writer is a true passion for what they're doing. If I can see that they are doing this day in, day out, simply for the love of it, then I can invest in them, can't I?

'No one is going to invest in you if all you're bringing to the table is your Eggberts uniform and a degree certificate with a coffee stain on it'.

Her exact words, I believe. She's right though, as per usual. The first item on our agenda today is to visit the dentist. After my incessant whinging last night, Renée offered to pay for my filling and she booked it in for 10 a.m. this morning – how kind of her.

***

I have escaped once again to the sanctuary of my toilet! One evening with my sister was amazing, but today she has been driving me insane!

First, she took me to be injected, prodded, and scratched by a dentist with an extremely heavy wrist watch. Then she brought me home, scrutinized my CV, and found ten jobs I'd enjoy. At the time of writing we've reached application 7! I know she means well, and I'm really grateful, but does all this good have to be done in one day?!

It doesn't even stop there. Once all the applications are filled in she said we would 'Order pizza and stay up late thinking of ways I can better organise my time' – won't that be fun?!

She's a nosey bugger too. When I went to get the takeaway menus she had her mitts on this diary! I feel violated. I think she's turning into Mum, but I don't dare say anything. She's scarier than my mum and she's my *baby* sister.

Oh God, she's knocking.

'Nothing you need to do in a bathroom should take longer than six minutes; especially if you have guests'.

Brill, so now she is timing my bathroom breaks.

15th June

Well, my sister has gone back to London. Not before dropping me off at work in a slick and sexy Audi that she rented just so she could drive herself to the train station.

That car's all everyone's been talking about all day. I've been given 6 phone numbers by desperate gold-diggers, two of which are from women who, as far as I know, are in pretty serious heterosexual relationships. And two from men in very homosexual relationships. So, that's another thing my sister beats me at: pulling. She's received 6 phone numbers through the tinted windows of an Audi, and I've received a perverted hug from Creepy Carl, and a sexual harassment case from Mr Y.

I do miss her though, despite what I said last night. Just being around her makes me feel more...alive. She's like one of those inspirational exercise adverts or something. I've got butterflies thinking about all of the jobs I've applied for. My sister even set up a job centre interview for me later on in the week, too. That's more than enough stuff to daydream about in order to get me through this nine hour shift.

Later in the day

Just received a seventh number for my sister. Creepy Carl handed me the sweaty piece of paper, 'Give that to your sis for me will you, babe *sniff sniff*'.

It's probably the first time he has said 'babe' in his entire life. It's better than 'sugar' though, I suppose.

'You didn't even see her, Carl. And where is this paper from? It reeks!'

‘Heard about her though. If your sis isn’t interested then feel free to keep hold of that for yourself. I ripped the paper from the back of a blue stilton wedge. Think about it’.

I threw the paper into a motorcyclist’s helmet, just waiting to see what happens from now.

18th June

To most girls, hair and make-up is kind of a big deal. For me, it never really has been. I always wear mascara, but that’s about it on a day-to-day basis. I’ll throw on a bit of foundation if my skin’s really bad, but I’ve never really cared for bronzer, blusher, eye shadow, nail varnish, or funky hair styles. Six years at Eggberts, however, and I crave them.

The rules for girls at work are: hair up, nails clean, subtle make up, and a maximum of two piercings (preferably one in each ear). I’ve tried so hard to disobey, but it just doesn’t work. They have everything: nail varnish remover, make-up wipes, elastic bands for your hair. They’re always one step ahead. If you ask me, it’s just another way for them to break our spirit. Another way to make us feel like just a number, and it works.

Sometimes I leave my nail varnish on, or slap on loads of make-up, just so I can have a ten minute delay before sitting down at my till. But Eggberts don’t mind. They’re smarter than that. Ten minutes is nothing to them because they have employed about seventy women (in this store alone) and told them that make-up and basic expression is forbidden. So now, thanks to reverse psychology, we *want* these things.

As soon as I have a day off, the nail varnish goes on, my hair gets let down, and I paint myself the colour of a tangerine. Nail varnish is now my crack cocaine – I need one in every colour, even though I can hardly ever wear it. Eggberts know this and they relish it, because where do desperate checkout girls like me buy our fixes from? Them, of course! It's a vicious circle:

Eggberts say, '*You are not allowed make-up*', which leads to...

Staff thinking, '*We really want make-up*', which then leads to...

Staff buying make-up from Eggberts, which leads to the one thing that this shop really cares about...

£££

How very clever and devious of them. Taking ordinary women like myself and turning us into make-up deprived junkies. Before I worked here, I was happy to lounge about in leggings and a vest top – no make-up, hair tied back. Now I want a nail in every colour, contours all over my face, seventeen piercings, blue highlights, and a Mike Tyson tattoo. There are so many negatives to this job!

***

Another thing I hate about this godforsaken place – in fact, the most hated aspect of all – is working from a rota. Ridiculous really, because it probably wouldn't even be that bad if that Rottweiler could do her bloody job properly!

The rule is that we are meant to receive our rotas two weeks in advance, so that we can at least plan our lives, but no, we have to beg for them. We have to plead for working hours that we don't really want to do, and then if we are persistent and lucky enough, we might get to find out what hours we're doing a few days before it's actually time to do them. Most times, it's not even complete and I don't know if I'm even working until the day before, which is just great when you have rent and bills to pay!

It's hands down one of the main reasons that people in supermarkets lose all of their friends. Plans turn into mission impossible:

‘Hey, coming out on 18th September for my birthday?’

‘I’ll have to tell you nearer the time because I don’t know if I will be working or not’ – sounds like the laziest excuse ever dreamt up, but of course, it’s totally true. And, in case you’re wondering, no I did not make that birthday, or any other birthdays after that.

It’s a piss-take too because, as you may remember, I’m only contracted to work Sunday 12-5, and Monday 4-9, that’s it. Yet, I haven’t had one Saturday off since Sharon Osborne was a judge on the x-factor.

Maybe you’re reading this and thinking ‘What are you complaining about? If you want to work your contracted hours then just do it!’

But, obviously I can’t because as I mentioned: bills need paying.

If I was ever so brash as to turn around and request a Saturday off, first I would be questioned: why/what/where. Then if I still persisted, I’d get the raised eyebrows and the ‘I’ll have to speak with the store manager speech’. If I dared go even further than that, then the store manager would come over and say, ‘Sure we can do that for you. But if you’re not going to be flexible enough we may have to find someone else’.

Of course, that’s when horrible images of me being homeless flash through my mind. When it comes to choosing between a roof over your head and going to the birthday party of the girl you’ve known since you were five – the one who knows everything about you and pinky swore that you could be her maid of honour when she grew up and got married – that bitch flies right out of the window.

In this economy, it’s a hell of a lot easier to make new friends than find a new job (although I seem to struggle with both). And so, you forget your friend’s birthday and spend another lonely evening on your checkout, daydreaming about the wonderful time you could be having, and that everyone is having without you.

I have a terrible feeling that is what is going to happen with Renée's hen do. I asked the Rottweiler if she could sort something out today, and she doesn't appreciate being asked the same question more than five times. She says if I ask her again before the actual rota is due, then I'll be working seven days a week. It's probably not an empty threat either.

20th June

I'm in the job centre. I've never been in here before, despite all my whinging about wanting a job.

It's such a depressing place. No one speaks, all that can be heard are keyboard keys tapping, and phones ringing. I'm waiting for my interview that Renée was kind enough to set up for me, although I wish she hadn't bothered. The sun is beaming today and I've spent the past eighteen minutes sitting on an itchy chair that appears to be made out of unwanted Christmas jumpers. And that's not the worst of it. I'm wearing the blouse that I bought for my first interview. It was the cheapest I could find, and after the second wash I can see why. It literally feels like I am wearing paper – low quality paper at that. I'm just so irritated. I wish the ground would swallow me up, or that I could run away. The silence makes it worse.

I had a play on the job finder machines they have here, but it didn't find any matches for me, so I doubt the advisor will. I should just leave.

My neck is starting to sweat. If I hear an ice cream van, I'm out of here.

***

I didn't hear any ice-cream van. Instead, I went through with my interview. Lord knows why I bothered. I'm going to kill Renée when I next see her.

The interview was with a girl about the same age is me. I could tell within seconds from her attitude that she was not going to help me. She was 'too good' for that, clearly. She had an expensive pantsuit, and hair that looked like it'd been styled by Nicky Clarke. Her make-up was immaculate, and she was wearing shiny black nail varnish, no chips. All of this I knew from the first handshake, and I already envied her.

As the interview progressed I just got greener, and greener.

She has her own desk, a big spacious one, and a comfy chair to sit back in, a computer that was made in this century, and a phone that she could '*put on hold*'. If that wasn't enough, she had a photograph of her and some guy (presumably her fiancé by the size of the rock on her finger) at Disneyland and one of those super-health smoothie things on her desk, meaning she has money to burn. Great – paid more than me, more successful than me, and I know for a fact that she gets weekends off.

But enough about my jealousy. Even if I wasn't envious of her, and had gone into the interview with high hopes and big dreams, I would still be in the foul mood that I am right now.

The interview began by the woman asking what jobs I am interested in. She held in a snigger when I told her I had a degree in Canine Training and Behaviour, God knows why that is so amusing. Next, she went on the job centre website and tried to find jobs suited to my skill set. There were no jobs even remotely related to canine care, and she seemed to think that this was because a job with dogs is unrealistic. I was quick to tell her that *actually*, the job centre website is just shit. I've found and applied for tons of canine related jobs, what I need is help with writing applications, my CV, and covering letters, so I can actually get these jobs.

She didn't take it well. Female dogs, or bitches as they're commonly known, will never start a fight with another bitch unless they know they are going to win. This is because when bitches fight, they fight to the death. I was in big trouble.

The job centre bitch refused to look at my CV, apparently that's 'not what she's paid for'. She is paid to set up realistic goals that can be met. She even talked about 'expanding' my career within retail. I could have strangled her. I stood my ground on dogs, telling her over and over again that I have a degree.

Do you know what I hate? If I'd have gone in there with a law degree, or a business degree, there would have been no sniggering or bitch-fighting, just a genuine, '*Let me see how I can help you*'. But, because I've got a degree in something that I'm interested in, instead of doing it just for money (not saying people with business and law degrees are in it for the money, but those subjects just send me to sleep!), I'm a laughing stock. She literally looked at me like my degree was given to me at my primary school graduation. And she's not the first to look at me like that either.

Anyway, I don't want to talk about this anymore, it's making my blood boil. She sent me off with one piece of advice – volunteer. Gee thanks, I'll be sure to do that when I get a minute.

P.S. I think Clare is avoiding me. She came home like, three days ago, at least I think she did, either that or a ghost has moved in. Maybe her interview didn't go so well. Not surprising with that cover letter poem she wrote. Still, I wish she felt comfortable enough to confide in me. I'd confide in me if I was her, she's not going to find a bigger failure than me to confess her troubles to.

22nd June

Well, after a lengthy chat with my sister about my horrible job centre interview she only went and agreed with the stuffy job centre woman! And I realise that she's right, even if I do hardly have any time to volunteer, I at least have to try. If it will get me out of Eggberts sooner, then I'll do it. I need something casual though, seeing as how the Rottweiler can't competently plan the rota in advance. My sister suggested asking around to see if any of my friends need their dogs walking. She never believes me when I tell her I have no friends, you know. The possibility is just so alien to her that she can't compute it. I'll pretend she told me to ask my colleagues seeing as they are the only people that I interact with. I'm going to ask June/Julie and the like, I know they've all got little lapdogs that they can't be bothered walking.

Clare is so avoiding me. I can see her over there on self-scan. I've been sat on my till for six hours now and normally she would have been over to chat at least four times, whether I wanted her to or not. Rejection must have hit her like a ton of bricks. I know the feeling.

***

I have some voluntary work! June/Julie, whose name I found out is actually June, has a Westie that I can walk three times a week. And her daughter has two pugs. Her daughter lives next door, so I've offered to do all three at the same time. It won't be that bad, especially with the weather getting warmer. The only problem is that I can't put either of them down as a reference. If I let slip that I am looking for a new job, I'll be even more of a pariah than I already am. But it can go on my CV and that's good enough. Dog walking: 2007 – present. Everyone stretches the truth on their CV right?

25th June

What is it with customers that will touch money that has been passed to millions of people, but get all squirmy and health-conscious when it comes to putting it in my hand?

The amount of times someone has given me the 'screwed-up face' look and then dropped the money on the counter, instead of my outstretched palm, is ridiculous

Coins that could have been anywhere from the bottom of a grubby pond, to the rim of a stripper's bum-hole, are considered so much cleaner than my own hands. The best part about this is, after I've picked up all of the coins, counted them and put them in the till; the customer will more than likely wait, hand-outstretched, for their change. I always make a point of giving them as much skin to skin contact as possible when giving the change back. So much so that a customer just complained about me inappropriately caressing his hand, a fact I'm strangely proud of...

4:25p.m.

My shift finishes in five minutes. I was on an early one for a change. It's rare that I get out of the shop before closing time, and today that still might not happen. Today I have to do the chore every checkout girl dreads – go shopping! As if I didn't spend enough time here already! Spending time *and* money here is even worse.

Still, it's much better than coming to the supermarket to go shopping on your day off. I can't think of anything more soul destroying. If I do it now, at least it will be over and done with and I can relax on my day off tomorrow (and when I say relax, I mean frantically apply for jobs).

Still, I wish I'd finished a bit earlier. This is the worst possible time to go shopping. All the mums nip in with their kids to get something for tea, and of course because their kids are with them it turns into a massive £80 junk food shop. Then, before those customers leave you get all the workers coming in clogging up the aisles.

But I've got the edge. I went round to each department and told people what I need to be waiting for me at half past four – and when I say 'I need', I mean 'Clare needs'. No one in here would ever want to do me a favour, but they all love Clare. So, they should be all ready and waiting with 'Clare's shopping', and I can be served and out of here in minutes. Hopefully.

29th June

Summer and ice cream go together like winter and hot chocolate, or autumn and tomato soup. It's payday, and I'm sat in the park eating a Mr Whippy. I think I'll make this a payday tradition. It's about the only one I can afford. It beats my old payday tradition of getting a cheap bottle of cider and drinking it in front of the TV. That can be my winter payday tradition, although, if I'm still working at Eggberts this winter I might just jump in front of a bus instead.

I've only got a thirty minute break, and by the time I sat down on the bench I was already down to twenty minutes. Normally I would play a game on my phone at break time, or ring my sister, but I'm determined to make these last fifteen minutes stretch for as long as possible, because when they're up I have to go back into Eggberts and stay there for another three hours and forty-five minutes.

I'm just looking around the park, from person to person. It's a sunny Saturday so it's quite busy. All these people have something in common, they look insanely happy. They're all cute couples holding hands, cute couples walking dogs, and cute couples playing with their kids. I've only just realised how single I feel. With Nick, we were so far apart at the end that I thought that was what a normal relationship felt like. I'm trying not to think about that though, I already have to be jealous of the fact that these people are off work on a Saturday; I don't want to be jealous of their relationships, too.

Oh great. Creepy Carl is approaching. So it's bye-bye relaxing break, and hello hell. Fuck's sake, I could hear him sniffling before I even saw him. Did you ever look at someone and just want to hurt them because you hate them that much? I'm going to tell myself that you answered yes to that question. It helps me feel like less of a monster.

July

2nd July

There was a reason Clare was avoiding me. Not because she was rejected from the job, the absolute opposite! She got it! I was so happy for her until I realised that in a few months she'll be off, living her life, finally, and I will still be here. Don't get me wrong, she deserves it more than anyone. I mean, she has been applying for jobs solidly for the past five years. Will I have to do that before something comes my way? I don't think the few shreds of hope I have will stretch that far.

When Clare told me the details of the job I was so emotional that I had to pretend I was crying tears of happiness, I doubt she bought it though. She starts in September – a three year contract with some fancy theatre company in London. She is moving there in August. I can't believe it. I don't have one thing lined up, except walking people's dogs for free, and Clare is an actress in a West End Show.

And you won't believe what won the casting director over: her ridiculous cover letter! He said that her poem was heartbreaking, and her performance even more so. Pass me a sick bucket!

I'm just jealous. As usual. I'll turn permanently green soon, like a modern day She Hulk. Maybe I could make some money from it?

I need to snap out of this negativity. It's a beautiful day and now I'm going to unwind whilst walking three dogs. For free.

***

I loved the walk. It didn't feel like working at all. It felt like relaxing - although the two Pugs were a bit rowdy, and it did rain for a bit whilst we were out. Still, if I did this all day every day for a living, I'd be happy. But of course, I don't. I've got scanning and more scanning to look forward to at my real job tomorrow.

Anyway, yes, the walk was good. The aftermath, not so much. I dropped the dogs off at June's and before I left she asked me for a favour. Have you ever said yes to a favour before even asking what it was? Of course you have. Why do we do that? Is it a British thing?

The favour was to pick up the dog poo from her back garden. I was fine with it, poo doesn't bother me, and it's more 'experience' I suppose. Plus, June has a bad back so I felt like I was doing something nice, and I needed good karma more than anything. But, when I got into the garden, bad karma was waiting for me, as usual. The garden was absolutely covered! June has had a bad back for a while now and when I took the dog out it was the first time it had been anywhere but the garden in seven months! I picked up a total of 74 Westie poos.

If that wasn't bad enough, I came home to find Clare looking at apartments in London. She asked if I would like to help her but funnily enough I don't feel like it. Instead, I'm locked in my room eating chocolate ice cream and trying not to compare it to dog poo.

5th July

Ugh. Some devoted Mama Bear just handed me a biscuit that her gumless baby had been sucking on all the way around the shop. She held on to the only dry section left of the biscuit, leaving me with the soggy, baby-spit side.

'Can you put this in your bin, please?'

It's not the first time this has happened either. Message to all the mothers out there: The way your baby sucks on Skips until they look like prawn porridge is not cute, it's repulsive.

Now, if you think being a checkout girl is a glamorous job, you're a moron. I can't think of a job that is worse, and even when I try, I always end up with something that my job remotely entails anyway. For example, I could think '*At least I don't work with kids'*. But I do hear them crying and screaming every day. And, as we've just established, I get baby food on me regularly.

I think the least glamorous thing about this job is the smelly food and drink products that can potentially end up all over you. To date, three wine bottles have combusted in my hands (not including the one I broke on purpose), all red. And I work in a place where your uniform isn't replaceable unless it is falling apart on your back. All of my shirts have stains on them, and I constantly smell like mayo because I spilled a dollop of it on my tabard back in 2010.

6th July

Ha-ha. You've got to laugh before you cry, right?

It's really ironic that yesterday I was talking about stenches and spillages, because I've just experienced the worst 'stinky spillage' of my life.

I'm going to refer to it as the 'off cat food incident'. If you've ever smelled out of date cat food, you've probably already gone to grab your sick bucket. If not, your life has been far too easy, and you'll never appreciate the sheer horror of this story. I envy you for that.

It was just a typical day: scan, scan, scan; moan, moan, moan; daydream about winning the lottery; fake laugh at customers' jokes, and so on. Then, just before lunchtime, a despicable smell filled the air. It was one of those smells that just gets everywhere and has you thinking, '*Oh shit. Is that me?*'

A few minutes later, a sweet, little old lady stopped her trolley alongside my till, and the smell was of an eye-watering potency. It was the smell of rot, of deep composition, and spoilage.

At first, I just watched the lady slowly unload her things, trying to spot what was making a smell like that. Then, as she freed up space in her trolley, and more air got to the problem item, I knew exactly what it was. Unfortunately, it was not my first time smelling such a smell. It took me a while to flag the woman down because I was retching so much.

'Excuse me. Have you got cat food in that trolley by any chance?'

She turned to me slowly, 'What's that, love?'

She had one of those feather-light voices that some old women have. I repeated the question.

'Oh, yes', she smiled proudly. 'My Billy and Benny are big eaters'.

She turned back to her trolley and started to unload more things. The more she unloaded, the stronger the stench. I raised my voice so she would hear me clearly, 'That smell that's lingering about, it's probably off cat food'.

She turned to me again. She seemed to find turning difficult, but she had no difficulty carrying huge chunks of beef that were probably for her precious kitties. 'Oh, I didn't realise. It always smells a bit funny in here'.

Well, she's right about that. But only off cat food can smell as horrendously bad as off cat food.

'Shall I get someone to collect it for you?' I was relishing the thought of the Rottweiler having to carry that stench all the way to the back.

'No', the lady turned back to her trolley. 'It was the last box. It won't have all gone bad'.

I could've said, *'I'll get someone to check the back for you'*, or *'there's another great brand that's even cheaper'*, but she looked like an old lady that would stand her ground. After all, the customer is always right.

I rushed her shopping through. The last thing she put on the belt was the cat food, and I'm glad really because it stopped any sort of queue forming behind her.

Just as I was about to scan the cat food the old lady said, 'Put that in a separate bag, will you? I don't want it to spoil anything'.

Even though the old lady was perfectly capable of packing the rest of her shopping, she left this one to me.

I'm sure you know that when packing a box that takes two hands to carry, you kind of have to lean it against your chest and shuffle it into the bag. So I did just that. Only, as I began shuffling, the soggy, aged cardboard gave way and the spoiled, warm, rotting, fish bits came spilling out all over my shirt, my tabard, some of it even went on my *skin*!

I did the only natural thing: vomited. Right there, right then – no time to move. My sick slid down the packaging side of the till and touched as many of the old lady's shopping bags as it could reach. I'm pretty sure a speck even landed on the woman's cheek, too. I'm not proud of the fact that I had cheese on toast for breakfast.

I retched all the way to the personnel office where I was told to: *'Go home and wash that off! Then get straight back here. And clock out whilst you do it, we aren't paying for your bloody water bill'*.

So I staggered home, throwing up twice on the way. I had a shower and rubbed make-up wipes on my uniform (I didn't have another clean one to wear), and still couldn't get rid of the smell. As a last resort, I rubbed some perfume under my nose so that at least *I* wouldn't have to smell off cat food all day. I was past caring what other people thought at this point!

It took me two hours to get home and back, and management are furious. I have to make the time up with no break. I started work at 8 a.m. today and I won't finish until 7 p.m. I've resorted to stealing grapes from people's shopping just to get by, and if a mother comes past with a soggy, half-eaten, baby biscuit, I'll probably eat that too.

9th July

My mum and dad dropped Jakey off last night. So I've spent my first day off all week looking after the little bugger. Not that I mind, he's not the spoilt lapdog I thought he was. I guess none of them are really when you get them on a muddy field with a ball or a stick. I'm not too sure my mum would be happy to see her fluffy little Poodle with knotty fur and muddy paws, but in my opinion, he's a dog, not an accessory. Mind you, the way my mum goes on you'd think he was a child.

My dad waited in the car last night because he knew that if he didn't, Mum would spend hours saying goodbye to her 'precious little man'. You'd think they were going away for one decade, not one week. Anyway, my mum carried all of his stuff in, explaining each and every one like I'd never seen a dog before: 'This is his bed, this is his food bowl, this is for his water...'

Honestly. Then she spent the next thirty minutes squeezing him and rocking him gently on her knee. I know it was half an hour because I decided to ignore her and watch Coronation Street. When the episode finished my dad beeped his horn loudly (he must have been watching Corrie on the tablet in his car, either that or he is a very *very* patient man). My mum finally stood up then, little pathetic tears in her eyes, like going on holiday is such a hardship.

‘Look after him, Suzie’. She said as she rushed out of the door. No hug for me, and no little tears, just an order shouted back over her shoulder. Cheers, Mum.

It’s been nice to have Jakey here. With Clare always occupied rushing around getting stuff sorted for her new life in London, Jakey has filled her space. Of course, he can’t drink vodka with me, or laugh at chick flicks, or empathise when I have a terrible shift. He can wag his tail though, and that’s more than enough for me.

11th July

Today I am on till 15, opposite my usual post.

Just a forewarning, this entry is going to be extremely fragmented because we’re super busy today, and till 15 is the bloody basket till.

No one likes the basket till. It’s like being on a non-stop fairground ride; except it’s no fun whatsoever.

The repetitive motion goes: look right, say hi, look down and scan, look left and take the money, spin around to put money in the drawer, spin the other way to hand the customer the receipt.

That all happens in the space of about thirty seconds. My head is seriously spinning.

We normally reserve this frantic till for the students (so believe me when I say I’ve done my fair share of shifts on here), but the summer holidays have started, meaning most of them have quit. It usually happens, and why shouldn’t they quit? They have no financial ties. I say good luck to them!

Only trouble is, we are probably going to be this busy until September now, when they all come sniffing around for jobs again.

I bloody hope I'm not going to be stuck on this till until then. I won't be able to walk in a straight line.

There are always arguments on this till too:

'*Excuse me, this lady has more than ten items*'.

'*He's got a trolley*'

'*One bag of compost wouldn't fit in a basket*'

'*Well, you should have thought of that before you came to the basket till*'.

Then there's that dagger look you get when you politely tell someone with a fully packed trolley that it's a basket-only till. Or the multi-dagger look from everyone else when you accidentally let a trolley go through.

I'm bloody sweating on this till. It's all go. And it's bloody torture looking across at my usual post only to see the Rottweiler sitting down scanning at her leisure. One of the proper managers told her to get on a till – we're that busy.

I don't want her evil, rota-writing fingers all over my till.

***

Checkout 14 has been empty for 23 minutes now. The Rottweiler is back to supervising and she still hasn't swapped me out for someone else.

I have to face it, I'm stuck here.

At least I don't have to make small talk with customers, there's not enough time.

***

Finally in bed and the room is spinning. This kind of side-effect just isn't worth it unless you're hammered. Oh well, another day, another dollar.

13th July

Kerching! June just asked if I would babysit the dogs whilst she and her daughter are on holiday. £50 a dog! That's £150 for doing something that I love - this must be what it's like to have a job you enjoy.

An added bonus is that I can add 'running my own boarding service' to my CV when I get home. I knew volunteering was a good idea. Well, actually Clare and Renée knew it, but I'm glad I listened to them.

I hope Clare will be alright with sharing the flat with three dogs. She's not been that keen on Jakey. Oh well, who cares? The bitch is moving out and leaving me soon anyway.

Maybe I'll buy her a leaving present with my money. She's been so good to me. It's great to be finally past the bitterness stage and just be happy for her. She deserves it too, anyone could see that. I can see her right now from my till. She's running around like a headless chicken on those self-scan tills. I wonder who they'll put on there when she's gone. I hope it's not me.

Another person that deserves a gift for being more than good to me is Renée. Maybe I'll split the money three ways, £50 each. I bet I could find myself a nice winter jacket on a sale rack for that.

I know it's July, but winter comes around fast, and last year I had to make do with an old cardy that had a massive hole in the back. I'm shivering just thinking about it.

Me and Clare could go out and do something as well. It'll be long over-due. I think the last time I went out to do something that didn't involve me drowning my sorrows with alcohol was my 'date' with Creepy Carl. Maybe I'll take Clare to that burger place that I went to on my 'date' (cringe). It wasn't too expensive, and that fit waiter might be working.

Bloody hell, listen to me, spending the money before I've even got it!

***

First June said she'd pay me £150 to watch her dogs, and now I've only just won a £25 gift voucher! The voucher is for Eggberts, but still.

I won it through a customer service award. I didn't even know they gave out awards! I was just sat in the canteen and I heard the manager call my name. I looked up, ready for a scolding, and found the manager to be smiling at me, along with everyone else in the room. Well, not everyone. There were a few mutters of '*as if*', and '*most undeserving winner*'.

Anyway, turns out once a month we can each nominate someone for the customer service award. All nominees are then placed in a hat and the winner is pulled out and gets a £25 gift voucher – easy as that!

At first I was like, '*who would nominate me?*' Then I saw Paul grinning from across the room, holding his peanut butter sandwiches in the air as some strange sign for 'you're welcome'.

I walked over to him, 'What did I do to deserve that?'

He told me that a customer had asked me where the decaff tea bags were, and I showed her. It's not something I remember, seeing as I get pestered by customers on a daily basis, but I could just picture it. Me, storming towards the canteen, determined to make the most of my measly fifteen minutes of peace, and then being stopped by a dear old lady that simply wants to cut down on her caffeine intake. Instead of making polite conversation, I probably rolled my eyes and lead the customer to the product without a sound, or maybe a loud sigh.

I wonder how that entire memory plays out in Paul's head, completely different to mine, no doubt.

I'm going to spend my voucher straight after work. I already know exactly what I'm going to buy. I'm going to use the first £15 to get Paul one of those Teenage Mutant Ninja Turtle lamps he's been after. He checks to see if they have been reduced every single day, sometimes twice a day, so I know he'll be made up when I get him one.

I'm going to spend the remaining £10 on an anorak that I saw on the sale pile down aisle 18. I figure if I wear it over this bubble jacket that I wear for work then I'll have a warm, waterproof jacket for winter. That way, I can spend more of my volunteering money on my sister and Clare.

I'm sure I'm coming across as very selfless today, but I can guarantee you, I'm not. I just know that having money and spending money doesn't make you happy. I spend 45 hours a week doing something that I viciously detest, so I'm definitely not naive enough to think a £50 jacket will make me feel better. At least, not anymore.

17th July

There was a crossover between June dropping off her three dogs and my mum coming to pick Jakey up. Jakey was in heaven. He rarely gets to interact with other dogs and suddenly three came along at once - and females at that! He couldn't have been happier. Of course, when my mum came she saw a completely different side of the story.

‘For goodness sake, they're so boisterous’. She grabbed Jakey and squeezed him in her arms. He barely had enough wiggle room to breathe.

‘They're playing, Mum’, I said.

‘Playing? Look at him, he's filthy. I didn't know you were going to turn your flat into a zoo whilst we were away’.

I decided to give up the fight. Sometimes it's best just to let her rant. The quicker she gets it all out, the quicker she shuts up.

My dad picked up one of the Pugs (Pugsy - terrible name, don't you think? The other Pug is called Lullaby and the Westie is called Jess) and started fussing over her. My mum continued, ‘Put that dog down, will you. I don't want your jacket to stink’.

‘You're holding Jakey’, my dad pointed out.

‘Yes, but he is a clean dog. Aren't you, Jakey-Wakey?’ She rubbed her face on his back and then recoiled, ‘At least he was clean before he came here. Suzie, I can't believe you'd be so irresponsible. You've no idea where these dogs have been’.

‘I didn't just pick them up off the street you know’.

She tutted and pulled at my dad's arm, ‘Come on, we'd better get home. Jakey needs a bath’.

Dad placed Pugsy back on the floor. ‘We haven't told Suzie about our holiday yet’.

‘Well, we'll be seeing her next week for Renée's birthday. We can talk to her then’. She was already halfway out of the door.

My dad rolled his eyes and shrugged. It's his '*you know what she's like*' gesture.

I walked him to the door and then waved them off. Clare showed up around the same time. ‘Who on earth are you waving at?’ she said.

‘My mum and dad; they've just been to collect Jakey’.

‘Thank God’, Clare said as she walked past me and into the flat, ‘no more staring competitions whilst I'm eating, no more sweaty dog smell on my clean washi - Suzie!’

I heard the dogs scurrying around her feet and went to face the music, tail between my legs. I picked up Lullaby and mustered a smile, ‘You did tell me to start volunteering’.

20th July

I’ve only just gone and forgot that I booked this week off as a holiday! It’s the best surprise I’ve had all year! I’ve planned it out perfectly as well. Today, I’m not getting up until after 12p.m. It’s 11:15 a.m. already, so I’ll easily complete that task.

Then, I’m going to walk into town and get a cappuccino and Nutella pancakes for breakfast – my mouth is watering just thinking about it! I’ll have to take the dogs with me because they haven’t had a walk yet. Terrible of me I know, but I just needed a few hours of me-time, alone in my room. I do that every now and then when I’m off work. I just lie in bed and do nothing. Time goes so much slower that way, and it reassures me.

After breakfast, I am going to come home and apply for all and any jobs (that pay well and interest me). It’s become less and less of a chore, applying for jobs. I suppose it’s because I’ve already seen some results from it, however minimal.

I saw this blog on the internet the other day. It was written by this successful millionaire and she was saying we must enjoy all the things that we will never have again once we reach our goals – easy for her to say in her position. Still, I kind of get what she means. When I had an interview, I got this exciting feeling in my stomach, like I was filled with optimism. I suppose it’s something I can enjoy about this miserable part of my life. My pre-life. I’m really really ready to start my real life now though, more than ready, in fact.

I've planned to apply for as many jobs as I can whilst I'm still watching the dogs. Then June will pick them up, hand me 150 smackaroos, and I'll have two fun-filled days off to enjoy it!

***

Worst day ever. Worst, worst, horrible day! It all started when I was in the queue for my breakfast. I could practically smell the chocolate, when I looked out of the window and saw it had started to rain. I couldn't leave the poor dogs out in that so I changed my order to take-out. The thought of cold coffee and even colder pancakes wasn't as tempting as what I had in mind this morning. But, I'm a professional when it comes to dogs, so I did the right thing.

You can imagine how puzzled I was, no, how bloody frantic I was, when I came out of the cafe and the dogs were nowhere to be seen. They'd vanished, leads and all.

From then, I ran. I ditched the delicious breakfast that cost me £6.30 (more than I usually spend on breakfast all month!), and I ran. I ran in all directions, calling their silly lapdog names, and asking people if they'd seen them. I even called the police, but they were far from helpful:

'This young girl's lost a Pug called Pugsy, you seen it lads?'

A rouge voice in the distance said, 'Pugsy Malone? He's a wanted gangster, isn't he?'

Then came an eruption of laughter.

I hung up on them. I hope that isn't a criminal offence.

It wasn't until one hour later that I stopped running because someone called me: June.

'What the bloody hell do you think you're playing at?! I thought you were qualified to look after dogs!'

'Where are they?'

'They're at Marie's. Not that you'd know. She found them tied up in the pissing rain!'

She was screaming at me. I could practically feel the heat from her breath. I turned apologetic, 'I literally just nipped in a cafe to get a coffee. I'm sorry. It had only just started raining when I paid for it –'

'Well, now my holiday is ruined. Marie can't look after all three of them by herself, and by the sounds of it, neither can you!'

'I can. I'm sorry. It won't happen again. I've been frantic looking for them'.

There was a long pause, but then she finally told me Marie's address to go and collect them. I was prepared to apologize so much more, but she didn't want to hear any of it.

I gave that cheeky cow Marie a right gobful when I finally had the leads back in my hand. She practically stole them; and she lives on the other side of bloody Leeds.

So, thanks to that meddling woman, it's almost 6 p.m. and I've only just got home and had breakfast. I had to settle for cheese on toast and black tea seeing as there's no milk in the fridge. I hope the pigeons enjoyed my soggy pancakes.

22nd July

Tell you what, if you have the post-grad blues (like me), and you're struggling to find a job (again, like me), then stay away from a little website called LinkedIn. I'm sure you've heard of it – 'The Professional Social Network'.

I made the mistake of going on it today. Just to update some details (make sure everyone knows that I now 'run my own boarding kennels'). Two hours later and I'm brimming with rage, jealousy, and tears. But mostly jealousy.

Absolutely everyone I knew at uni, that I'm connected with on LinkedIn, has an excellent career. Most of them have had several jobs since uni. They're climbing the bloody ladder, meanwhile, I can't even get on it!

There's Chloe, who started off as a dog walker for the RSPCA, now she's an Animal Care Assistant. Zach, who barely scraped by on the course, is a dog warden. And Xander is writing for Heart Your Dog magazine.

Meanwhile, my LinkedIn page is dotted with odd jobs that weren't really jobs at all, including this so-called 'running a boarding kennel' thing. I'm never going to get headhunted with a profile like that.

***

I've had time to think about the LinkedIn binge I went on earlier, and I've realised something that's cheered me up: I don't even want any of the jobs that my ex-friends have. Sure, all of them would absolutely annihilate Eggberts in a game of Top Trumps, but I wouldn't want them for the long run. I mean, none of them really involve dog training, which is what we're all qualified to do. They get to interact with dogs, sure, but none of them are building the bond that I want to. I want to train dogs, that's why I went to uni in the first place. I don't want to write about them, or return stray ones to their owners – I don't even know why I was so jealous.

I bet if I go on LinkedIn again now I'll look at it all in a whole new light…

Scratch that. Just been on one girl's profile, Gemma, and found out that she trains dogs for films. Bitch.

25th July

Today has been such a busy day. June came to collect her precious pooches at around 10 a.m. She still had her suitcases in the car, clearly desperate to get her dogs away from me as quickly as possible. She even docked my wages by £25 for the international calls she had to make, and made a quick jibe about her dogs looking skinnier. I already had the money in my pocket at this point, so I couldn't resist saying, 'That's because they weren't sharing a Twix with you every evening'.

I don't think I'll be doing any more volunteer work for a while.

After June left, I went straight to town to look for an amazing birthday present for Renée with my newfound riches. Her birthday is today. I completely forgot – I'm such a bad sister. To ease my guilt, I searched everywhere for something really special. I was torn between a white gold necklace with the word 'sister' engraved into a heart pendant, or a rose gold Michael Kors watch that was 1/3 off for one day only.

I had to take some time out to make my mind up, so I nipped to the bakery and got a sausage roll. When there was nothing but pastry crumbs left I had made up my mind. I decided on the watch because Renée knows how much they cost, and she'll never know I got it on offer. I know it's the thought that counts, but I want to make sure that Renée knows my thought is: '*I don't have much money, but I want to spend it on my sister because she's great*'.

So, by the time I'd done all that and got ready, my dad was beeping his horn outside. Renée chose to have her birthday meal up here so we could all be together. On the one hand it's sweet, but on the other, it's like I'm some burden that everyone has to make accountabilities for.

The evening started well. Mum didn't mention anything about me needing to try harder with my job applications, and Dad paid for everything, so I drank more than enough wine. We gave Renée her presents before dessert. We were supposed to wait until the end of the meal, but I couldn't. My mum and dad got her and her fiancé, Claude, tickets to France to have a mini-break at Grandma's house (much better than my birthday presents, if you remember. I think they were just trying to show off in front of Claude).

Then it was my turn. I knew everyone had low expectations, especially when I realised I'd forgotten to get her a card – I earned a huge sigh from my mum for that little *fo-pah*[*].

When Renée unwrapped it, I felt like the whole room went silent. My dad spoke first. Being the big bargain hunter that he is, he didn't have a bloody clue how much it was worth. 'That's lovely, Suzie. Isn't it Renée?'

Renée turned to me. She looked angry. I wasn't prepared for that. 'How could you afford this?'

'I made some money...volunteering'. I winked at her, but she didn't laugh.

'What are you talking about? Prostitution?!' Mum blurted out (she was on her fourth G&T).

'Jesus', said my dad.

'I've heard about it. Young women struggling for money. It's an easy path to take', Mum continued.

'Bloody hell', I said. 'I earned the money babysitting someone's dogs whilst they went on holiday. What do you take me for?'

It was only then that we realised the waiter had been stood over us for the past five minutes. He handed us our melted ice creams and scuttled back to the kitchen.

Renée eventually said, 'Thanks, you shouldn't have', and then we went back to a somewhat normal form of conversation.

Renée badgered me to get a confirmed 'yes' on my days off for her hen do (which is happening next week!) as she needs to book the plane tickets to Greece.

Mum couldn't resist chirping in with, 'She could've bought her own plane ticket if she'd got you a normal birthday present and saved her money'.

---

* My French side coming out again!

Everyone ignored her, as it's sometimes best to do. I told Renée I'd get it sorted as soon as I'm back in work. I can't believe I've only got one more day off. Time off goes so much quicker than time in work. Funny that.

26th July

Do you feel thinner, dear Diary?

I forgot to mention that Renée asked to take a chapter back to London with her. She said when she read it briefly last time it was 'comedy gold', she quickly added, 'no offence' as she saw the rising steam coming out of my ears. I know my life is a joke, but I'd prefer if people didn't point it out. She's right anyway. I re-read a few entries this morning and they did make me laugh. Like my time in the Cake Shop with ashtray Kathy, or how much of a stupid break down I had over Nick. I suppose it's easy to laugh in retrospect.

Anyway, she reckons she can give it to someone at her work and see if it's worth publishing. She said I'd get some money if they did, and let's face it, I can't turn that down, even if it means facing public humiliation.

Gotta go now, I'm going to the park with Clare. It's scorching out. Probably the only hot day we'll get all summer, and I'm off work to enjoy it! Yippee!

***

Am I a doctor? A fireman? The Queen? No. So why is it that the Rottweiler thinks it's okay to call me on my holiday and ask if I can come in and cover a shift?

It's not like it's a one off either. All of us checkout girls spend half our lives being told by our managers how indispensible we are, yet as soon as we have a day off they're begging for us back.

They even ring you on private numbers too, so you can't tell that it's them calling. They rang whilst me and Clare were at the park, which is a frighteningly close three minute walk from the store.

I binned what was left of my ice cream and answered on the first ring, naively thinking it would be about a job interview or something.

'Hello?' I said in my best telephone voice.

'Suzanne, is that you?' The Rottweiler grunted.

I sighed, 'No, it's Suzie'.

'No time for games. It's chock-a-bloc in here, can you come in for a few hours?' No 'please'. No 'thank you'.

'Can't sorry, I'm busy'.

'Doing what?'

'Enjoying my last day off', I snapped before cutting her off. I'm really going to pay for that tomorrow. It's so unfair too. She invades my privacy, and I'm the one that gets a slap on the wrist, or in this case, a bite.

Clare's phone rang minutes later. I told her not to answer it, but you know how much of a 'goody goody' she is.

'Hello?' She said, sounding more innocent than I've ever been since I was newborn.

'Okay...well...'

Hesitation is never a good thing in a situation like this. I started miming excuses to help her out: sore throat, Grandma's funeral, cystitis, anything!

'Okay, I can do a few hours'.

I could have smacked her. I waited until she hung up the phone and then grabbed the ice cream I'd bought her with my money. 'What the hell? I thought we were going to have a nice day together?' I sounded like a possessive boyfriend.

'Sorry, Suz. I need all the money I can get before the move. We'll have to go to that burger bar another time, make it my leaving do'.

I've been sat in the burger bar by myself for the past hour. I was determined to enjoy my last day off, even if my only friend had been kidnapped by a Rottweiler.

The fit waiter isn't working, and the burgers aren't as good as I remember. Maybe it's because I'm going back to checkout 14 tomorrow, even my taste buds are depressed.

30th July

Remember the other day when I hung up on the Rottweiler and said she was going to make me pay for that when I'm back at work?

Well, I'm back, and I'm paying, big time. I can't go to Renée's hen do.

We got the rotas today. It's the earliest the Rottweiler has ever given them to us, and I'm sure it was just so she could prolong my disappointment. I looked at it, and obviously she had marked me down to work on the 3rd August, the Saturday that I should be spending in Greece celebrating with my sister. A funny twist was that she made my days off for that week the 2nd and the 4th, bookending the special event nicely. I asked her to change it immediately. I hate to admit this, but I was as kiss-assey as I could possibly be, it's the only way to get what you want in a supermarket, and even then, it hardly ever works.

I started, 'Christine, you probably just forgot, but it's my sister's hen do on the 3rd and you've put me down for a shift'.

'I didn't forget', she said, handing me some pads and remover to take my chipped nail varnish off. 'We're just busy. There's meant to be a heat wave, and no one likes queuing in a heat wave'.

I hadn't heard anything about a bloody heat wave, but I bit my tongue and carried on with the polite approach even though I knew she could probably see right through it. 'Can't you swap me for Caroline or Sarah? They've not seen the rota yet so they won't know any different'.

'Nope, it's too much hassle. I'd have to get Geoff to look through it again, and he'll want to know why I didn't get it right the first time. It's too much effort'.

Geoff is the personnel manager, and she's right, he would question the change.

Geoff is the world's biggest bloody liar. I still remember him telling me about the company in my interview all those years ago: '...and we're proud to be the most family-orientated supermarket out there. That's mainly why we offer such low contracts, so that you can tell us when you're free to work, rather than be tied to the same working hours every week'.

What a stupid cow I was to believe him. I was about to continue my protest to the Rottweiler when she said, 'Your nails look clean enough now. Till 14, off you go'.

So, off I went and here I am. My mind has been ticking away all day trying to find ways to make it to that hen do. I have a few ideas:

1. Ask Sarah and Caroline if one of them will swap shifts with me. It'll be a hard bargain to push; there aren't many people that will swap a Friday day shift for a Saturday evening. Still, I have to try.
2. Ask Clare if she can talk the Rottweiler into changing the rota (I can't ask Clare to cover for me because she is also down for a shift – it's like the Rottweiler planned this on purpose).
3. Finally, if all else fails I could flirt with Creepy Carl (what a disgusting sentence). I'm sure he's till trained and he might cover for me if he thinks there's a chance. In fact, he'd do just about anything if he thought there was a chance.

It's break time in a minute. When I come back to this till I'm determined I will have that Saturday off.

***

Well, despite my best efforts, I failed. And now I'm crying like an idiot. Thankfully, my tear-soaked cheeks are scaring customers away so I can have some time to myself to calm down.

It was all sorted. I didn't even have to flirt with Carl or anything. Sarah said she'd cover for me. It was perfect. She's saving up for a trip to America or something, so she was just going to work my Saturday shift for me, without me having to work her Friday. Meaning I would get 3 days off to celebrate my sister's hen do in Greece. Amazing!

At least it was amazing until the Rottweiler burst my bubble with those sharp teeth of hers. She went off her head at me like the psycho bitch she is.

'Who's the manager? Me. So when I make a rota, it's final. When I sit there on my couch, when I should be watching Corrie, organising the shifts of 40 different people who all want to swap their hours, my say is final. Can you get that through your thick skull?'

The tears started around the first time she yelled 'final'. Not because she was shouting at me, but because I knew then that I definitely wasn't going to Renée's hen do. It would just be another family event I'd have to miss, like every bloody Christmas.

The Rottweiler caught a glimpse of me and decided to twist the knife, 'Oh, that's right, turn on the water works, Suzanne'.

'It's hay fever!' I screamed as I stormed back to my till where I've been sat ever since

I feel a little better after writing it all down. Well, I'm still gutted, but at least I've stopped crying.

August

3rd Aug

It's August 3rd, the day that will go down in our family's history as Renée's hen do, and I'm sat behind a grotty till, as per usual. They'll have all landed in Greece by now. Maybe they've even hit the first cocktail bar. I, on the other hand, have spent the last half hour trying not to touch my own skin after accidentally putting my finger into someone's wet chewing gum. I bloody hate it when people use my till on my days off. Is that sad? Probably.

I'm glad I'm not at the hen do anyway. Not because I don't want to be there, I'm desperate to be, but it all comes down to what it always comes down to – money.

I know my sister would have paid for me, but imagine the humiliation? All her posh London friends thinking, 'Poor Renée, she's had to pay to bring her skanky, Northern sister to her own hen do'.

And Mum would be worse than anyone! I know exactly what she'd do. She would get accidentally drunk on gin and tonic and then say repeatedly, 'Oh, Suzie. I wanted so much more for you'.

This would sober me up quicker than a ton of bricks landing on my forehead and I'd have to spend the entire night listening to her drunken disappointment.

Just re-read that part about my mum, it makes her sound like a right bitch, and me sound like I'm looking for excuses. Well, she's not, and I'm not.

Like I said before, it is about the money. It always will be whilst I'm working here. Well, the money, and the shit rota.

I currently have £24.53 in my bank account. That would be fine if all of my living expenses were dealt with, but unfortunately, I have a £69 bus pass that runs out at midnight tonight. I'm off on Sunday, but Lord knows how I am going to get here on Monday. It would be about an hour's walk, maybe longer. Meaning that instead of spending 9 hours 40 minutes getting to work, working, and getting home, I'd spend a total of eleven hours doing it.

Usually I'd ask my sister for cash, but I can't bring myself to do it whilst she's away enjoying herself. And I can't ask Clare because she is saving up for the '*big move*', as she keeps calling it.

That only leaves my dad, but nothing is ever straight forward with him. So, here's to finding a big bag of cash on the way home!

4th Aug

Well, it got to about 6:30 p.m. before I had to call my dad and ask for help. That was after telling myself all day that I'll just walk to work in the morning. It'll do me good. Fresh air and exercise.

Then I realised it's almost two weeks until pay day. That's a lot of fresh air and exercise. In fact, it's 20 hours of fresh air and exercise. 20 hours of my life, on top of the 90 I will waste at work. Equalling a total of 110 hours of my life wasted in two short weeks. How disgusting.

So, I caved and told my dad about my problem. I really wish I hadn't bothered. I called him at 6:32 p.m. and said something along the lines of: 'Dad, I'm really sorry, I know I've left it last minute, but I don't have any money for my bus pass tomorrow'.

He replied: 'Oh, Suzie'.

Then, after a short pause: 'I think I have something to help you. I'll set off to yours now'.

That was at 6:34 p.m. It was another hour and twenty minutes before he knocked on my door. So, from 6:34 p.m. until 8:02 p.m., I was pacing my bedroom floor wondering what the hell my dad meant by '*I think I have something to help you*'.

I eventually settled on telling myself that he was bringing me some cash, and that he didn't want to transfer it online because he was lonely at home without my mum. *Wishful thinking.*

I opened my front door to find my dad and a red push-bike. Not just any red push-bike, a kid's red push-bike.

'Well, what do you think?' My dad grinned from ear to ear.

After him driving all that way on a Sunday evening what could I possibly say? I settled for, 'Great. Isn't it a bit small though?'

'Nah', my dad said, 'the guy at the auction house said it was a women's bike. I knew, I just knew it would come in handy. Your mum was nagging about it taking up too much space and being good for nothing. I knew otherwise though. Lucky, eh?'

Before I could even reply he came out with the classic '*Guess how much it cost me?*' I always double the price I'm actually thinking, just so he can be even more chuffed when he tells me the answer.

'Forty quid?'

'Tenner!'

I smiled and put my hand out to touch the bike. I knew I was going to have problems riding it when I had to stoop down just to reach the seat.

All night my dad couldn't shut up about the bloody thing. There's some rust over here, it'll need a light on it in winter, the seat's well padded...

He's not used to goodbyes. My mum is the one that always cuts their visits short. I always thought it was a bit bossy of her, until tonight. At 10:23 p.m. I finally told my dad he had better leave.

He has work in the morning as well as me. God knows what time he'll get to bed. Oh god, I'm starting to sound like my mum.

Anyway, back on to the real problem: it's half ten, and the only way I can get to work tomorrow is by a bike that is too small for me. Looks like I'm setting an early alarm.

5th Aug

Today was a new low. The bike that my dad got me was far too small, but of course, I knew that before I got on it, didn't I?

Still, desperate moron that I am, I rode it all the way to my desperate, moronic job. A forty minute bike ride in an August shower. By the time I arrived at the supermarket entrance, my legs ached (mainly from my knees scraping the ground each time I pedalled), and my bubble jacket was stuck to me – I couldn't tell if it was with sweat or rain water.

I know that big people on tiny bikes are hilarious. Everyone knows that I suppose, those idiots at the circus make a living out of it. I also know that sticks and stones will break my bones, but names will never hurt me.

Working on a checkout, I've been called so many names that I've worked up a pretty thick skin. But today, it pains me to say, I couldn't hack the name calling. There was hardly any name calling really, just a lot of snickering, pointing, one or two looks of confusion, and a lot of car horns.

It was when I got to work that the heckling really began, and by that time I was tired, wet, and had 40 minutes of hard thinking time. A customer started it: 'They definitely aren't paying you enough, love'.

Then a parking attendant: 'It's free parking for staff you know. You didn't have to nick a kid's bike'.

Then, as I was chaining the bike up, a few of Clare's friends walked past and spotted me as they made their way into the store.

'That is fucking tragic', one of them started, and then they all burst into a fit of laughter.

Just before they were out of earshot I heard another one say, 'I bet it's even got a little bell and everything!'

I finally locked the bike up, trying my best to ignore them. Then I turned to go into the store and Paul the Basket Guy was stood directly behind me.

'Oh, it has got a little bell. Ha-ha, silly Suzie'.

And then, from nowhere, floods of tears started running from my eyes. I ran straight to the toilets, avoiding everyone's gaze, and then when I was finally in the cubicle, I let all of the sobs burst out. I arrived at my till twenty minutes late. Luckily, no one had seen or heard me crying, and even more luckily, I clocked in for my shift before my crying fit, so I won't be docked for being late.

All day I've had little digs from people, and all day I've had a lump in my throat. It's like my body is ready and waiting to start crying for the slightest reason. Now I really do know the truth behind the expression: 'The straw that broke the camel's back'. Or rather, 'the bike that broke the checkout girl's front'. Maybe I'm having some kind of emotional breakdown – again.

The worst thing about it is – and my eyes are literally threatening to overflow as I write this – I have to ride that ridiculous bike all the way home again in four hours and fifty three bloody minutes.

7th Aug

Miracles do happen! Well, sort of. After two more humiliating days of riding that circus bike to and from work,

I decided to sit down and check my online banking. I've no idea why, because I knew I had no money, still, I checked anyway. My balance, instead of being £24.53, was £124.53! I'd had a cash transfer from the one and only, Renée Quesnell.

After the initial burst of happiness, I felt quite angry. Surely the only explanation was that my dad had told my mum about my situation, and she in turn told Renée, which ruined her hen do! Great!

I decided against ringing her, mainly because I couldn't afford an international call. But she's finally home today, so I can get an explanation. I hope she doesn't want the money back though, I spent it immediately on a bus pass. I've never appreciated that smelly, itchy-seated contraption more.

I've just got three more hours of my shift left, which is timed almost perfectly with Renée getting home in about 4 hours. So, that's approximately sixty customers left to serve before home-time. It's very upsetting that I am able to calculate that.

***

I'm the worst big sister in the world. I rang Renée to ask about the money, and it turns out she set a direct debit up months ago because she knows I always need cash about two weeks before my next wages are due.

She wasn't her upbeat self when she told me about it. She just sort of shrugged it off instead. I thought if I shifted the conversation towards wedding talk she'd chirp up. She's turned into a proper girly-girl since she started planning her wedding, or maybe she has always been one and I never paid attention.

'So, how was your hen do?'

'Great'.

'Great? Is that it? No juicy stripper stories? No tales about Mum getting drunk and embarrassing herself?'

‘Yeah, all that. It was amazing. I just don’t fancy reciting it word for word’.

‘Oh, okay’. I decided that her mood must be down to jet lag and thought it best to leave her be, ‘Well, I’ll talk to you soon then’.

‘Actually, there is something I want to talk about’.

She went silent for what felt like an hour. I had my fingers crossed that it would be about that extract of my diary she took to work.

‘I don’t think you’ll be able to be a bridesmaid. It’s just, your working hours are so unreliable...I’d hate to buy the dress and everything and then find out that you won’t be able to come’.

I really didn’t know what to say. I don’t think I would’ve been all that bothered if she just wanted someone else as a bridesmaid, but it hurt to know she wanted me to be one and I couldn’t. I tried to find a solution, ‘When are you getting married? My holidays renew in March. I’ll book the day off’.

‘We were thinking of getting married at the beginning of next year, maybe January’.

‘Oh’. That wouldn’t work for two reasons. One: I have no holidays left until March. Two: No one is allowed to book time off in January. My sister and I both had to face facts, ‘I guess I won’t be able to be one of your bridesmaids then’.

We both knew that I was really saying, ‘I probably won’t be able come to your wedding’.

It’s one thing for this job to turn my friends against me, but not my bloody sister.

9th Aug

I have an interview! I can’t cope with the excitement bubbling up inside me! I’ve not told anyone about it. I can’t, it’s too much pressure. This is my second interview in less than six months! I must be getting my applications right, so now all I have to do is nail this interview.

Instead of telling anyone, I've just been walking around tight-lipped and sweating. It's possible that people think I've got diarrhoea or something. When I flashed my light, the Rottweiler ran towards me faster than she ever has done, even when a drugged up pregnant woman was threatening to kill me (long story). If she asks me if I want to go home early, I'm not going to say no.

I received two rejection emails today and then the interview voicemail. It's a good job it was a voicemail because I choked on my noodles when I heard it.

My interview is next week. I need to tell the Rottweiler that I've got a dentist appointment, but I can't ask her today, I'm too excited. I might say the wrong thing. Today I'm just going to do my job and go home. I need to try not to daydream about how amazing life would be if I got this job. The salary alone is making my hands sweat so much that I keep dropping whatever I'm scanning. £20,000 starting! That's £7000 more than I get here, £8000 even!

When I get home tonight I need to write down all of the skills I obtained in my short time in the admin department. I forgot to change my CV when I got moved back to checkouts, so it still says I'm an admin assistant, which is probably the only reason that I got the interview in the first place. It's a receptionist job at a boarding kennels in Manchester. Thankfully I have enough spare money to buy the train tickets. I've decided I'm not going to tell anyone that I'm going for this interview. That way I can't jinx it, and I won't be nervous about having to tell people I was rejected. The only people I would normally tell are Clare and Renée anyway, and since Clare already has a job now I don't feel obligated to share with her. I don't want to tell Renée because she will get too excited for me, and I'm already beyond excited, believe me.

Wow, how amazing would it be to do something I'd enjoy? Something I'd be good at. Something I would be proud to tell people. No more pretending I'd swallowed a fly when asked: '*So, what do you do?*'

I'm going to get this one, I've got a feeling. It's like, just when I'm feeling low something is going to swoop down and rescue me, and that something will be a full-time job surrounded by dogs. It'd be perfect for me and Clare to leave Eggberts around the same time – like the end of a cheesy film. The satisfying full circle from us crying in an alleyway whilst singing the F.R.I.E.N.D.S theme tune.

12th Aug

If there was one thing that I could wish for to make my life as a checkout girl easier, it wouldn't be more money. It wouldn't even be for the rotas to be given to us on time. It would be for a mute button on the till. If I could just mute that beeping I'd be so much happier, or at least ten percent happier. I feel like they use it as a kind of mind control technique: Beep. Beep. Beep. You. Are. Our. Slave. Scan. Scan. Scan.

If I lose my mind one day, the checkout sound will be wholly to blame.

Even if nothing can keep me sane, the old people that come in to the shop are managing to put a smile on my face.

I don't know if this is a well-known fact in the outside world, but in supermarkets, it's universal: Lonely, old people who have reached an age where they've been widowed so long that no one cares anymore, and/or they've got too old to go on day trips with the family, visit the supermarket on a daily basis, just for some company. Visiting a supermarket every day sounds like voluntary torture to me, but I suppose it's better than sitting around patiently waiting for death.

Lonely old people come into Eggberts every day without fail. They purposefully only buy what they will use in the next twenty-four hours: a small tin of beans, 1 pint of milk, 1 travel-sized box of cornflakes, and a chocolate bar or cream cake (don't old people have a right sweet tooth on them?).

I think it's nice. The whole thing is like a day trip for them. I'd say, with just going to Eggberts and home they get themselves out of the house for about three hours a day. I've calculated it like so:

Walk to Eggberts: 20 mins

Have a cheap brew in the cafe and talk to the girls in there: 1 hour

Fill basket with shopping: 40 mins

Stand in the longest queue and make small talk with the other customers (always insisting that they don't need to jump to the front, even if they only have three items – *'Well, you know at this age, I've nowhere else to be'*): 30 mins

Pack shopping very slowly and chat to the checkout girl: 20 mins

A trip to the kiosk for some fags and/or to the loo before walking home: 30 mins

Walk home: 40 mins (because they have weight in their trolley)

They're funny those little trolley-things that old people drag about, aren't they? I wonder why they're called trolleys. They look more like mini-suitcases to me.

Anyway, I guess what I'm trying to say is that it's nice to know you're wanted. And it's also nice to make someone else feel wanted.

Okay, that's enough stalling for one day. I've been quiet all day, and pinched my cheek every time I got the chance. It's time to pretend I need an emergency dentist appointment.

16th Aug

My interview went so well today! I really think I may have got the job!

I walked in and just the smell of dog made me ecstatic that this might soon be my place of work – not a trolley in sight, or a beeping till to be heard for miles. The place is really in the middle of nowhere, like most kennels are, so I would definitely have to move nearby if I got it. It was a forty minute walk just from Piccadilly Station, so I don't really want to be making a commute like that every day. Anyway, I need to stop getting ahead of myself!

I was interviewed by two women, one was the kennel manager. She was in her late forties and looked like one of those posh women you see at Crufts, you know, with the tweed jackets and immaculately clean wellies. I found out later that she does actually show dogs at Crufts – great intuition or what?

The other woman was just a bit younger than me. She was like the deputy, for when the manager wasn't in. Her duties were split between the office and caring for the dogs, whereas my role (if I were to get it) would be solely in the office so that the other girl, Amy, could spend more time with the dogs. I did a good job at disguising my disappointment here. I know that no matter how many weeks, months, or years, I work in the office, there will come a time when I will be needed in the kennels. It's much closer than I would ever be in that stupid supermarket.

When they called me about the interview they told me it would take around 40 minutes, but I was there for well over an hour. We just chatted and chatted about dogs. They were really happy about how much knowledge I had on dogs, and pleased that I was certified in dog first aid (I was gutted when I had to turn down a foam party for that course, not so gutted now though!) They introduced me to all the dogs too, and I was great with them, as usual. I just felt so at home being there. I told them about all of the work I did with kennel dogs at university and they were eager to listen. They didn't even ask me about office skills, or my role at Eggberts, and I was glad because being out there in the countryside, with the sound of barking to distract me, I forgot that I even worked in such a hell hole.

Oh, I really hope I get the job! After my interview I wandered around the fields for a bit. Far away from the kennels, so they didn't think I was some weirdo staking it out. It was nice to walk around quiet fields, the city is so loud, and Eggberts, even louder.

After that, I got the train home and I've just been sitting in front of my phone ever since. Sitting in front of my phone and binge eating. So far I've had a packet of Jaffa Cakes, a bagel slathered in peanut butter, a bowl of strawberry ice cream, and I'm onto my second bag of ready salted. I'm not worried about the calories. I must be burning off around 100 per minute with the amount of nervous sweating I'm doing.

It's weird - when I was at uni I did not think I would care this much about a receptionist job in a kennels. I assumed that when I got my degree I wouldn't get out of bed for less that £30,000. So naive. They should definitely teach a life skills course on the side at uni, or even as early as college.

Shit, shit. The phone is ringing. It's them.

I GOT IT! Oh my God. Oh my days with a cherry on top! I got it! I've been jumping up and down on my bed for the past twenty minutes! This is unreal. I am leaving Eggberts! I knew it! I knew it would happen for me this year and it has! Oh wow! Only my second interview and I *got* the job. If only I'd done this years ago – oh well, best not to think about that. Clare keeps calling me a 'lucky cow', but even she can't help giggling and hugging me, she even had a little jump on the bed too.

Wow. We're leaving. I'm leaving. I'm going to write my notice letter right now. I've dreamt about writing my notice so many times. A lot of the times it's been a huge rant, like:

Please take this letter as notice that I will be resigning from my position. The reasons for this resignation are plentiful, and the pain that I have felt over the years of my employment with this supermarket is far too much to document in words.

However, I would like to make it clear that I am leaving because of mistreatment. It is unfair to work full-time on a part-time contract, the stress of not being able to make rent has sometimes been unbearable. Not to mention the lack of holidays I have been able to take over the past six years.

It is unfair to make your employees work under conditions where they have no drinking water, no authority to go to the bathroom, and have to work with cat food or red wine clinging to their skin – both I have experienced.

Not to mention, a most recent sexual harassment issue that I felt I had no one to turn to and talk about.

And never a thank you, and never an apology.

So, please take my resignation, without a thank you, and without an apology.

Suzie Quesnell (not Suzanne).

Then other times I think, what's the point? No matter what I say in my resignation, the supermarket will never change. People will always be treated despicably, so I might as well just say:

I resign, see you later.

I'll call my sister for her help on it. She's had more jobs than me, and definitely has more tact.

17th Aug

Hello dear Diary,

I didn't hand my notice in.

It all started when I rang my sister and told her I got the job. She was thrilled and started making plans for me, like she does. Only, when we started making plans we realised that I can't afford to work there. The flats to rent around the kennels are ridiculously priced, like double what I'm paying now. We looked as far out as we could get, even near Piccadilly Station (a 40 minute commute would be heaven compared to working at Eggberts), but they were even more expensive. There was nothing that could be done, apart from sleeping on the streets, and my sister didn't sound too happy when I suggested that.

'Just be more realistic next time. Something amazing will come along before you know it', she said.

So, with that, it was final. I couldn't go for my new amazing job. I had a little cry about it, and then another little cry when I told Clare. But I'm over it now. Well, not totally over it. I haven't called the kennels to let them know yet. How can I? It's too embarrassing – *'Er, I just wanted to let you know I can't take this job because you don't pay enough for me to make rent'.*

Ugh! I hate life!

19th Aug

Just had a ridiculous telling off in the manager's office, oh well, at least it breaks my day up a bit. It has been a very interesting Tuesday morning indeed.

I started at 8 a.m. after working until 10 p.m. last night, so I was kind of sleeping with my eyes open when a group of workmen came in the store. Not unusual, loads of similar people come in each morning to buy their dinners for work.

What *was* unusual was that instead of putting their items in baskets, these guys were putting them in their pockets. I watched them whilst my brain woke up and they continued to steal, as brazen as can be.

The next thing I knew, the Rottweiler had clocked on to them and gave chase, but she was all bark and no bite. It was brilliant to watch! The Rottweiler chased them for about twenty yards, at which time the largest of the workmen turned around and growled in her face – like, a full-on dog growl! Even strangers think she is a mutt! The Rottweiler was so frightened that she tripped over her own feet and landed flat on her face, mere inches from my checkout.

The builders continued towards the exit at a leisurely pace, laughing and howling. I watched them happily until I heard her screaming from beneath me, 'After them, Suzanne! Stop them! Suzanne, move it, now!'

The Tuesday morning thieves had just about disappeared when the senior management team arrived – always perfect timing! They helped the Rottweiler to her hefty feet and she instantly made a beeline for me. 'Wipe that smug look from your face, girl! That little stunt you just pulled is more than your job's worth'.

'If anyone's a bloody jobsworth love, it's you'.

Of course, I didn't say that. I stayed put, served a few customers, and watched out of the corner of my eye as the managers took the Rottweiler's details of the incident and helped her fill in an accident assessment form. I noticed that the two store managers also resemble so-called 'bully' dog breeds. Maybe it's a requirement of moving up the supermarket ladder – a squashed face and a bad temper. Well, they're setting a bad example if it is. It's dogs like them that give the rest of the breed a bad name - sorry, people! I mean people like them...

Once the managers were done taking down the Rottweiler's story they turned to me. I was given the '*come with me'* death stare from the big boss, and the *'you're gonna get it'* smirk from the deputy.

The managers' offices in supermarkets, or at least in this supermarket, are truly a testament to how far cheap and tacky corporations will go to save a few pennies. The Eggberts' management team, the *crème-de-la-crème* (that's my French side coming out again), share an office smaller than a disabled toilet cubicle. It has one desk and two chairs, (despite there being four managers – God only knows why they need four, jobs cuts and the lark, but that's the truth of it) and their favourite toy: The CCTV Monitor. I was shown the footage of the Rottweiler falling over until it wasn't funny anymore. They zoomed in on my grinning face until every pore was visible.

'This is not the face of a helpful member of staff', I was told. 'This is the face of someone who doesn't value their job'.

Hit the nail on the head there, didn't they?

When they finally put down the remote and pulled their eyes away from their magical, out-of-date, black and white screen, I was shown my contract. My contract clearly states: 'It is your duty to always pursue thieves unless you feel that you are in personal danger'. They underlined 'your duty' three times in red pen, just in case I was deaf. Then, thankfully, it was my turn to speak.

I politely informed them that:

1. The Rottweiler asked for help from Suzanne – that is not me.
2. I *did* feel in danger – Hello? A group of huge men howling like hooligans. What kind of woman would approach that by herself?
3. I was told that the last time I was attacked by a customer I no longer needed to become involved in difficult situations if I didn't want to.

The managers considered the first point quickly and challenged it defensively.

'If you wore your name badge then you wouldn't be mistaken for someone else'.

'My name badge says Suzanne. I've been trying to get it changed for six years'.

'Yes, well... we'll see that it's sorted by the end of the day'.

Yep. I've heard that one before.

The other points were discussed for quite some time, until I asked for my break. So here I am, eating dry crackers and waiting for the verdict.

When I left them they were fighting over the CCTV remote, trying to find evidence of my previous 'attack'.

It wasn't as grim as it sounds, and I wasn't in any *real* danger, I think. But I'll write it down anyway because it's one of those traumatic things that, unless you've worked in retail, you will never know happens to normal people like me and the other girls. It's just one of those wrong place-wrong time kind of stories, and checkout girls have a lot of them, because we're always in the wrong bloody place.

I was on my way back to till fourteen after gulping down a disgusting Eggberts ready meal on my pathetic fifteen minute break. I was struggling to keep it down and so focused on holding back my vomit that I walked right into the middle of a domestic – A tiny woman and a man, no, a giant, having a disagreement down the chocolate aisle. I quickly scurried out of their way, managing to notice the root of the disagreement within seconds: the man (who had learning difficulties) wanted chocolate, and the woman (who I later found out was his carer) had told him no. Now, 'no' was not what the giant wanted to hear. He took one of his tree trunk arms and swept an entire shelf of Cadburys onto the floor.

A couple of bars hit me on the back and I turned to face the carer, 'I hope you're going to clean that up'.

Me and my big mouth. Apparently, no one is allowed to give cheek to the giant's tiny carer, except him. He ran towards me like a human tornado, arms outstretched, knocking everything that he could reach from the shelves. For a millisecond I stood my ground, waiting for his carer to do something. Then I looked at the size of her, and the size of him, and I did what any normal person would do, I legged it.

***

The managers got back to me after letting me sit in the canteen for forty minutes – not that I'm complaining. I would much rather sit and watch a blank wall than sit on my checkout, and that's the truth. I think time actually passes more quickly when I'm doing nothing, than when I'm scanning shopping. Anyway, they let me off the hook because they'd seen the previous incident and deemed that enough to put anyone off being a hero. However, I was informed that I need to take more actions when incidents occur, for example scream '*help!*' or run to get one of the managers off their backside.

So, all in all a strange morning, but at least it went quick. Oh, and my name badge still says Suzanne.

21st Aug

Bent down to get some more bags from underneath the till. Found a £2 coin. Keeping it.

24th Aug

Some customers just live to annoy checkout girls. I'm sure of it. It's just their absolute goal in life. You know the type I'm on about. They queue up and you can hear them sighing and huffing and puffing until it's finally their turn to be served and then they say, 'It's bloody ridiculous this, you should have more staff on'. Like it's the checkout girl's sole responsibility to choose which staff go where.

Oh, and our responsibilities don't end there according to some customers. Apparently, it's also my fault that we don't have enough stock on the shelves, or in the case of the crazy witch that's just been screaming at me, ice cream in the freezers.

You see, there's a promotion on at the minute, buy one box of Eggberts' ice-cream cones, get two free. Great offer, right? That's why it sold out within the first hour of the store opening. But this customer couldn't possibly believe that. Her theory was that we advertised that great offer to get people to the store, then when they realised the offer was a fake they would have no choice but to buy the more expensive branded ice cream cones because they'd already promised their kid's ice cream.

So, not only am I solely responsible for queues, stock control, and advertising, I'm now in charge of pricing! I wish someone had told me that.

She finished her rant with the classic, 'I'm shopping elsewhere from now on'.

As if that is going to cause me any sort of personal offence. Even if it did hurt my feelings, they wouldn't hurt for long because she'll be in here again next week, along with all the other complainers and I'll think, 'Damn it! I thought they were going to piss off and annoy some other checkout girls!'

28th Aug

It's Clare's last day as a checkout girl today. Her and her friends have already started sobbing. God knows why. If that was me I'd be skipping out of here. The last thing they'd see of me would be my middle finger. Except Paul, he'd get a hug.

Speaking of Paul, he loves his Teenage Mutant Ninja Turtle lamp. He's told everyone about it at least five times. Even I'm sick of hearing the story, and it makes me sound like a saint.

There's a party in the staff canteen today for Clare. Stupid really, seeing as everyone has different break times. Still, it's free cake. If there's any left by the time I get my break. If there's ever anything remotely exciting going on in the canteen then breaks are always given in order of favouritism. So, as you can imagine, I'm always last.

It reminds me of how dogs live in packs. The lowest member always eats last and is totally fine with it. Since when did I roll over and accept being anything but the alpha? Probably the day I put this disgusting uniform on.

Finally cake time! Whoops, I mean, break time.

***

Life is like baking a cake. All of the ingredients would be terrible if you ate them individually: raw eggs, a chunk of butter, flour. But they all come together to make something amazing.

Believe it or not, I heard that from Paul at lunchtime – Paul! We were each eating a slice of Clare's leaving cake and he saw that I was feeling down (when am I not?) and he just blurted it out. It's wonderful isn't it?

I asked him where he heard it but he just shrugged his shoulders. Apparently he likes to read a lot, but forgets what he's read.

I love sayings like that. They really cheer you up. It's like, at the minute my degree is just a lump of flour, and my job at Eggberts is like two raw eggs, the volunteering I've done is a lump of butter, and one day all of that (along with a few other ingredients) will come together to make a delicious cake.

The broken pieces of my life will come together if I work hard enough, and I'll finally be happy. If I keep on whisking the ingredients together it is just inevitable that I *will* be happy. One day. One delicious day.

September

1st Sept

Supermarkets have just hit a new low, and not just Eggberts, this new scheme is nationwide. How they think they'll keep it from customers, I don't know. Us checkout girls aren't exactly being paid enough to keep our mouths shut.

This new scheme, or policy, as the personnel manager put it, regards plastic bags. I learnt about it less than an hour ago at a training meeting. If you absolutely detest your job, like me, then I bet you love training meetings just as much as I do. An hour away from my mind numbingly boring reality – yes!

We have training meetings every four months at Eggberts because they have to make sure we still remember all of the complicated parts of our role – like being able to tell the difference between someone who is 14 and someone who is 26; or knowing what to do when the fire alarm goes off. We usually play games like 'guess the customer's age' for about twenty minutes and then we watch a 40 minute video that I have seen about 30 times. It's one of those cheesy, made in the eighties, training videos. I feel sorry for all the old cronies that work here, they must know it by heart.

Watching the video is the best and worst part of the training meeting. It's the best part because the lights get turned off and you can have a brief nap. It's also the worst part because the last thing you want to do after a nice, little nap is go back to work.

But this time we didn't go straight back to work. We learnt about this new bags ~~scheme~~, sorry, policy.

The bags ~~scheme~~ policy is a 'Green' strategy that is taking effect in supermarkets all over the country. The plastic used for supermarket bags is non-recyclable, and landfills are getting pretty full. So, to cut down future use we are now only allowed to offer customers one bag for a basket and three for a trolley. Yes, just three bags for an entire trolley load! The idea is that the Great British public will be too polite to ask for more bags, and so usage will be reduced.

But, unlike the wrapped-in-cotton-wool office workers that thought up this brilliant ~~scheme~~ policy, I actually work with the Great British public day in, day out, and they aren't as polite as they're cracked up to be.

Can you imagine me handing a busy mum three bags to pack the entirety of her weekly shop? That wouldn't even cover nappies and baby wipes – I'd get my head bitten off!

Of course, the Personnel Manager so cleverly pointed out that if we ever run in to any trouble we can always offer the customer one of our reusable bags for 10p. That's when it clicked. They want to make even more money from the everyman by practically forcing them to buy recyclable bags as part of their 'Green' strategy. Making the supermarket look like it's run by saints, and the customers feel like they are solely responsible for climate change.

Sounds like a great ~~scheme~~ policy.

4th Sept

I have two job interviews: one at the end of this week, and one at the beginning of next. But I don't even have enough optimism left inside me to look forward to them. Don't get me wrong, they are amazing jobs. The best jobs I've ever got interviews for.

One is a role as a canine training assistant for a woman called Meryl Bleekman. Meryl judges the Springer Spaniels every year at Crufts, and she owns her own dog training facility right here in Leeds. It would be the opportunity of a lifetime to work with someone like her. So would the second job, too. The second job is a dog day care manager position in a posh London apartment block. The dog day care facility is built-in to the building, for all the rich people that don't have time to spend with their dogs (not something I particularly agree with, but if it gets me a job I can't complain). It would be pretty great too, as part of the job I would get my own flat on the premises. That one is just a telephone interview though, so I'll probably get rejected on my Northern accent alone.

Anyway, bottom line is, I have two amazing interviews lined up and I'm sat at my checkout, happy with the familiarity of scanning food items, and dreading the thought of putting myself through the gruelling interview process, yet again.

I suppose I've already told myself I won't get the jobs. Why would I? I didn't get any of the previous jobs I applied for (bar one) and they were for jobs way shitter than these.

Maybe I'm just getting used to everything rolling down hill. It would make sense. In the space of a month Clare has moved out, I've got a job I couldn't take, and I've been kicked off my sister's bridesmaid list. When stuff like that happens in your home life, the sticky floor and grimy smell of Eggberts doesn't seem half bad. Maybe this is what the acceptance stage feels like, and now I'll spend the next fifty years content with scanning other people's shopping. Good God, don't let that be true.

7th Sept

This is the quietest Sunday in the history of man. Apparently there's an important football match, or rugby match or something, so everyone's at the pub watching that. I haven't served one customer in the past 40 minutes. I haven't looked at the clock in that time either – I know that 40 minutes has passed because the dreaded Eggberts CD has started from the beginning. Eight songs on a loop, all day, every day.

It's sending me insane. Thanks to Eggberts, now when I'm at parties and Bon Jovi comes on screaming: *'It's my liiiiiife!'* instead of rocking out with everyone else I have to hide in the toilets. Well, let's face it; I never go to parties anymore. But it is strange how even great songs can be ruined by being overplayed. Too much of a good thing.

Here are the songs from the Eggberts CD, so you know that all of these songs are completely ruined for me. As soon as one of these comes on the radio, in my mind I get transported back to this clammy supermarket.

I've already mentioned Bon Jovi, but I never really liked him that much anyway. Dolly Parton's '*9-5*', I did like. It's cheery and funny. But now, it just mocks me. In fact I'm sure they only play it for the sole purpose of tormenting us. The truth is, there is no such thing as 9-5 in a supermarket! There is a 5-9 – that was a popular shift for me to get on a Friday and Saturday night when I was a student. A four hour shift, just enough time so that they don't have to let you have a paid break. So yeah, the song should be 5-9, or 8-5 (the supermarket equivalent of 9-5 – you have to work your dinner hour back, you see), but never 9-5.

The third song on the CD is '*Closing Time*' by Semisonic. Pretty self-explanatory. The most annoying thing about it is every time it comes on I automatically calculate how many hours I have left until it's actually closing time.

It's even worse when it plays at closing time because idiot customers think it's funny and try to make a joke about it, instead of getting the hell out so I can go home.

Next on is, '*Your own personal Jesus*'. This song is just offensive to everyone. Sort of like Marilyn Manson's face. Customers have actually complained about it. Every time I hear him say *'Reach out and touch faith'* I want to throw a punch at the closest thing to me – we're in a supermarket, we have no faith.

'*Every day is a Winding Road*' by Sheryl Crow is probably the happiest song we have. I'm sure it makes most shoppers feel nostalgic – ooh, summer in the nineties, those were the days. Maybe it even subliminally makes people buy some cherryade and a few extra chocolate bars.

The lyrics that stick out to me are: '*I'm just wondering why I feel so all alone, why I'm a stranger in my own life'*. This is the part of the song that was made for checkout girls. I'm alone in a huge crowd of people that I must serve tirelessly, lest I be jobless. And I'm convinced that my real life hasn't started yet. My biggest problem with this song is that Sheryl Crow manages to sound so happy whilst singing lyrics like that. The reality is anything but.

The next song is quite a contrast, '*Time of your Life*' by Greenday. I'd love to know the reasoning behind playing this particular song. I heard once that supermarkets pick their songs carefully to encourage people to buy things. I get it with the Sheryl Crow song making people buy nineties sweets or whatever, but what would this make you buy? Razor blades and vodka?

'*The world is just a great big onion!*' Of all the amazing Marvin Gaye songs, Eggberts thought they would choose this one for their eternal playing CD. And now, I hate Marvin Gaye. This song tries so hard to tell people to love each other, plant love seeds until there are no hate-filled onions, and all that. Well, I want to be an onion. I want to stick out like a smelly, eye-sore in protestation to this job.

Next up, you guessed it, the epitome of work songs: '*Manic Monday*'. I could probably deal with it, if they played it once on a Monday, but of course they don't. It's just not relevant to be hearing '*it's just another manic Monday'* on a Friday morning. Or, worse still, hearing *'I wish it were Sunday, that's my fun day'* when you're scanning pickled eggs on a Sunday instead of eating a home cooked Sunday roast.

8th Sept

Paul the Basket Guy brought a book in for me the other day. It's his mum's, but he's read it a few times apparently. I'm not much of a reader, but I've skimmed it, and actually, it's pretty good. It's one of those self-help books. It has a really obscure name that I can't bring to mind right now, like '*Awakening*' or '*Shine*'. It's all about how if you think positively, positive things will happen to you. At first I was like, '*Yes! This is the key to me winning the lottery and leaving Eggberts!*' But after more thought, I don't think things can work like that. You have to appreciate the little things, no matter just how tiny they may be.

So, I've been appreciating every little detail of life: the fact that I can afford to buy and make myself a hot meal (even if it is Eggberts value noodles on toast), the sun shines, birds tweet, I get two whole days off a week to myself. All of these little things that have always been there, and I've been walking around like I was owed more than this. But we aren't owed anything, are we? We have to think positively and work hard and then we will get what we desire – or so this book says. So, I've been thinking positively all yesterday, and all today, and I really do feel better for it.

I mean, it's a gorgeous day outside and I'm stuck in here scanning, but hey, I'm earning money, I'm helping people out with their shopping, and I get burnt in the sun anyway, so it shouldn't really bother me. And yes, five people have called in sick and the shop is crammed with customers saying things like:

'You need to put more staff on'.

'These queues are ridiculous'.

'Eggberts is getting worse every time I come in'.

But, I have to take in to account that they are frustrated and they don't really mean to be shouting at me. So I've just been smiling and thinking positively and trying to do right, even when a customer said, 'What you smirking at?!'

I'm not going to lie, it is difficult to stay this positive, I mean, I am still me. And the book can't be that good at improving your life seeing as Paul is still lugging baskets about for a living. But, maybe it can improve your state of mind, and I really need that. Honestly, I feel like I'm losing it. Never has the phrase 'emotional rollercoaster' been so apt as to when it is applied to this diary. One day I'm up, one day I'm down, and nothing changes does it? So, I figured I'll just remain 'up', all the time, regardless of what happens. Plus, I've got my job interview with Meryl Bleekman tomorrow so if I continue to think positively I might just land myself a job!

9th Sept

Who was I kidding?! I'll never get a bloody job. No one wants supermarket leftovers.

I was so numb when I received my rejection phone call that I didn't even listen to the feedback, so now I have nothing to improve on for my interview with the dog day care centre tomorrow. It doesn't matter anyway, I won't get it. I'll never leave here. As soon as you sit down behind one of these grimy tills you get tarred with a brush that says 'UNEMPLOYABLE' in bright red letters.

Who was it that started this rumour about us checkout girls anyway? Who was it that spread the universal message: supermarket workers are stupid and lazy?

I know there are a lot of freakshows that work here, but most of us are degree-educated nonetheless. Most of us started out with drive, ambition, passion, we just made a little pit-stop to earn some cash and the world treats us as lazy, stupid, and unemployable!

It's really not on. I'm going to write to someone about it – the council or whoever it is that deals with this kind of thing. Employers aren't allowed to judge on sex, race, age, disability, so why the hell can they discriminate against those of us that had to take a rough job?

***

I feel a little calmer now. I guess I just needed to get the initial disappointment out of my system. I should never have read that stupid book, all it did was get my hopes up. Anyway, I found a better way to feel good, instead of forcing myself to feel positive about ridiculous things, I am going to vent. Today I vented on the personnel manager, and I feel pretty great for it.

I was on my way to the canteen when I heard the personnel manager stressing at someone in his office. I hovered around for a bit, excited by the prospect of some minor entertainment.

'You've been to the doctors five times for the same problem. I will not grant anymore time off for it. If you want to get it checked out, go in your own time'.

I was grinning to myself, thinking it was going to get interesting, when I heard Paul the Basket Guy's quivering voice, 'B-b-but, I don't know when my days off will be to book an appointment. It's h-hard to get appointments these d-d-days'.

'Well Paul, maybe you should just quit your job all together and go on the sick if your varicose vein is that troubling. You'd probably get some disability allowance as well for that mashed up brain of yours –'

I stormed in at precisely that moment. Who the hell does he think he is, talking to staff like that?! He was only doing it because he knew Paul wouldn't talk back, he doesn't know the policies well enough. Luckily, I do. I've read them a thousand times, once for every time I've been screwed over by the small print.

'I heard all that you know. Just because you're a member of management doesn't mean the big boss can't throw you out on your arse for comments like that!'

He went red in the face, I couldn't tell whether it was because I caught him red-handed, shouted at him, or because I'd said 'arse'.

'This is a private meeting. Get out or you'll be in serious trouble'.

'It didn't sound private. We can hear you all the way down at the checkouts. So that's more than enough witnesses to get you done for discrimination'.

I could feel the anger bubbling up inside me Everywhere I look it seems like discrimination is there, turns out supermarket workers have 'MUG' printed on their forehead as well as 'UNEMPLOYABLE'. Before the personnel manager could retaliate, the real manager came in, the big boss.

'What's going on in here?'

Paul and I both looked at the managers, one to the other. I was just about to open my mouth when the personnel manager said, 'Nothing. Paul, make sure you get a letter from your doctor so that you get paid for the time off. And Suzie, that holiday you asked about for tomorrow is approved'.

Wow. He called me Suzie *and* gave me an extra paid holiday. Ranting and raving does pay off. Still, I wish I could be there to see him explain my absence to the Rottweiler.

12th Sept

Remember those students that quit at the start of summer? Well, after having lots of fun in the sun they are now skint and back looking for work, as I predicted. Eggberts have taken them back without batting an eyelid. Staff that have already been trained are a bargain, and we all know just how much supermarkets love a bargain. But, not all of the students came back – good for them – so we've had to get seven brand new starters. They are all under 20, bright eyed and bushy tailed. They can't see anything but the £££ signs – they have no idea what they are getting themselves into.

One of them was put with me for a few hours. They have to watch you for a bit, then they take a turn on the till, and boom! Training is complete.

The new starter I was training was a girl called Cherry, and that's her real name too, as in, it's on her birth certificate! Cherry is sixteen, fresh out of school, and as thick as two short planks. I already know she'll be here until retirement – poor cow.

Anyway, she watched me for a while. She didn't ask any questions, but she watched intently. She reminded me of a golden lab, fixating its gaze on the ball, motionless, unblinking, ready for you to throw it. It's cute in dogs, but very unnerving in humans. After an hour, I felt like I could feel her gaze burning the back of my neck, so I told her it was her turn to use the till.

Despite staring at me like her life depended on it, she hadn't taken any of what I'd said in. So, I told her for the fiftieth time: Find the barcode, scan it, push it towards the customer. Take the money, give the change. It's not rocket science. I even found myself giving her tips like, '*Look the customer in the eye, and always ask if they want help packing*'. Then I realised how much of a jobsworth I sounded, so I stopped. She got the hang of it soon enough, so I was free to just take a look around, daydream, and occasionally say what was on my mind. I wasn't even aware of what I was saying and who to, until Cherry chirped up, 'What did you say?'

I looked up and realised we had no customers. I repeated what I'd said, '91% of people that hang themselves have jobs they don't enjoy'. Then I saw her childish eyes widening and I realised who I'd been blabbering on to, 'But, that's a small percentage anyway. And, I'm not saying I'm going to hang myself. Are you? No. Course you're not'.

Unfortunately, the word vomit didn't stop there. 'There's no connection directly to checkout girls. Although, there was a girl that used to work here who tried to top herself a few times. But she had stuff going on at home.

'Supermarket jobs do cause depression, 37.5% of people with depression work in supermarkets, so I've heard. But that means that 62.5% of people with depression don't work in supermarkets. I mean, I don't have depression. I hate my job and my life, sure, but, you know...'

I didn't know what else to say, and I could swear she was tearing up so I just finished with, '...you'll be fine'.

Literally one second after that, no earlier, the Rottweiler came over. 'I'm glad you're helping Cherry settle in, Suzanne'.

'It's Suzie'.

She gave me a quick look up and down and then turned back towards Cherry. 'You can go home now. We'll see you tomorrow evening. You're on a 4-9 shift'.

Cherry got up to leave and walked off without a word. I wonder if we actually will see her tomorrow.

15th Sept

Currently hiding in my room with the chest of drawers in front of the door for protection. Imagine my sheer horror at coming home after a hard shift to find the door to the flat wide open. My new roommate had arrived with no word of warning from my landlord. My new roommate: Creepy Carl.

I've smacked myself in the face a few times just to check that I'm not having a nightmare. But he is still here. This is real. This is worse than the bike incident. I'd ride that little clown bike non-stop for the rest of my life if it meant that that creep would disappear.

We had our first roommate row within seconds. I started it:

'What the fuck are you doing in my house?'

'I think you mean *sniff sniff* *our* flat'.

'Do you think this is funny? I'll get you done for harassment'.

'I'm not harassing you *sniffle*, if anything you're harassing me'.

It was only then that I realised every time he unpacked something I was throwing it back in the box. I took a step back. 'You knew this was my address. Why on earth would you move in? And why the bloody hell wouldn't you tell me about it?! We've seen each other a million times since Clare moved out'.

'I thought it would be a nice surprise. A friendly face'.

'Did Clare know about this?'

'No, *sniff sniff* I didn't want to make her feel uncomfortable'.

'Oh yeah, God forbid poor Clare to feel a little bit uncomfortable! What about me?!'

I thought my rant was over, until I saw a Star Wars poster, 'This isn't going up in any communal areas!'

Creepy Carl nodded and then began to advance towards me. 'Sorry I didn't tell you. I didn't realise you were so bad with surprises. Need a hug?'

That's when I ran to my room and barricaded the door. He's been past twice since, and both times he didn't try the handle – at least that's something. The first time he said, 'Just think, I can give you lifts to work when we're on similar shifts'. The second time he asked if we had toilet roll. I didn't reply to either comment.

It's been almost five hours and I'm desperate for a wee. I guess it's time to make peace. The first thing out of my mouth when I open that door will be, 'So, how about these lifts?'

18th Sept

Why is it that when the reduced stickers come out, all the customers turn into vultures? Well, that's an exaggeration.

It's not all of the customers, just a select few weirdos. I've just come back from my break, and I had to take a detour down the pet aisle to get back to my till, because of said vultures.

They were all gathered around Tom, this weedy, frail looking guy. He looks like the milky bar kid if he'd grown up with a calcium deficiency – ha! Irony.

Anyway, Tom set up camp with his trolley of products to be reduced down aisle 16, and the flock of vultures followed him there. Cluttering the aisle with their trolleys and baskets, licking their lips. I feel kind of sorry for the people that actually wanted to browse the aisle.

They're so impatient as well, these 'reduction vultures'. Before Tom had even labelled things they were picking them up and fighting over them. 'How much is this, mate?'

Some people just love a bargain – they don't even care what it is or how reduced it is for that matter! I've just served a customer and all he bought were multiple packets of ready to eat tripe. A basketful of the stuff, and it all goes out of date tomorrow. Customers are so numb to so-called 'bargains' that he probably didn't even check the summary of his receipt. If he did, he would have found out that he only saved 33p.

Just on the off chance that anyone is reading this and actually feeling sorry for the bugger, '*Oh leave him alone, he might be on a tight budget, blah, blah, blah*'. None of the people that buy reduced stuff are on a tight budget. They're buying things they don't bloody need just because the product has a little bit knocked off the price – they've got more money than sense! Quite literally.

Another woman has just come along and bought 12 donuts for a £1. I suppose that is quite a bargain actually...But, she'd still have to eat them all before tomorrow and it's 7 p.m. already!

I'm convinced some of these reduction vultures only buy this stuff so they can sell it on. Why else would you come to the supermarket and buy 13 macaroni cheese ready meals, and three bags of carrots all with today as an expiry date.

If you're a reduction vulture, or you know one, here's a secret for you. When you see guys like Tom getting they're reduction gun ready, you're not lucky, you're a mug. The first reduction is never more than 10%, in fact, more often than not it is just 5%. So, you should either come back in four hours when the item will be reduced by 60%, or in eight hours when it will be reduced by 90%, or my advice would be to buy that item for the extra 5% more and enjoy eating it without the risk of food poisoning. But, what do I know? I'm just a checkout girl.

21st Sept

The Londoners finally got back to me about my telephone interview. It went well. Surprisingly well. They've asked me to go to the day care facility next month for a more formal interview. I'd be really excited, if I actually had the money to get there.

They've asked me to go down on 2nd October, which might not even be one of my days off, and if I tell the Rottweiler I've got another dentist appointment she will probably want to inspect my teeth herself. So, I'm going to wait it out. If I have the day off, and I have money then I will go to the interview, if not, no big deal. I've missed out on opportunities before because of Eggberts and this will be no different.

They phoned me with the good news at 9 a.m. – not a time I normally wake up at on my days off. It's now 10:02 a.m. and I'm *so* bored!

I don't want to go out anywhere because that would mean spending money, and I have to at least *try* to save money to go down to London, even if I know it's next to impossible. Train fares are ridiculous aren't they? It's like £200 to get from Leeds to London and back. I will need a miracle to have that much money spare in the next two weeks. I don't even have a pay day in between. I guess I have to face facts: I won't be going on that interview.

I guess I could ring Clare to pass some time. I haven't had any contact with her since she moved. She could be crippled by loneliness for all I know, bless her. It's horrible to move to a place where you know no one. Well, I've never personally done it, apart from to come to uni. But when all the friends I made at uni left Leeds that was pretty crushing. I'll give her a call.

***

Well, dear Diary. I rang Clare and then I watched White Chicks – hilarious film, never gets old. But now I'm bored once again. I'm even considering asking Creepy Carl if I can do one of his Star Wars jigsaws with him when he gets back from work. I suppose I could have spent today applying for jobs instead of moping about and being bored, but oh well, what's done is done.

My phone call with Clare was far from enjoyable. She was out for 'brunch' with her actor friends. She stayed on the phone for all of three minutes. Her accent has totally changed already, it's all Southern and posh, and she laughs at the stupidest things. For example, I said: 'Hey, how's life down under?'

She laughed for three quarters of the entire phone call at that one interjection. It wasn't her usual laugh either. It was horsey and middle-aged, like moving to London has made her a middle-classed forty year old. She eventually answered, 'It's fine, dear. Wonderful. Can't talk now though, having a quick brunch. Call you soon'.

Then she did a kiss sound effect, like 'Mwah', and hung up! I feel like maybe I got the wrong number or something. I don't remember Renée changing that much when she moved to London. Mind you, I was too busy getting drunk off my face at uni to notice.

I'm quite glad I won't be able to make it to that London interview now. I mean, Clare sounded like she was having fun and all, but she did not sound like Clare. Not one bit. Maybe she was staying in character. She had to do that sometimes at uni, it was beyond weird. Her and the rest of her performing arts buddies would have to walk around campus pretending to be butlers and maids from the Victorian era, or alien hunters from the future. Oh well, whatever floats your boat I guess.

24th Sept

Just been playing an Ab Fab rerun in my head. I was so into it that when a customer spoke to me I blurted out, '*Why not just have stupidy tax? Just tax the stupid people!*'

Mortified.

27th Sept

It's 2 a.m., and no, I haven't been out on the lash – unfortunately. I'm in Eggberts. Of course I am, where else would I bloody be?

I'm doing a night shift. The only prior warning I got about it was a phone call yesterday on my day off. I need to stop thinking that when the phone rings it's going to be someone offering me a job. It just makes all other news received via telephone seem worse than it is. Anyway, it was the Rottweiler - the worst thing is, she got me to volunteer for it. It's so crafty of her in hindsight. She was all, 'Ooh, it'll be like having an extra day off because you won't need to come in until 9p.m.'. And just like that, I agreed. Anything to keep me away from this place for a few more hours.

But now I'm halfway through and struggling to keep my eyes open.

Have you ever been so tired that it makes you feel physically sick? That's how I feel right now. I'm on my lunch hour, at first I thought I'd try and have a nap, but the minutes dwindled down fast. Now I've only got 37 minutes left and there's no point having a nap that short. Especially on a plastic chair in a drafty canteen. I'll wake up with a stiffer neck than Frankenstein's monster.

I've seen a lot of monsters tonight, and werewolves, and ghosts. We're decorating the store for Halloween. Last year, all of the other supermarkets beat Eggberts tremendously at Halloween sales – they had things like spider cupcakes in their bakeries, staff dress up days, and lots of cool costumes for kids. All we sold were witches noses and broomsticks, and they were well over-priced.

So this year we're going all out. We've dedicated two entire aisles to Halloween stock, and are putting decorations everywhere.

I'm not a fan of Halloween. Dressing up like an idiot so you can get a measly bit of cash? I do that for a living. The one thing I do like is pumpkin carving. Me and my sister carved one together every year until I left for uni. I still do one every year by myself though, I wonder if she does.

30th Sept

Creepy Carl and I are experiencing our first day off together as roommates. It's not fun. He's spent the first three hours of the day leaning over his Star Wars jigsaw puzzle, sniffling. The worst thing is, I've spent the first three hours of the day watching him. Every now and then, snot drips from his nose onto the pieces and he wipes at them vigorously with his sleeve.

I'm in my room now. My own four walls – that I rent. Sometimes I hate this room. I hate that it's all I have, all I can afford, even though I work nine hour days in worse conditions than battery hens.

I would go out somewhere, but I don't have any money. I've given up on making it to that London interview, even though I've got the day off on the 2nd – typical!

I suppose I could apply for some more jobs today. I need...

...sorry, forgot what I was talking about. I heard Creepy Carl answer the door, so I poked my head out of my room to find out that he's only gone and got a date with the hottest 40-something I've ever seen.

He was pouring them both a glass of wine. He asked if I want one, and I'm not one to refuse a drink, so I crept out of my room to get it.

At first I thought she was like his sister or something, but she started messing with his hair and said something suggestive like, 'So, what have you got planned for me today?'

She speaks in that husky, sexy way, like Scarlett Johansson – only with a Yorkshire accent. The tone of her voice made me blush, let alone him. I grabbed my drink and scampered back to my room.

They've been talking for the past few minutes. I can't make out what they're saying but she's laughing every other minute. He isn't even funny.

I can't believe Creepy Carl has had a date around here before me. I haven't even thought about guys in ages, this must be what it's like when you're career driven. All I think about is getting the hell out of Eggberts. Relationships can be put on hold until then. God knows the rest of my life is.

Still, I can't think what a girl like that is doing with someone like him. Oh God...what if she's a prostitute?

Oh my God, I bet she is. Shit, prozzies are dangerous, aren't they? Maybe I should go out somewhere. Scratch that. It's just started pouring down. Thanks, British weather.

I'll just stay here and wait it out. Then I'll give him an absolute rollocking when she's gone. The dirty bastard. Mind you, it's about time he popped his cherry. It's probably the only reason he moved out from his mum and dad's.

Oh no, it's happening. I can hear the bed squeaking. Thankfully, that's all I can hear. Oh, it's stopped now. Maybe I'm just imagining it. That's one thing I do not want to be imagining. The front door has just opened and closed. Surely she can't be gone already.

Oh no, maybe she's invited friends. I'm going to go and investigate.

***

He is one disgusting human being. I left my room and he was sat on the corner of the sofa wearing nothing but his dressing gown, and a horrible smirk on his face.

I didn't mince my words, 'Did you just bring a prostitute to our flat?'

'Suzie! Don't be so rude. Anna is a call-girl'.

Whatever she was, and whatever she had done had cleared his congestion right up. Somehow, that made it feel even more wrong. 'Well, if you ever do that again I'm telling the landlord. She could've robbed us or anything'.

'She doesn't need to rob us. She sees more money in one day than we see all week'.

'I bet she sees a whole lot more than that'.

'Oh Suzie, you are funny'.

'I don't find prostitution funny. You're taking those sheets to the launderette as well. I'm not mixing my washing with anything that's had a naked prostitute on it'.

'I told you, her name is Anna'.

‘Whatever’.

I started walking back towards my room when he called me. I turned to look.

‘I just lost my virginity!’ He shouted as loud as he could and then did a celebratory dance that involved thrusting. I hate men.

October

2nd Oct

It's 11 p.m., and I'm currently on the train home after spending an entire 24 hours in London. You didn't see that coming did you?

Seeing as I have another two hours left of my journey (and I'm on an 8 a.m. start tomorrow – *great*), I might as well start from the top.

I got a call from my sister yesterday at around 1ish. She sometimes calls me on her dinner hour because I'm the only person she knows who is never too busy for a pointless chat. The main reason she called was because she still felt bad about the whole bridesmaid thing and the fact I couldn't take that job I was offered. I reassured her that Eggberts is 100% to blame for both instances, not her. Then we got on to my job hunt, and I happened to mention the London interview I landed. I just mentioned it in passing, sort of a joke, like, 'I've only gone and got myself a job interview that I can't afford to go to'.

Renée started asking more and more questions about it, and the minute I told her it came with free accommodation in The Howard building, she practically squealed.

'I would kill for a place there! Do you know how much they charge a month?!'

If her question wasn't rhetorical my answer would have been: 'A ridiculous amount that is pretentious enough to make people think it's worth it?'

Good job I didn't come out with that smart cow remark because in the next minute she was transferring £200 into my bank account.

'Jesus, Renée. They pay you too much!'

'Oh, you're very welcome. Now hurry up and get your ass on a train'.

She ended the call after that, probably for effect like they do in films.

Important journeys always look nice in films don't they? Beautiful scenery, a pleasant soundtrack, the comfort of knowing that the journey will be worthwhile because in films they always are. In real life, I squandered £200 to sit across from a heavy snorer that absolutely stank of cigs and had a flatulence problem.

I arrived in London at 1 a.m. Renée was waiting for me at the station in her PJs and slippers. She showed me The Howard building on the way to her house. It's only around the corner from her, which would be nice; more than nice actually.

After sleeping for six good hours on the comfiest mattress I have ever laid on, I ate breakfast with Renée and Claude. We had croissants – very French of them. Then it was time for my interview.

The interview went great, at least the first part of it did. The first part was a discussion about my past experience and skills – usual interview stuff really, only without the bullshit questions like, '*On a scale of 1-10, how efficient would you say you are?*'

After that, they took me on a tour of the doggy day care centre. The rich residents of The Howard building must really love their dogs. An entire floor is dedicated to the happiness of their furry friends. There was a spa, an agility course, a living room setting, a green area, and, wait for it, a bloody pool. I had to bite my tongue to stop myself from telling everyone that this dog babysitting club was nicer than any of the hotels I'd ever been to.

The staff were really nice too. It was all going great. I was so comfortable I practically forgot I was at a job interview. Maybe that was the problem.

Before leaving, they took me on a quick tour of the flat, or 'apartment', as they called it. And you know me well enough by now to know that it all went wrong from there.

The flat, oh God, I can still picture it now. It was stunning. Each room was bigger than my entire flat in Leeds. It was furnished with gorgeous, expensive things – not one Ikea table in sight. The sofa was so comfy it was like sitting on a cloud, and it faced a real wood fire and a 50 inch tele. The flat even came with its very own balcony, complete with a water fountain and BBQ. On the way out they asked me, 'How would you feel about living here?'

To which I replied, still in a trance from the enormity of the place, 'Holy shit. I could *live* here?'

I snapped out of my trance just in time to see the awkwardness etching itself upon my interviewers' faces. I tried to salvage the situation, 'What I meant to say was, living here, and working here, would be a dream come true'.

They seemed satisfied enough by that answer, but then an angry neighbour burst out of her flat. Apparently, hearing 'holy shit' in what she described as a 'farmer's accent' was not why she paid £5,000 a month to live there. I was going to say, 'you've been ripped off, love'. But, as I caught sight of my interviewers, I realised that this stupid bitch of a neighbour had actually ripped me off.

I waved goodbye to the perfect flat and the perfect job and went to meet Renée for dinner. She introduced me to all her posh, publisher colleagues. They were nice enough, but they pissed themselves laughing every time I spoke – apparently, my accent is as broad as the tube is packed, whatever that means.

I told Renée that the interview went okay because I didn't want to give the Londoners another reason to laugh at me.

I actually started to feel a little home-sick before I got on the train. I still do. Strange, I thought you were only supposed to get home-sick if you had something, or someone to miss. I'm going back to the possibility that my flatmate and a boatload of prostitutes are having an orgy in the living room.

4th Oct

I got my rejection phone call this morning. Well, rejection voicemail. They said they decided to offer the position to someone with more experience.

Where have I heard that before?

Oh yeah, every job rejection since forever! At least now I know that it's not actually true. What the posh Southerners were actually thinking was, 'We decided to go with someone with a much smaller gob'. I just wish they had the guts to say it to my face, or at least to my voicemail.

I tell you what would make me feel better: a tan. Everywhere I look people are positively glowing from their summer holidays. I even overheard one customer say, 'We could only afford to go to Majorca this year...'

My jaw almost touched the floor. Talk about a first world problem! I can't even afford to take a trip to the sunbeds!

I think everyone should work on a checkout for at least one week of their life, just so they can appreciate what they actually have. Even though I don't sound grateful a lot of the time, since I started working here I've really grown to appreciate things that most people take for granted. Like steak dinners. I haven't eaten steak since I got my last student loan payment. And yet, some people feed it to their dogs! Oh no, is that right? Are there really dogs out there that are higher up in the world than I am? Well, I think my trip to The Howard Building is proof that there are.

Wow. That's enough reflecting for today.

8th Oct

You ever look at the clock and think that it's stopped, but then you realise time is just moving *so* slowly? I do it all the time in this place. Eggberts must be more like purgatory than the real thing.

11th Oct

Just woken up from a terrible, terrible dream. Scratch that, nightmare. Yep, it was definitely a nightmare.

I was a seventy year old woman. I could feel my old bones creak and ache when I moved, and the tightness of my weathered skin. The worst part was, I was still scanning items on checkout 14. Every time I turned to pick up an item I felt a sharp pain in my back. The only thing that seemed to have improved was my hearing, which was torturous because it made that bloody beeping sound of till worse than ever.

Anyway, this customer complained about me being too slow, and the Rottweiler came over (she hadn't aged a bit). She told me that it was time I retired. But this made me feel sick. I knew that if I retired from Eggberts I'd have no money to live on, and no reason to live for. I started to panic. I felt a desperate need for fresh air. I tried to leave my checkout, but it was blocked by an invisible force field. I was trapped in this 4x4 square forever. My breathing started to get shorter and shorter, until I eventually woke up in bed, sweating.

Thank God I don't have to go in to work today.

Today is definitely a job applications day. I am going to apply for every job I see, or at least keep applying until I no longer have terrifying nightmare flashbacks. The worse kinds of nightmares are the ones that feel *so* real. But that will never be my reality! I'm going to get up, and apply, apply, apply! See you in a few hours.

***

Successfully applied for twelve jobs! Doesn't sound like a big accomplishment, but three of them were via application form – and those things take time, believe me!

I applied to three kennel cleaner jobs, one kennel receptionist, six general receptionist jobs, a job in a clothes shop, and another as a cattery assistant (I'm getting desperate).

I hope I hear from them, any of them. Preferably very soon. Creepy Carl caught me applying, and it's like a crime to apply for other jobs when you work at Eggberts. Once, the manager of the beers, wines, and spirits section showed the slightest interest in opening her own wine tasting place one day – she's been segregated for about three years.

The same will happen to me if Creepy Carl blabs – not that I have many acquaintances at work anyway.

He's such a bloody nuisance. I didn't even know how long he had been stood over me. I only spotted him when a chunk of apple fell on my keyboard. I looked up and all he had to say for himself was 'whoops' or 'oops' – I couldn't tell exactly because his cheeks were filled with Granny Smith.

'Why are you leaning over me?'

'Job sites caught my attention', he said. 'Why do you wanna be a *sniff* receptionist?'

I closed the lid of my laptop. 'I don't. I just want to get out of Eggberts'.

'It's not that bad'.

I didn't even dignify him with a response.

***

Well, Creepy Carl and I are more than even. I doubt he'll tell anyone about my job applications now.

I came out of my room to get some vodka. Creepy Carl got a posh bottle for his 18th birthday and never opened it, so I've been trying to put it to good use.

Anyway, before I got to the kitchen I was stopped in my tracks by a naked woman on TV, screaming her heart out. My eyes wandered over to the sofa where I found Carl, pants around his ankles. In case I'm not being clear enough, he was watching a porno, in a communal area of the bloody house! Not even the decency to do it in his own room!

'Turn it off!' I shouted. I wanted to let my presence be known before I saw anything more.

Thankfully he got dressed and turned the TV off – I think that's the first socially acceptable thing I've ever seen him do. He turned to me, unsure of what to say.

To be honest, I didn't know what to say either. I grabbed the vodka, and went back to my room. I forgot the mixer, so I'm just drinking it straight. I've gone through a quarter of the bottle already. I think it's safe to say I'll be having a dreamless sleep tonight.

12th Oct

I've been officially segregated at work for the second time this year. Ugh. It's the Mr Y thing all over again. Well, except it's absolutely not. This time I'm being shunned for something that in any normal workplace would not be a big deal. Or even a tiny deal.

I was in the canteen, minding my own business, when Carl stormed in, 'Where's my laptop?'

I looked up at him. It was the first time I'd seen him frowning, it wasn't an improvement.

'What are you on about?' I said. 'And why are you twenty-five minutes early for your shift?'

He sat down opposite me, 'I came early to find out where you've hidden my laptop. It's not funny'.

I wasn't even laughing. I turned back to my beans on toast, 'Shut up, Carl. I haven't touched your laptop'.

'Oh really? So why isn't it on my bedside table like always?'

He raised his voice. So I matched his volume, 'As if I would go anywhere near your room'.

Some idiot from across the canteen nudged his friend and said, 'Ooh, a domestic'. This made everyone think it was alright to start gawking.

'Stop lying, Suzie! Even though we live together, I can still get you done for stealing!'

Everyone was silent from then, apart from a few whispers – *'Stealing?'*

I lowered my tone, 'Shut it. You're making us both look like prats'.

That just spurred him on further. He said something that he knew would make everyone hate me. 'What do you care what this bunch of apes think of you? 'Cause that's what we are to you, aren't we Suzie-Q? You're 'too good' to work here. That's why you're applying for other jobs'.

The entire canteen had turned into the set of a soap opera. One woman gasped, and then I got hit with a million questions, a lot of them rhetorical:

'Is that true?'

'You think you can find better than here? Good luck'.

'Who do you think you are? God's gift?'

Creepy Carl smirked and got up to walk away. But I wasn't about to let him get away with it that easily. I joined in with the tacky soap opera. I stood up and shouted, 'At least I don't watch porn in communal living areas!'

He was so mortified that his face turned plum purple. But as I looked around at everyone else, I realised I hadn't had the effect I'd hoped for. They were still talking about me:

'Applying for "other jobs"?'

'She must think she's "too good" to scan other people's shopping'.

‘She needs to get her head tested’.

Seriously, these are the kinds of comments people were coming out with. I had to spend the rest of my dinner hour in a toilet cubicle. And it only got worse.

For the rest of my shift I got daggers from whoever I dared to look at. Whenever I asked for something the answer was always something sarcastic like, ‘Oh, you’re talking to me? I thought you were too high and mighty for that’.

In what universe is watching porn in a communal area more socially acceptable than applying for jobs??! I feel like I’m losing my mind. If I stay here much longer, I will lose my bloody mind!

The worst part is, I went home to find that idiot’s laptop on the coffee table in the front room. But because I got home before him, he’s insisting I planted it there so that I wouldn’t look like a thief.

I can’t escape the madness!

14th Oct

I’m still hated by all: the Rottweiler’s put me on terrible shifts for next week; I’m getting the tiniest portions of food in the canteen; even Paul the Basket Guy has had a go at me.

I saw him in the car park yesterday morning. He was putting some trolleys away. Sometimes I see him on my way in, and it’s not uncommon for us to have a quick chat. Only, yesterday he completely ignored me. So I stood squarely in front of him, ‘What’s up this time, Paul?’

I thought one of the lads had taken the piss out of him or something – also not an uncommon occurrence.

He just shrugged and muttered, ‘People have been saying you think it’s rubbish here, and that we’re all idiots’.

‘And you believe ‘em?’

He shrugged again.

‘I’m looking for other jobs because I don’t enjoy working here. I wouldn’t call you an idiot, I’m your friend’.

Paul locked up the trolleys and started to plod away slowly, like he does. 'Seems to me like looking for another job is something you'd tell your friend'.

I didn't follow him. If he wants to join the herd with the rest of them then so be it. But I'd rather be the lone sheepdog than the ignorant sheep.

15th Oct

Even though I'm not in the least bit popular here, I *am* popular with Renée's publisher friends. Apparently, after meeting me in person they now want to see my full diary. Of course they do. Imagine having the power to do that: ask anyone you want if you can read their diary and have them just hand it over without a second thought. Well, they're not getting cheap laughs out of my misery. I gave them February to read because Renée said they might give me money for it, but the more they want to see, the more I think they just want someone to laugh at. They're bored of reading tacky horror stories and *fifty shades of what's it* rip offs, so they've come to the stupid little checkout girl to brighten their day. Renée is too naive to see it, but I'm a girl of the world – even if I've never been travelling.

It's surprising what you can learn about life when you're sat watching the world go by from behind a till. Sure, most of it is depressing as hell, but at least if your glass is always half empty, you'll be happier when something else lands in it. If something else lands in it. Until then, those posh London snobs can keep their hands off my dignity – it's not for sale.

***

Turns out you can put a price on dignity, and that price is £50,000!

I had two missed calls from Renée when I finished my shift. So I rang her back and she started banging on about my diary again. She said her friends seem really excited about it, she hasn't seen them this enthusiastic in ages. I was about to tell her to stuff it when she said those two magic words that made my head spin.

'Say that again?' I said when I'd regained my balance.

'I said the last time they got this excited about a book, they paid the author fifty grand'.

'Fifty grand'.

'I'm not saying you'll get the same, or anywhere near. You might get nothing, but...'

'Fifty grand'. I couldn't stop saying it. If I had that much money I could really quit Eggberts, and not even have to worry about getting another job for at least a year, maybe two. And I could move out of my flat, and get away from that cheese mongering weirdo. My sister cut my daydreaming short...

'So, are you going to send it?'

'Well yeah, but it's not typed or anything'.

'Can't you go to the library and scan it onto a computer?'

'Yeah, okay. I'll do it right now'.

'Okay. But just carry on as normal, yeah? Like I said, they might decide against publishing it. And even if they do, they'll probably want the full year, January to December. So just keep doing what you're doing'.

Well, it's not like I've got anything else to do, is it?

18th Oct

Don't know about you, but I love correcting people – especially when I'm dressed in this 'dunce' uniform. Yes, checkout girls know full well that the rest of the world thinks we're thick. Some of us are, but that goes for any profession. Anyway, I love to show off my knowledge, and I especially love being extra-sarcastic about it too.

I mainly correct people on what pet food they're buying, or their terminology when talking about dogs.

There's another girl here, Kayleigh, she has an English degree, and she's always correcting the way customers speak. She's even had a verbal warning about it. She loves telling people the story – in perfect English of course. Sometimes I feel a little bit sorry for her. I mean, a language buff like that stuck in Leeds? She's always correcting the same old Yorkshire sayings. Changing *'Goin' t'werk'* to *'Going to work'*. *'Ge-or'* to *'Give over'*.

I don't feel sorry for her when I see her face though. She *loves* doing it. It's probably the only thing that keeps her going – I know how she feels.

One woman that I corrected today really stuck in my mind. She was one of those people that you just know are going to be excruciatingly annoying before they even open their mouths. And when she did open her mouth, she couldn't stop harping on about her 'designer' dog, Sweetums. Hate her already, don't you?

'Sweetums is a cockapoo', she was saying. 'Sweetums is so clever. Very expensive, mind, but I suppose it's alright to pay a bit extra for a designer breed'.

As much as I love correcting people, on any normal day I would've let Sweetums' owner get away with it, just because she was so bloody irritating and I didn't want to give her an excuse to talk more. But, when she said 'designer' for the second time, I couldn't stifle my laughter. I have nothing against crossbreeds. A lot of them are beautiful, striking dogs, and all of them are loving. What I *am* against is people purposely crossing dogs just to make a few bob, not even considering the possible health implications. I also can't stand the gullible idiots that fall for the hype, like this woman.

She looked at me for an explanation of my laughter, so I gave her one. 'There's no such thing as a 'designer' dog breed, people just made that up so they could get more money for cross breeds. See, a ‘cockapoo’ is actually a cocker spaniel crossed with a poodle’.

At first, she looked confused, ‘But, I saw Sweetums’ mum and dad, they were both cockapoos like him’.

I carried on scanning her shopping. ‘Well, Sweetums’ mum and dad’s parents were likely not both cockapoos’.

She did not look happy to hear that. I thought I was going to get an earful, but she just said, ‘Really? That’s awful. They charged me £600 for that dog’.

I didn’t like the way she said ‘*that dog*’ so I tried to put a positive spin on the conversation. ‘Well, you and Sweetums sound like the perfect match, and you can’t put a price on that’.

‘Yeah’, she said absent-mindedly, ‘but, he does have a dodgy ticker. Do you think that’s because he’s a...’ she swallowed and whispered, ‘...crossbreed?’

‘It could be. The kennel club advices against crossbreeding because of certain health problems’.

‘Hmm’, she said as she put the last of her bags in the trolley, ‘perhaps I shall have a word with that so-called breeder’.

‘Don’t tell them I sent you’, I said. That made her laugh, and the whole conversation earned me a five quid tip. I’ve never had a tip before. I guess it pays to actually talk to customers. It feels a bit weird though, like I’m stealing from the till or something. Suppose the best way to deal with that is to get rid of it immediately. Cookie dough ice cream and raspberry cider, here I come.

***

P.S. Today was good for another reason. My colleagues no longer avoid me like the plague. They found someone else to bitch about and hate. Apparently, this lad from the produce dept. was caught satisfying an unusual itch with a pineapple – I didn’t ask any more.

22nd Oct

It all started with an unexpected phone call from my mum.

'Hi love. How are you?'

'Fine', I said cautiously. My mum never rings me.

'I just spotted something on the internet that might be of use to you. A career opportunity...'

For about two years after I graduated, my mum would ring me non-stop about these so called '*career opportunities*' she'd found for me. It's a sweet enough thought, but she never found anything useful. They were always jobs that were, at a stretch, only remotely related to canine behaviour: taking tickets at the zoo, working in a pet shop, helping out on a farm. I think the closest she ever got was dog groomer; even then, she couldn't wrap her head around the fact that my degree did not qualify me to cut dogs hair.

'I cut Jakey's hair myself', she said.

'Yeah, and it's the worst part of his year. Even worse than going for his booster injection', I laughed.

My mum didn't, and she stopped calling.

But now I feared it was about to start all over again. I was right. Only, her suggestions had got worse:

'...it's a graduate scheme with Eggberts'.

'Huh?' Was all I could muster.

'You can climb the supermarket ladder. Become a store manager in two years, it says here. You'll even get a company car.

'I'll get your dad to send you the details'.

'No, Mum. I don't want the details. There's no way in hell I'm doing that'.

'Well, why on earth not? You work there anyway, so you might as well put your degree towards *something*'.

I couldn't be bothered arguing with her. So I swallowed a big ball of anger (probably not good for my already crumbling mental health) and said, 'You're right. Thanks Mum. I'll take a look'.

I received the email from my dad's address a few minutes later. I deleted it without reading.

***

What the hell is it with people today?! First my mum and now the Rottweiler. She came over to my till today and started to make small talk. First she started talking about the weather and I let her go on, after all, she is my manager and I do, on occasion, try to show respect. But then she just started to pull things from thin air.

'So, erm, how do you get your uniform to be so, you know, not creased?'

'I iron it', I said, whilst giving a customer his change.

'Oh, that makes sense'.

I started on the next customer's shopping when I heard the Rottweiler take in breath, meaning she had thought of another stupid question to ask. I stopped scanning. 'What do you want, Christine?'

At first she rolled her eyes, but then she looked glad to have an opportunity to get to the point. 'It's no secret that you're looking for another job. And we're obligated to ask a few staff members if they'll apply for the Eggberts graduate scheme'.

It was my turn to roll my eyes. I turned back to the customer and continued scanning.

'No thanks, Christine'.

'You're always whinging about that 'wasted degree' of yours. Why not use it for something?'

She sounded just like my mum. And since when do I complain about my wasted degree? Well, okay, I complain a lot in this diary, but never to people at work. I barely say two words to the rest of the staff.

'I will use it for something...eventually'.

‘But this opportunity is now’.

I stopped scanning and squeezed the product I was holding to stop myself from screaming. I took a deep breath and said, ‘I’m not interested. So go and find your stupid commission somewhere else’.

Turns out, the product I was holding was a tub of ice cream, and I squeezed it so hard that it became misshapen and the lid popped off. I handed it to the Rottweiler, ‘I need another one of these’.

26th Oct

I don’t normally read the paper. But today, a headline practically screamed at me. I just turned my head slightly whilst picking a seat for the bus ride home and there it was: **‘Supermarket shifts ‘cause anxiety and insecurity’**. It was in The Guardian too, so you know it’s legit. Of course, I know it’s legit through terrible daily experience, but I felt elated to finally see my struggle getting media attention. I snatched the paper before anyone else could, and started to read.

Apparently, some research on a major supermarket chain has revealed that low contracts, especially the dreaded zero-hour contract, impact the mental health of supermarket workers. My favourite part of the article is this:

‘So-called 'flexi-contracts', whether that's zero, eight or 10 hours – none of which can provide a living – allow low-level management unaccountable power to dictate workers' hours and consequent income to a damaging extent that is open to incompetence and abuse’.

I didn’t think anyone else cared that I was on a ten hour contract and having my work hours dictated to me by an incompetent psycho-bitch. I was truly touched by this article, and my stomach even did a little somersault when I found out that the research was to be complied into a report and sent to the government to review.

But this is my diary – and nothing ever has a happy ending. Having read the article three times, I went home to show Creepy Carl who pointed out that the newspaper was over two years old. I'm sure that smug bus driver planted it there on purpose.

31st Oct

Today marks the beginning of my last holiday until they get renewed again in March. I've got everything I need to enjoy Halloween in peace: two DVDs (*The Ring*, and *Hocus Pocus* to watch afterwards, you know, calm my nerves), a mountain of chocolate, and a pumpkin to carve. As an added bonus, Creepy Carl has gone to a family Halloween party and won't be home until tomorrow. He left some sweets for me to hand out to trick or treaters, so I can add those to my mountain of chocolate – kids don't need more sugar.

It's going to be great. Just me spending quality time with me.

***

Turns out, a few hours of quality time with me is more than enough. I've watched *The Ring*, eaten my body weight in chocolate, and I got halfway through carving my pumpkin whilst watching *Hocus Pocus*. I stopped because I'm not having fun.

I thought to myself, 'Why are you carving a pumpkin?' And my reply was: 'I don't know'.

It's something I've always done. When I was a kid I carved one with Renée. When I was at uni, I carved one with my roommates. Then, up until last year, I carved one with Nick.

After carving out one eye and half a mouth, I realised pumpkin carving isn't a solo sport. I think I'm just going to throw it in the bin and go to bed. Bed is probably the best place for me to be because it's getting harder and harder to ignore the trick or treaters whilst I've still got the lights on.

Yep. I'm going to go to bed and hopefully I'll wake up in a more optimistic mood - or at least feeling less lonely.

Goodnight Diary.

November

3rd Nov

From here on out, my days will start to go faster. That's because it's event, after event, after event until January 2nd. Coming up is: Bonfire night, Remembrance Sunday, Diwali, Black Friday, Hanukkah, Christmas, and finally, New Years.

Eggberts likes to celebrate each and every one, which is fine by me because the job starts to get more varied. For instance, today I am selling fireworks at the front of the shop. It's nice to have a change of scenery. The queues never get too bad either, because usually if someone sees me with another customer, they just get on with their shopping and come back later.

Being at the front of the store also means that I get to chat to Paul every now and again when he comes in to fill up the baskets. He's told me seventeen times that he doesn't agree with fireworks. A few times he's scared customers off with it. It's hilarious.

On the contrary, he's a big fan of Guy Fawkes, is Paul. I know a lot of people are, V for Vendetta and all that. Paul loves that film, his favourite part is: *'Remember, remember, the Fifth of November, the Gunpowder Treason and Plot. I know of no reason why the Gunpowder Treason should ever be forgot...'*

Pretty cool.

I don't really celebrate Bonfire night. It's a big waste of money if you ask me. Some of the fireworks we're selling are £50+. That's a lot of money for a tacky little light show that lasts less than half an hour. Sparklers are the same. I know they're only cheap, but it's still a waste. Holding a sparkler once is enough for a lifetime. I suppose it's all for kids though. If Eggberts has taught me one thing it's that kids are expensive. Very expensive. I think I'll stick to dogs.

4th Nov

Sick of people saying stupid things, like: '*Live each day as if it's your last*'.

What a ridiculous thing to say. No one can do that; well, unless they're a millionaire. The cold hard truth is that bills need paying, work needs doing, and life is just like that.

If we really did live each day as if it was our last, we'd all be bank robbers riddled with countless sexually transmitted diseases.

8th Nov

If you don't have a job where you're constantly I.D-ing people, then I feel like it's hard to appreciate how tricky it is. But I'm going to try and explain it anyway.

You know yourself, you know your age, you look at yourself everyday in the mirror. To you, you're just an average [insert age here] year old. But, how is a stranger supposed to know that?

It's pretty easy to tell if someone is over or under 18. But when the law brought the I.D. age up to 25, it got a lot harder.

There are all kinds of 25 year olds: people that have lost their hair, people that are going grey, people that look like they're still in high school. And, with a £5000 fine hanging over my head, there's a lot of pressure to get it right. But of course, customers don't give a shit about that, do they? They just want to nip in, get their shopping, and go. I.D. is an inconvenience when you're 25.

Some customers are alright with getting I.D.-ed, and I love them for it. They just say something like, '*Oh wow. I haven't been asked for I.D. in years*' and hand over their driver's licence, gushing.

Some people aren't alright with it. I served one a few minutes ago, and my heart is still racing with the adrenaline from the argument.

He put a bottle of wine and an 18-marked DVD on the belt. He was all over this girl that was with him, so I couldn't see his face properly. The girl alone, I wouldn't ask for I.D. I guessed her to be 27-ish. She had a bit of make-up on, and wore one of those posh pantsuits. The guy, what I could see of him, had thick, fawny hair, and wore a t-shirt with a cartoon character on it.

When he stepped forward to pay, I had about two seconds to glance at his face before I needed to speak. Depending on what he looked like, I would say, 'That's £18.99 please', or, 'Please can I see your I.D.?'

He was clean shaven, had smooth skin, and bright eyes. So I said, 'Please can I see your I.D.?'

He shrugged it off and laughed, 'You 'avin' me on?'

'You look under 25, so I need to see your I.D. please'.

'I'm 33. You need to get your eyes tested, love'.

This is when it starts to get awkward. There's a queue of people judging you, a customer insulting you, and it makes you doubt yourself – '*Does he really look under 25?*'

Now that I had more time to look at him, I could see a few greys on the side of his head, and crow's feet around his eyes, but it was too late. Once you've asked, you have to keep going – stupid policy.

'Sorry, but I still need to see your I.D.'.

'Just show it to her', his girlfriend said.

The guy showed me his I.D., and sure enough it showed him as 33. He paid for the shopping and muttered 'ridiculous' as he walked off. Clearly never worked in customer service in his life. Lucky bastard.

The next customer was an old man with some whisky. He couldn't help himself from making the obvious joke, 'You wanna see my I.D. as well?'

It's been one of those days.

10th Nov

It's the most ~~wonderful~~ depressing time of the year – and, as you may have noticed, it's arrived very early. It always does when you work in a supermarket.

Today we were handed our old, itchy, Christmas hats that we will now be obligated to wear until Boxing Day. There are two kinds: Santa and Elf. I got Santa, thankfully. I couldn't be arsed having a jingly bell on my head for a month and a half.

I used to *love* Christmas. I loved everything about it: spending time with family, watching films, building snowmen, giving presents, receiving presents, decorating the tree, making gingerbread – all that cheesy stuff.

But when you work in a supermarket, Christmas is anything but traditional. It's the busiest, most stressful time of the year. Not to mention the non-stop working whilst everyone is enjoying themselves just makes me feel lonely as hell.

When I watch Christmas films now, I can't enjoy them. Every time someone rushes to buy a present last minute, or sits on Santa's knee, I'm thinking about the poor sap behind the counter, or the fat guy with a beard that doesn't feel the least bit jolly inside.

When I found out Santa wasn't real, I was eight years old and punched my cousin in the stomach for saying such a thing. Then I got sent to my room where I cried over my loss. First the tooth fairy, then Santa. It wasn't my best year.

Now though, I'm glad he isn't real. I couldn't think of a job worse than Santa's: flying around all Christmas Eve/Day, alone in the cold and the dark. I know he only works one day out of the year, but Christmas is a special day. Or at least it used to be. I think everyone's forgotten that now. Eggberts certainly has.

12th Nov

With Christmas, comes the 'Collect the Voucher' campaign. I'm sure you've heard of it by one name or another. At Eggberts it always starts exactly eight weeks before Christmas. Within those eight weeks, customers have to spend £80 or more per week for 6 weeks in order to collect six vouchers. With those vouchers, the customers can come in on the week running up to Christmas and get an £80 shop for £40.

On paper I'm sure it sounds like a brilliant idea, which must be why so many people go mental for it. But if you add everything up, it's not that great at all. Eggberts are saying: 'Spend a minimum of £480 in our stores in less than two months and we'll give you £40 back'.

Now, I don't know much about family shopping (mainly because I live alone) but, I doubt the average family will spend £480 on food in eight weeks. Maybe I'm wrong. When you're as skint as me anything over £20 is a lot of money.

Anyway, the voucher campaign doesn't bother me much. It brings more customers in, which makes the days go quicker. What does bother me is that when the campaign begins, checkout girls turn into the promoters.

I'm just back from standing at the front of the store for five and a half hours. Yes, that's right, an hour and a half longer than is allowed by law. We're supposed to take it in turns doing two hour shifts handing out leaflets at the doors, but the Rottweiler has her favourites and clearly I am not one of them. Someone eventually came to swap with me after I begged customer services to put a call out over the tannoy.

I'm just sat in the canteen trying to enjoy the last 15 minutes of my dinner hour. I spent the first 45 leaning over a sink trying to dab myself clean with wet paper towels.

See, when promoting the Christmas voucher campaign, we have to wear this t-shirt. It's bright yellow, it's size XXL, and it must be over ten years old – at least! God knows if it's ever been washed. It reeks of age-old sweat and depression. To make matters worse, the guy who wore it directly before me has little to no personal hygiene. Plus, he said standing at the front of the shop made him feel self-conscious, so the top was dripping with his sweat, and I had no choice but to slip it on. Straight off his back and on to mine.

13th Nov

It's always embarrassing when your card gets declined, even when you know there's more than enough money on it. You notice that people are suddenly judging everything about you: your clothes, your hair, how you handle the situation.

Sometimes it's hard to handle the situation with dignity because a smug little checkout girl will be grinning up at you, 'Card's declined, mate'.

That bitch is me. You have to understand that working as a checkout operator is duller than sitting in a room and watching paint dry whilst the radio plays one eternal song: Beep. Beep. Beep. Seeing people becoming uncomfortable is a sick pleasure of the checkout girl because we are normally the ones under scrutiny.

Think about it. We sit on a chair in our stuffy, itchy uniform all day, and sometimes all night. Hundreds of people come by all day, and sometimes all night, and the majority of them judge your life – it's like being in a zoo for failed human beings. These people will occasionally judge you openly. For example, a good looking guy saying, ‘This isn’t your *full*-time job, is it?’

Or a sweet, old lady whispering, ‘I bet some bad choices brought you here, petal’.

Once, I even had a guy hold out change and ask if we had a charity box, when I said yes and took the money he raised one of his eyebrows and said in all seriousness, ‘You aren’t the charity box, are you?’

Thankfully, more often than not, people will judge you with their trap shut and use their facial expressions instead. There’s the *‘I understand but don’t care head tilt’*; the upturned nose and flared nostrils that say *‘something smells bad, and it’s probably you*’; the smug smile that says ‘*I’m standing up here, and you are sitting down there*’; and the *‘you’re such a stupid bitch’* eye roll.

I’m not going to take this opportunity to say something patronising like, ‘*the next time you go shopping, see the person, not the occupation*’, because that is bullshit. We’re all judged by our occupations, and we all do at least one of things mentioned above, even me. Especially me! I’m ruthless to checkout girls, I don’t sympathise with their position just because I know what it feels like. Truth is, when I’m shopping there’s no time to feel sympathy. I want to pay for my over-priced food and leave. So if that means blaming the checkout girl when a barcode doesn’t work, I do it. I sigh, do the ‘*you’re such a stupid bitch*’ eye roll, and then, when the shoe is on the other foot, I let someone behave like that towards me. This way, balance is restored in the universe.

So go ahead, glare at me like I’m a pile of cow pat that you made the mistake of stepping in with your Gucci heels, because I’m sure as hell going to give you the same stare when you can’t get a plastic bag open, or when your *supposedly* platinum card gets declined.

16th Nov

Lost count of how many customers have looked at my festive hat in disgust and said: ‘It’s not even December yet’.

I’ve told each one to take it up with management because if anyone can change this ‘*let’s milk Christmas for all it’s worth*’ attitude in supermarkets, it’s customers. None of them took me seriously though. Gee, with a hat like this on, I wonder why.

18th Nov

Just vomited in my mouth a little bit. I got a letter through the door today from Eggberts. It’s my day off and I still can’t escape them. It’s about a bloody retirement scheme. The mere thought of being there until retirement makes me want to smack my head against a wall until the lights go out.

The letter is to inform me that as of January 1st, I will be paying £50.82 towards a pension with Eggberts, unless I opt-out by replying to the letter.

There are so many things wrong with that. First off, as if I have a spare fifty quid to give them. They must be mad. Do they even know how much they pay their staff?

Secondly, I’m way too young to be thinking about any pension.

And finally, why the hell do I have to ‘opt-out’? I have to go through the hassle of writing them a letter and buying a stamp and walking to the post box just to say no thanks to their poxy retirement scheme. Haven’t they heard of the internet?

Oh, I’m bloody fuming. I was going to go Christmas shopping today, but I think I’ll leave it for another time. When I’m in a mood like this there is only one positive thing I can do to blow off steam: apply for jobs.

I’ve just got to keep telling myself it’s not too late. I can still escape this year. I will not live out the rest of my life as a checkout girl. No matter how many signs the universe seems to send me.

20th Nov

Christmas shopping with no money is no fun. Oh well, at least it's over and done with now. It took a total of six hours to shop for four people and one dog. Thank God I don't have any friends to buy for.

The reason it took so long is because I kept picking things up that were perfect, walking around the shop with them, realising they were too expensive, and putting them back.

Shopping in real life is so much more expensive than it is online! I suppose you have to pay extra for the 'experience', or whatever. But walking around in the freezing cold trying to stretch £20 out to buy five gifts wasn't quite the experience I was hoping for. I should've just stuck with Amazon.

The annoying thing is, I know my family so well but I can't show it through the presents I get them. A great example is my mum. I saw tons of great things for her today: a cookbook, a poodle ornament, earrings with her Birthstone in. Do you know what I eventually settled on? Chocolate.

I settled on chocolate for everyone – dog chocolate for Jakey. Just like I have every year since I started working at Eggberts. And every year, when my family call me on Christmas day to thank me for their presents, I can't stop myself from saying, 'I really wanted to get you [insert expensive gift here], but I couldn't afford it'.

Then I get, 'Oh never mind, Suzie. It's the thought that counts'.

I wish I could surprise them one year. Save up and get them something they'd all love, like an antique for my dad and a nice dress for Renée. Every year I plan to save up, but it's impossible. There's never enough left at the end of the month. This is what I'm dealing with:

Wages: £904.36 (After tax and N.I – I'm too poor to pay off my student loan. Yay!)
Rent: £325 (dirt cheap for the city centre)
Bills: £170
Food: £60
Payday Takeaway: £20 (which I regret deeply)
Monthly Bus Pass (to get to work): £70
Money I Owe my Sister: £150
What's left (emergency money): £109.36

A measly £109 left. It may sound like a lot on paper, but it doesn't stretch well over four weeks, let me tell you. There's always something popping up. Take last month as a prime example: Creepy Carl broke the shower head (doing God only knows what) and because it was our, or should I say *his* fault, the Landlord said we had to pay for it.

Even if Carl didn't break the shower head, there would have been something else:

- More food
- Bus fair to an interview
- Ant repellent
- A blind man asking for charity towards Guide dogs

All of these things that other people can pay for without a second thought.

Well, now we've proved the harsh reality of my finances, but the question still remains: why the hell did I go out Christmas shopping with every intention of coming back with state of the art goods? I couldn't even afford state of the art wrapping paper!

I'm deluded, that's why. It's the only explanation. If this diary ever gets published, I'm going to end up in a padded room.

21st Nov

So, it's been just over a month since Renée made my head spin talking about £50,000 of cold hard cash in exchange for me baring my soul in print.

I figured it was about time to chase her up on that – 'cause I could use fifty grand about now. I rang her up on my way home from work last night, but she didn't answer. I waited for her to call me back, but then she didn't, and that's weird for her. So, I tried again on my way to work this morning. Still ringing out. I decided to send a text, and I checked my phone as soon as my dinner break started - still not a word.

Anyway, she finally answered on my last break of the day. I've just got off the phone with her. It wasn't the best conversation we've ever had. In fact, we probably had much more coherent conversations when she was one and I was three.

'Just those two, and that one, oh and that please', she said to someone next to her and then she turned to the speaker, 'What's up?'

'Not much. What you up to?' I said, spinning cold tinned spaghetti around on my plate.

'We're just looking at some centrepieces for the wedding, but we're running late...' she turned away from the phone again, 'that one is a bit tacky-looking, don't you think, Claude? And that one is too big, too loud. I think we'll have to come back another time'. She turned back to me, 'Sorry Suz. I forgot what I was saying'.

'You were saying you're running late'.

'Oh right, yeah. We're off to taste food for the wedding'. She turned to Claude and said 'It's Suzie'. I couldn't hear his response but Renée turned back to me and said, 'Do you want something? I'm going to have to go'.

'I just wanted to know if you'd had any word on the book. My diary, I mean'.

‘No. No word yet. I’ll let you know as soon as. Talk soon, sis. Bye’.

Then she was gone, and it was just me, my cold spaghetti, and the cook in the staff canteen once more.

How can two sister’s lives turn out so differently?

She’s running around London, making extravagant wedding arrangements with her French hunk, and I’m here. Same uniform, same place, same cold spaghetti I have every Wednesday.

Wonder what Renée is eating right now. I bet they’re thinking of a creamy pate to start, probably a fish dish for the main (Renée is obsessed with fish). Wonder what they’ll have for dessert. Maybe something French like, Crème Brûlée. But, from what I remember, Renée isn’t the Crème Brûlée type. It might be something like a mini melt-in-the-middle chocolate cake, with milk chocolate sauce and raspberry coulis...

That does it. I’m going to the vending machine.

24th Nov

It’s official: I’m going to be stuck working at Eggberts for another year. I knew the chances of me getting out before the New Year started were slim (considering there’s only 37 days of the year left), but now I definitely know I’m going to have to stay put.

I just sat down to do my fortnightly, frantic, ‘*I’ve had enough of that place*’ job search and there is absolutely nothing available in the entire country. Zilch. Well, I’m stretching the truth there a bit. What I mean is, the only jobs that I am qualified for, and/or interested in, are temporary Christmas vacancies.

In fact, most positions were. I suppose it makes sense. No employer wants the hassle of hiring someone over the Christmas period unless they desperately need them specifically for the Christmas period. I think most kennels and training schools take a break over Christmas anyway. Alright for some.

It's times like this when I feel like binning this diary. It just doesn't make sense for me to carry around pages and pages of misery. Literally, nothing has improved since I started writing on New Year's Day.

Although, I did move into this nice flat with Clare – but of course, she left me and now I live with Mr. Sneezalot.

Renée's engagement dinner was pretty special, but I missed out on the hen do, just like I'll miss out on the wedding.

Bottom line is, there's more bad in this diary than good. So why am I still writing?

It's comforting, I guess. It helps to let someone know what I'm truly going through, even if that 'someone' is a blank page. Plus, it passes the time when I'm sat on my till doing nothing. Keeps me sane, I suppose you could say. Or maybe I'm not that sane at all, considering the closest thing I have to a friend is this diary. Either way, I'll probably keep on writing. It's not like I've got much else to do.

25th Nov

Today has been great so far. Scratch that. Today has been good. I don't think you can ever have a *great* day on a checkout.

We've had little brownies, or scouts, or whatever they're called, doing all the bag packing today. So I've had a bit of a break, and someone to talk to.

My brownie/scout is called Annie. She is eight, she loves German Shepherds, and has a First Aid qualification. It's great to finally have an intelligent conversation with someone in the work place. Yes, that's right. Annie is 8 and she is more mature and knowledgeable than half of the staff in here, and that's including quite a hefty amount of those that managed to scrape through uni and come out the other side with a degree!

Annie's just gone home. She only had to work 9-1, alright for some!

I have to admit, I did *not* put money in her bucket – and not just because I'm skint. I mean, I *am* skint, but I could've spared her 10p and I didn't.

Don't get me wrong, Annie was nice enough, but she didn't fool me. They're never collecting for charity you know, these kids. They are collecting for their own selfish gain. They *are* the charity. Whether it is a holiday to Butlins, or a trip to the cinema, they march down to the local supermarket, pack a few bags, and hey presto, they have the cash they need to enjoy themselves. If only we could all do that every time we fancied a little treat, eh?

I bet you're thinking I'm just being cynical, but I know it as an absolute fact. Sure, they've got the talk:

'We're collecting to go on a four day trek in Nepal'

That actually sounds like charity work, especially if you're only half listening because they're packing bleach on top of your eggs.

Another good one is:

'We're collecting for an end of year ceremony'.

It's not as good as trekking in Nepal, but it still sounds like if you give them money you'll be doing a good deed. But don't be fooled. The 'four day trek' is just a mini-break for them, and the 'end of year ceremony' is in fact a junk food indulged Marvel movie marathon.

I discovered this because after a bag packing session a few years ago, the scout/brownie leader came to my till and bought an abundance of crisps, chocolate, and fizzy pop, along with a Marvel box set. He paid in change, straight out of the bucket, and not one ounce of guilt was felt.

Since that day I've stopped giving them money. I just admire their schemes from a safe distance. Little hustlers, living the dream.

30th Nov

Well, the hideous Christmas rotas are in. They're the only ones ever to arrive on time. I don't want to bore you with it, but here's a sneak preview:

23rd Dec: 1 p.m. – 10 p.m.
24th Dec: 9 a.m. – 6 p.m.
25th Dec: Day off. Wow.
26th Dec: 7 a.m. – 4 p.m.

I know, I know. Other people have it equally as bad, or maybe even worse. But I don't know any of those people so I'm going to wallow in self pity and complain.

Checkout girls are such an integral part of supermarkets, and yet we get treated the worst. In the month of December, the shop opens one hour earlier and closes two hours later for the convenience of customers. But the only department that has to work those extended hours is, you guessed it: Checkouts (and Admin, but they don't count because they get to sneak into their posh little office and scoff Celebrations). All of the fresh food counters, shelf stackers, and so on, aren't needed at these times. But checkout girls are – which means a lot of starting work before the sun is up and finishing the day waiting at an icicle covered bus stop in the pitch black.

Christmas Eve and Boxing Day will be extra fun because the buses aren't running. I wonder if my dad still has that ridiculously tiny bike he let me borrow in August. God, riding to and from work in 6 inch deep snow on that clown bike doesn't bear thinking about.

That's right – 6 inches of snow. That's how much fell over night and it's supposed to stay like that until February. Worst winter every recorded, or something like that. But they tell you that every year.

Creepy Carl has been out playing in it since we both got home from work two hours ago. God knows what he's doing, building snow girlfriends probably.

Speak of the devil – he's just come back in the house. And he's managed to drag in mountains of grey slush on his feet too. Great.

***

Just had a moment with Creepy Carl. Not a '*moment*', like, '*our eyes met across the room and we realised we belonged together*'. A nice roommate moment. For about half a second, then he started giving me the creeps again.

He came in from building a snow cheerleading squad (what did I tell you?) and asked if I wanted to help him put the decorations up. At first I protested, we see enough baubles and tinsel at work. But he used some sort of reverse psychology to trick me into doing it.

'Fine. Be a grump all your life', he said as he brought a huge box of decorations out from his room.

I sighed, knowing he was right about the grumpy thing, and tried to force myself into enjoying it. I loved Christmas before Eggberts, and I felt sick of thinking about that horrible place twenty-four seven. So, I blocked out Eggberts and thought only about decorating.

The decorations were Creepy Carl's parents' old ones, so they weren't much good - a few decorative plates with snowmen on that we put on the living room window sills; some stringy-looking tinsel that we cello taped to the TV; a reef that we put on the door; and some fairy lights for the window.

It didn't take long, and I felt so much better for doing it. I was finally enjoying Christmas again.

Neither of us had a tree, so Carl suggested we make one. I agreed a lot more readily this time, and he went to collect some 'materials' from his room whilst I made hot chocolates.

It all sounds so cheesy now that I'm writing it down, but I swear it wasn't! At least I didn't feel like it was.

Creepy Carl came back with some green card and a tub of Roses chocolates.

'You eat those *sniff sniff* whilst I cut this card into a tree shape'.

'No problem', I said whilst my teeth had a fight with a toffee penny.

He cut the card into a tree shape and then tacked it to the wall. Then he pointed at the Roses wrappers, 'We can use these as baubles'.

So, we stuck all the used wrappers to the makeshift tree, and used loads of the gold toffee wrappers as the star – I'm going to need another filling before this year is out.

When all the wrappers had been stuck and all of the hot chocolate had been drank, we stood back and admired our work. It looked pretty amazing.

We stood looking at our one decorated room and felt genuinely happy to be there. We looked at each other and smiled. Just a non-committal, simple gesture. But then Creepy Carl's eyes widened. He'd never seen me smile before. He cleared his throat and said, 'Shall I make us another hot chocolate? *Sniffle* We can watch Santa Baby'.

He reached his arm out to touch me and I jumped back. 'Nope'. Then I ran to my room.

And here I am. Door closed. Listening to him watch that bloody film for the second time this week. All that roommate bonding, ruined.

December

1st Dec

Remember the 'Collect the Voucher' campaign? Well, it's still going strong and it's making customers dimmer each week.

The saving on the week of Christmas is £40 – so yes, a lot of money. But what's the point in it if you're scrimping and scraping each week to get your shopping to reach the £80 mark, just to get the voucher?

At least one in three customers are asking things like, 'How much does it come to?'

Sheer panic in their eyes, and not because they think they've spent too much. The complete opposite.

My response will be along the lines of, '£74.53', and then they'll start to panic even more, looking for the nearest thing to shove in their trolley.

'Can I just grab six of these Cadburys bars?' They'll say; one corner of their eye on the queue of impatient customers behind them.

Obviously I say yes, even though the customer has more than likely bought three Cadburys bars already.

I don't know how these people can't see the amount of unnecessary spending they're doing. People really are blinded when it comes to 'special offers'.

The worst case of this I've seen so far is a woman that spent £63.12. She really wanted to spend that extra £18, just to get that stupid piece of paper – the one that is equivalent to one sixth of £40, which, thanks to the calculator on my phone, I know is a measly £6.60.

She grabbed one of those posh Christmas cakes by the till. 'How much is it now?'

'£74.12'

‘Crap’, she said, as other people in the queue started to mutter and sigh.

I actually felt sorry for her, so I tried to give her some advice. ‘You know, it’s only six vouchers you need to collect, so you can just miss this week and catch up next time’.

‘I know. But I only bought the wine so that I could bring the shopping up to £80’.

I glanced at the wine. She’d bought six bottles.

‘Can I just run and get another one of them?’

I nodded and she ran to get it. Her shopping eventually came to £81.11. So, she left happy, clutching her precious voucher, along with seven bottles of wine she doesn’t need, and a Christmas cake that will be out of date by the time she’s opened the fifth window of her advent calendar.

4th Dec

I’ve been in the shop less than two hours and I’ve already scanned about 50 packets of mince pies. We’ve been selling them since September. I don’t know how people aren’t bored of them yet.

The real Christmas rush is finally here. The customers must’ve been using November as a time to do some warm-up shopping.

I do wonder if people actually eat everything they buy in the winter months. Trolleys seem to be twice as full. £120 food shop for a family of three seems to be the record at my checkout so far. You’d think we hibernate for the winter the way some people go on. Mind you, all this snow is probably adding to the panic...

***

Sorry about that. The Rottweiler interrupted me. She said she can tolerate me scribbling when I’ve nothing better to do, but not on a busy day like this. It's probably the most reasonable way she's ever told me off. She must be full of Christmas cheer, or she's just thrilled at how a little snow can bring in so many customers. Either way, I'm not sure I like the idea that she knows I write. It raises all sorts of questions:

'How long has she known?'

'Why doesn't she care?'

'Does she know what I'm writing about?'

On second thought, I think that last question can be ruled out. If she knew what I was writing about I'd be out of a job.

***

Okay, I think I'm out of a job. The Rottweiler just sent me home with a disciplinary letter. She must've been waiting for this day for months, years even. The wretched cow.

She came over to my till and put a closing sign on it. So I assumed, early break - fine by me. Only, when I closed off she called me over to her petty manager's podium. She held out her hand. 'Hand it over'.

'Hand what over?' I said.

'That notepad, diary, whatever it is, I'm confiscating it until the end of your shift'.

I instinctively shoved my hand in my pocket, clutching the pages. There was no way in hell I was letting her see what I'd written.

'Suzanne, hand it over. You can have it back when your shift is finished'.

'How many more years do I have to work here before you realise that my name is actually Suzie?'

'Don't change the subject'.

'Look, I'm not giving it to you. I'll stop writing in it, but there's no way I'm handing it over'.

'You've already been asked to stop writing in it and you didn't'. She was so calm, like a serial killer or something. 'This is your last chance. Give it to me'.

'No'.

'Fine'. She took a letter out of her drawer that was addressed to me. 'Get out of my sight'.

I took it, but didn't open it. 'What's this?'

'It's a disciplinary. I'm surprised you haven't had one already. Take it and get lost'.

'You're sending me home?'

'For the day. It's procedure'. She went off to help one of the other checkout girls take a security tag off a bottle of vodka. I was still stood there when she came back. I looked around at the queues, each one was ten trolleys long, at least.

'You've got to be taking the piss. You can't send me home. Look how busy we are'.

'Well, hopefully that will show you how serious I am'.

She was right, it did show me. And now I'm sat at home trying to stop myself from having palpitations, and also trying to come to terms with the fact that, as bad as things are, they could so easily become worse.

5th Dec

Another day off ruined by worry, doubt, and a boatload of '*what ifs*'.

What if they sack me?

What if I can't afford the flat?

What if I have to start sleeping on my parents' couch?

I didn't tell you what the letter said, did I? Well, here it is. It's short and terrifying:

Miss Quesnell,

In recent months, you have displayed behaviour which breaches The Eggberts' Code of Conduct.

Please accept this letter as written warning that disciplinary action will be taken shortly, beginning with a meeting to discuss your future employment with the company.

Sincerely,

Personnel Dept.

Wonder when they'll want to have the meeting? Surely not this month, we're too busy. But does that mean I have to stay off work unpaid until they want to see me? No, surely not. I mean, it's not clear in the letter, but I don't think they'd be stupid enough to lose a checkout girl on the run up to Christmas. I'll just go in as normal tomorrow and see what happens.

I wish I knew my rights. My mum and dad would probably be able to help, but I don't want them to know. They'd just make an even bigger deal out of it. I need someone who can keep a cool head. I need Renée. But she's probably still busy with wedding stuff. I haven't even spoken to her since last time I called and she was running around looking at flowers or whatever. Still, maybe she's sorted it all now. I'll give her a ring...

***

Well, she answered first time so she must be a little less busy. But not much, she only stayed on the phone for two minutes.

'Hi Suzie', she answered, cheery enough.

'Hey, you still busy with wedding stuff?'

'No, no. Now I'm busy with work stuff. I let it get away from me with all the wedding planning'. She sounded like she had a pen in her mouth, and there was a lot of paper shuffling. I was going to tell her about my disciplinary when she cut me off.

‘If you’re ringing about your manuscript, there’s been no word yet’. Manuscript is what she calls my diary. ‘Still working on it, I presume?’

‘Well, yeah. But...’

‘Good. I’m sure one of the girls will read it when there’s time. It’s on the pile, just not at the top’.

I heard a crash as she dropped something. She spat the pen out of her mouth, ‘Oh no. Look Suz, I’m going to have to call you back’.

The line went dead before I could say anything. So, looks like I’ll have to get my advice the good old lonely way – from the internet.

8th Dec

Well, I’m back behind the till. But I’m not breathing easy just yet. The Rottweiler has set my meeting up for the 7th January. A day before my birthday. My 28th birthday – ugh. She said she’ll be watching me like a hawk until then. I believed her at first, but the Christmas rush has her so busy she’s resembling a headless chicken more than a hawk. She had her eye on me earlier today though, and it’s a good job she did because I’d probably have gotten myself sacked by now if not.

I had a nasty customer, and I mean nasty. But, because the Rottweiler was watching me I played it calm and patient. Like a model worker. Here’s what happened...

I was serving this guy. A typical office worker type buying a few ready meals and some beers. Before opening the bag to pack his shopping he let out a huge sigh and then loosened his tie.

‘Rough day?’ I asked him. *Rough day?* I’ve never said that to anyone in my life. I still don’t know what possessed me. Maybe I was more bored than usual.

He looked at me with cold eyes. He had the look of a wolf that had just spotted a lone dear – an easy target. 'Yeah. But I suppose you wouldn't know anything about that'.

'What?' I spat, and then I felt the Rottweiler's eyes on me and pasted a polite smile on my face.

'You wouldn't know a hard day's work if it smacked you in the arse, love. Of course, it would never be able to hit your arse 'cause you're always sat on it'. He got his card out to pay. I prayed that it would get declined.

I kept my face neutral as I said, 'This is actually a demanding job, and we work nine hour shifts'.

He snatched his receipt and whispered, 'Cry me a river', before storming off.

He's nothing special. We get customers like that every now and again, people that like to use us as human punch bags – in the verbal sense anyway. It feels shitty not being able to give any cheek back.

When you walk around to our side of the checkout you make a choice to be considered a lesser human being by assholes like him. And it's just a choice you have to live with.

12th Dec

I've hit rock bottom. In some ways, it's not that different from almost-rock bottom – I'm still sitting in the flat that I share with a pervert, wearing my fusty Eggberts uniform. And in other ways, it's completely different – I'm applying for jobs as a checkout girl.

I've got to cover my back in case this meeting in January turns out to be as horrible as it is in my nightmares. It's the responsible thing to do. Clare would be proud.

If I'm sacked and I have another job as a checkout girl lined up, at least I won't be any more worse off than I am now. And let's face it, it's highly probable that I'm going to be sacked. I've punched a co-worker in the face; came in drunk on more than one occasion; poured red wine all over myself; screamed at co-workers; got myself involved in a sexual harassment scandal; oh, and I've written down everything that happens behind the scenes and given it to my sister's friends to read. I'm screwed.

The good thing, the *only* good thing, about applying for a checkouts job is that supermarkets seem to be hiring all the time. And with the amount of experience I have, I'll definitely get a job somewhere.

There's one that I might take even if Eggberts don't sack me. It's only a two minute walk from the flat and they give employees 10% discount. Fingers crossed!

I've applied for four in total. One of them was for a checkout supervisor role, so who knows, I might even get a pay rise. All I can do now is wait and see what happens.

In the meantime, I'm going to watch Christmas films that have dogs as main characters because that's the only thing that can cheer me up right now.

15th Dec

My mum and dad came to do a present swap today. They almost couldn't come at all because of this bloody snow (yes, it's still snowing. The weatherman was right for once!) But they made it. It just took them double the time. They'll wish they hadn't bothered when they open their presents from me on Christmas day.

Renée was supposed to be coming with them but she didn't. The first thing I said to them when they walked through the door was, 'Where's Renée?'

'Let us get in the door first', my mum said.

So, we sat down and my dad explained that Renée was too busy to come down and she'll be leaving my present at their house when she goes for Christmas dinner.

After a hot chocolate, we swapped gifts. My parents gave me a gift bag full of presents, as always.

‘Now, no peeking until Christmas day!’ My dad said.

I promised I wouldn’t. I don’t need to. I know exactly what they’ve got me: some chocolates, some fluffy socks, some perfume, a DVD, a dog teddy, and something random from the auction house. It’s the same every year. Not to say I’m not grateful. I like the routine of it. Renée’s present is always more of a guessing game, and that’s not as fun – remember the pocket organiser she got me for my birthday?

‘So, what are you doing for Christmas day?’ My mum asked, like she does every year.

‘Are you sure you can’t come down and see us for a few hours?’ My dad asked, like he does every year.

‘When I learn to drive, I’ll come down for Christmas, but until then it looks like I’m stuck here. I’ll just do the usual: presents, food, films’.

‘Is your friend going to be here?’ Mum said, meaning Creepy Carl.

‘No. His parents only live around the corner. He’s going there’.

‘So you’ll be alone then?’

At the time I just shrugged and said ‘Yeah’. But the question has been ringing in my ears since they left.

I’m going to be completely alone on Christmas day, for the first time ever.

I usually spend it with Nick. It shouldn’t make much of a difference considering he wasn’t much company, but it will. That’s a *long* twenty-four hours of seeing no one. Nothing will be open either. I suppose I could find a pub, they’re always open. I’d feel a bit weird going in by myself though. Oh well, maybe I’ll get some free drinks out of pity.

17th Dec

A while back, I wrote about the annoying songs I have to listen to on repeat, day in, day out. At this moment in time, I’d give my right ear to have them back. Well actually, if it was up for bargaining I'd get rid of both ears and just be done with it. Or better yet, leave my ears at home when I come to work. How blissful would that be?

Anyway, the songs have changed. They changed weeks ago, but then it was fresh and new. Now, it's a strange form of slow torture. Eggberts has dug up a cheap Christmas C.D. from somewhere. A cheap, shop friendly one. Every classic has been covered by some idiot that can't sing. There's a rumour going around that it's Mr Eggberts' daughter trying to break into the music industry. Well, it just goes to show that money can't make all of your dreams come true. No amount of cash could make her hit that Mariah Carey high note.

Oh yeah, that old classic is on there: '*All I want for Christmas is youuuu*'.

Other classics ruined by this nightmarish singer are:

Dean Martin's '*Let it Snow*'

Boney M's '*Mary's Boy Child*'

Wizard's '*Well I wish it could be Christmas every day*'

And, my personal favourite, or at least it was until she butchered it, '*Here comes Santa Claus*' by Gene Autry.

So, that's just five songs. Imagine listening to the same five songs over and over again for nine hours straight, five days a week. Oh, and they're all sang by a singer so bad she has the power to make ears bleed. Believe me, I've seen it.

19th Dec

My life changed today.

I finished work at 10 p.m. I felt like the walking dead after working the busiest shift so far this year. The beeping of the till was still ringing in my ears when I glanced at my phone on the way home. I had seventeen missed calls from Renée. Instantly, I rang her back, my stomach heavy with that sick feeling you get when you think something really bad has happened. She didn't answer. So I rang my mum.

'Hello?' She said, normal as ever (well, as she ever will be). I felt a weight lift from my body then – nothing that serious could have happened.

'Have you heard from Renée?'

'No love, I haven't. Do you know what time it is? I'm in bed you know. Have you been drinking?'

I heard the muffled sound of my dad's voice, and my mum turned to him and said, 'It's Suzie. She's been drinking again'.

'Mum, I'm not drunk. I've just finished work'.

That gave the bus driver a little chuckle as I stepped off the bus. At least someone was jolly.

'You've only just finished work? At this time?'

'Yeah. Look, has Renée called you today?'

'They shouldn't have women working this late. It's dangerous. Are you home now?'

'I'm just walking through the door now'. It wasn't a lie. I nodded in greeting to Creepy Carl, who was watching Santa Baby yet again; and then I went to my room.

'You should tell them you don't want to work that late anymore'.

I hate it when my mum behaves like a moron, which is, let's face it, most of the time. After the shitty day I'd had, I couldn't stop myself from snapping at her. 'Or maybe, I should just tell them I don't want to work at all!'

My phone started to vibrate then, and I heard my mum say to my dad, 'You talk to her. She's in one of her moods', as I pulled the phone away from my ear and looked at it. Incoming call: Renée Quesnell.

I cut off my mum and answered Renée.

'Sit down', she said.

The heavy set feeling was back. She sounded excited and I thought, 'I hope she's not pregnant'. I'm not ready to lose my sister to aquanatal classes and playgroup yet.

'I am', I gulped.

'Okay, good'. She let out a little squeal. 'I'm just trying to think of the best way to do this. Is your laptop nearby?'

'Yeah', I said.

'Go on your internet banking'.

That was the exact point when I switched from nervous to excited. I quickly entered all my passwords and then looked at my account balance.

'Have you done it?' I heard Renée say, but she seemed far away in the distance somewhere.

'Yeah', I said.

'Merry Christmas!'

My account balance was: £20,053. I started to cry without realising.

'Have you won the lottery?' I said.

'No. You have, Suz. Your diary, they want to publish it. That money in your account is an advance. It's yours'.

'It's twenty grand'.

'Yep. And another twenty when you send them the finished product'.

I felt a lump forming in my throat. I started to cry even more, 'I don't get it, Renée'.

She laughed. 'If a publisher likes your book then they pay you an advance to finish it for them. If the book sells more than the advance then you start to earn money, but even if it doesn't, the advance is still yours.

'There's usually loads of legal mumbo jumbo, but I pulled some strings to get it sorted today before the office closed for Christmas.

'Meaning, you can sack that job off, come home for Christmas, *and* be a bridesmaid at my wedding'.

She had to repeat that last bit about three times because I just couldn't stop muttering, 'Is this a joke? It has to be a joke'.

But it's not a joke, and now I'm sat in bed, holding my letter of resignation. I'm leaving. I'm actually leaving. Oh god, I think I'm going to be sick.

20th Dec

Sorry for getting all emotional on you last night. I feel one hundred percent better now. In fact, I feel invincible. With £20,000 in my account I can afford to volunteer until I get a job. Or, if I make even more money like Renée said, I could open my own dog training facility.

But first, I have to kiss Eggberts goodbye. And on the busiest week of the year, no less! I cannot wait to see the Rottweiler's face.

***

Well, I'm rid of Eggberts. I've walked on those sticky tiles and donned that blue bubble jacket and tabard for the last time.

My notice period was supposed to be one week, but the Rottweiler practically exploded with anger when I handed in my resignation and told me, in her own words: 'Get the shit out of my sight!'

So I did, happily.

I didn't mess around with goodbyes. After all, I've no one to say goodbye too. Paul the Basket Guy wasn't in, so I left him a card and a little Christmas present in the canteen. Hopefully no one will nick it.

I've told Creepy Carl too, but he thinks I've had a mental breakdown. He's asked me if I'm okay, like, sixteen times. But I won't have to listen to him much longer, because I'll be driving home for Christmas! (And when I say driving, I mean falling asleep in the back of Renée's car).

But first, I have to do two things:

1. Buy my family some nice gifts
2. Throw my 'Suzanne' name badge in the canal.

25th Dec

Merry Christmas! Truly, I have never meant two words more than I mean those, so treasure them with your life.

I'm slightly drunk. We've been drinking champagne since 10 a.m. this morning. We have a lot to celebrate:

1. I left Eggberts
2. I got a book deal
3. I'm spending Christmas with my family

What a difference a week makes! Never forget that. Never forget that things can change so quickly. If you're at your lowest point today, then that's good because at least tomorrow can only be better. And, who knows, tomorrow might be the best day of your life.

All you need to know is that it's possible. I'm proof of that.

We've just finished Christmas dinner. It was great. We had real turkey and real gravy – two things I haven't tasted in a long time. My mum is just doing the dishes and then we're going to play board games. She loved her present, as did everyone.

Did I mention I got everyone new gifts? I think I did, but I'll say it again.

I got my mum those birthstone earrings I spotted last month. I got my dad a signed Only Fools and Horses promotional photo – one of only 500 in the world according to the guy in the shop. I got Jakey a squeaky toy. And I got Renée and Claude some His and Hers towels.

Renée! That reminds me! My bridesmaid dress is hideous. Awful! It's lime green and figure hugging to the point of suffocation. But I couldn't care less! At least I'm going to the wedding, whether I'm dressed like an unripe banana or not makes no difference.

Oh, Mum is back now. And she has Monopoly. Wish me luck!

Afterword

New Year's Day

Happy New Year!

My name is Suzie Quesnell. It's French, and my dad did teach me a little: *'Mange tout, Rodney, mange tout'*. I forget what it means.

Last year, I looked around at my life and said: 'I am not happy'. And I changed that. I might have needed many pushes, prods, and shoves along the way. But I can finally say I am happy now.

It's not the money from the publishers that has made me happy. Money can't make you happy, I still stand by that. What has made me happy is that I made the choice to leave Eggberts, and fought tooth and nail to make it happen. I've still got a lot of fighting to do in order to get my dream job, but I know that I will get it sooner or later.

So, if you related to the very sad, yet occasionally hilarious desperation in this book, then it's not too late to change your life. *Did you hear me?*

It's not too late to change your life. If you're willing to work your arse off, it's never too late.

And if you're trying, and nothing is going your way, and you feel like giving up, read page 131, or page 233. In fact, reread the whole book, and know that good things will come. And until they do, there's always laughter. Family, friends, and laughter.

Bonjour,
Suzie Quesnell.

On February 2nd, Suzie Quesnell began working as a Guide Dog Trainer. She has dreams of opening her own dog training facility one day.